SAINTS+SINNERS

2025
NEW FICTION
FROM THE FESTIVAL

SAINTS+SINNERS

2025
NEW FICTION
FROM THE FESTIVAL

edited by

Morgan Hufstader and Paul J. Willis

Saints+Sinners
2025

Published in the United States of America by
REBEL SATORI PRESS
rebelsatori.com

ISBN: 978-1-60864-365-3

Credits
Editors: Morgan Hufstader and Paul J. Willis
Production Design: Paul J. Willis
Cover Art by Timothy Cummings
Cover Design by Toan Nguyen
Book Design by Sven Davisson

CONTENTS

* Winner, 2024 Saints+Sinners Fiction Contest
** Runner-Up, 2024 Saints+Sinners Fiction Contest

ACKNOWLEDGMENTS

We'd like to thank:

The John Burton Harter Foundation for their continued support of the fiction contest and their generous support of the Saints+Sinners Literary Festival program.

Sven Davisson and **Rebel Satori Press** for lending their talents to helping us publish our anthology.

Timothy Cummings, cover artist for the 2025 Saints+Sinners Literary Festival anthology.

Tracy Cunningham, whose editorial contributions over the years have informed and shaped the quality of these anthologies.

Everyone who has entered the contest and/or attended the Saints+Sinners LGBTQ+ Literary Festival over the last 20 years for their energy, ideas, and dedication in keeping the written LGBTQ+ word alive.

OUR PAST CONTEST WINNERS

Charlie J. Stephens "For the Birds" (2024)

Ariadne Blayde "Minor Difficulties in BigEasyWorld" (2023)

J. Duncan Davison "My Elijah" (2022)

Colby Byrne "The Fog House" (2021)

Matthew Cherry "Big House" (2020)

J. Marshall Freeman "The Grove of Mohini" (2019)

Jeremy Schnotala "Sand Angels" (2018)

J. Marshall Freeman "Curo the Filthmonger" (2017)

Jerry Rabushka "Trumpet in D" (2016)

Maureen Brady "Basketball Fever" (2015)

Sally Bellerose "Corset" (2014)

Sandra Gail Lambert "In a Chamber of My Heart" (2013)

Jerry Rabushka "Wasted Courage" (2012)

Sally Bellerose "Fishwives" (2011)

Wayne Lee Gay "Ondine" (2010)

INTRODUCTION

Greg Herren, 2025 Fiction Finalist Judge

I find writing short stories harder than writing a novel.

Whenever I say this, other writers often look at me like I've lost my mind. How can anyone think a short story is harder to write than a novel? For one thing, while they are both forms of literature, the mindset for writing a short story is vastly different from the one you need to write a novel. Writing a novel is like climbing a mountain—there's an end to get to, but when you're starting, it's very far in the distance. It's more physical work to type out eighty thousand words than five thousand, of course. A novel may have more than one story going, and there are any number of characters, themes, locations, and subplots to map out and work through into one single cohesive story.

Just because a short story is shorter doesn't make it easier to write.

For me, it's about having to pare down things you can expand on in a novel and deciding what's necessary to the story and what isn't. I tend to overwrite and over-create; there are so many things I want to say in the story to give a full picture of the characters and their situations, but without the luxury of length. I also didn't read short stories much when I was in school; I read books, and the short stories I was forced to read for school were so tedious or dull that I never had any desire to write them—I always thought in terms of novels when I had an idea—so it was a challenge for me when I got to writing classes and had to start writing them.

It didn't go well. My first creative writing professor told me I'd never be published…yet here I am, with over forty books and over fifty short stories to my credit. The short stories we were assigned to read in that class were equally dreadful; if it had been written by a dead straight white guy, it was "serious" literature we should emulate with our own work, while anything else was dismissed outright as having no real value.

But I always remember that dreadful professor whenever I am editing an anthology of short stories, going through the slush pile of submissions to select the ones that work best as well as go together. I remember to be kind, and to never forget how it felt to have my dreams shattered by an authority figure when I was eighteen.

Picking out stories for an anthology, however, is not nearly as difficult as judging and evaluating stories for a contest *because I want everyone to win.* I know all too well the high hopes with which a writer sends off a story to be judged and evaluated and placed in order; had this task required me to place the stories in ranked order, I would have begged off! I also always want to be fair—but there are no rubrics or standards for judging and evaluating a story. A story can be perfect in every respect but not stick the landing. Another story can be so-so and then have an ending worthy of "The Lottery." Should it be an overall impression? To make things even more difficult for your weary judge, the stories are also not limited to or by genre—so the reading and judging experience was wonderful in all the marvelous creativity on display by our writers, but not so easy to judge.

Ultimately, it had to come down to what I enjoyed the most for picking the winner and the runners-up.

This is such a marvelous collection—you're really going to enjoy every story.

I selected "Beaver Moon" by Laura Corin primarily because it kept surprising me as the story went on, and every shift in the story reinvented not just the story itself but the characters themselves, and the surprises kept coming until the very end. I thought it was one thing, then another, and finally it turned out as something else from what I originally thought—what a lovely gem of a story.

The runner-ups, "Our Finest Gifts" by David Pratt and "Bubbles" by Reggie Kent, were also wonderful surprises and highly original. I won't say much about "Our Finest Gifts" because I don't want to spoil anything, but there's a certain Christmas carol I won't ever hear in the same way ever again… in fact, I can honestly say I am looking forward to hearing it again (and I've been sick of it since I was a teenager). Reggie Kent's "Bubbles" is an interesting look at self-confidence and coming to terms with one's sexuality as a young man, while also exploring a bathhouse with his best friend.

Izzy Beach has an entirely new approach to the world of the queer vampire in "When Henry Bit Shelby"—what is love, desire and pleasure to the undead? Can they feel love, as they do in Anne Rice's fictions, or are they, to quote her character, "dead inside"?

John Copenhaver's "Werewolves" takes us back to the not-so-distant past, when being queer was a crime and bars were hidden away yet still raided, lives ruined. John's novels are fantastic journeys into the past, and "Werewolves" stands as yet another stark reminder of how bad things were and why we can never go back. Tom Semmes writes about the jungle that is childhood for queer kids with his character Ezra, who is smarter and more analytical than his bullies—as he thinks and calculates the best ways to adapt and fit in. He reminded me a bit of either Brains Benton or Jupiter Jones, two of my favorite characters from children's series. "After the Storm" by Mina Manchester is a painfully honest story about grief and going on after a horrible loss—made even worse when you find out what happened to Anders, the young trans man. Beautifully written and very powerful, J. Duncan Davidson's "The Hundred Year Man" aches with the melancholy of what might have been had things been different in the past.

Charlie J. Stephens grabs their reader by the throat with the first sentence in "Those Coyote Teeth," and doesn't let go until you finish their last sentence—and take a moment. Wistful with an almost unbearable sense of longing, like Shirley Jackson they never have to raise their voice to get to their reader. Anil Classon's "Snow Cranes" is also gentle, with a soft voice that lulls the reader into this tale of a Japanese mother discovering truths about her son that she needs to know but doesn't want to think about; it's a tender and touching tale of what family means.

"Fry Shack" by Meagan Perry was an absolute delight. Hasn't every queer born in a small town—or some oppressive area, at any rate—dreamed of getting away from that boring little burg and moving to the big city to finally start living? I know I used to dream of escaping Kansas when I was flipping Quarter Pounders at McDonalds, so it was easy for me to identify with Josh and Matt; I would love to read more about their lives once they do get to the city.

Miah Jeffra's "Epicenter" opens with an earthquake and Jeffra plays their cards deftly as the story takes a very different track that is not only fascinating but thought-provoking. Lewis DeSimone's intriguing tale of a gay man who left his life in New York behind and is being visited by a friend from the life he left behind, "Typhoid Harry," is stylishly literate with a touch of the noir and is an incredibly fun read. Alfred P. Doblin's "Last Call for Don" takes on the changing of queer communities over the passage of time, with some slight wistful regrets for the past through scenes from the club they frequented, The Edwardian.

Last but definitely not least is Marcy Rae Henry's cleverly titled "Martini (How I Ended Sleeping with My Friend Alex and Their Ex)", which is a heart-tugging tale of loss, dealing with loss—and the importance of snacks after a connection.

What a terrific and marvelous collection of stories. Why are you still here? Turn the page! READ!

BUBBLES

Reginald Kent

In the small gym, next to the partition separating the reception from the inner world, a silver daddy is doing deadlifts in a jockstrap with his sneakers on, for safety. Behind him are rows of red lockers; I look for the one that my key will open. I start stripping. To get here, I cut through Pagoda Street, buffeted by white tourists. Some stop to gawk at tchotchkes imported en masse from China. Serving staff at entrances hand out flyers, beckoning them to patronize their overpriced restaurants. Most locals head to their usual dinner haunts, little eateries tucked into the smaller streets. I am local, but I don't eat dinner. I turn left onto New Bridge Road. The shophouse I'm looking for has been completely gutted and retrofitted. I push the heavy bulwarks open, then flash the attendant my expired membership card. A man with the straggly mustache asks me to fill out a form. Silently, he checks my pink national identity card, updating my file. New year, same old me, still at my old haunts. I'm young, so it's twelve dollars annually, a steal. The establishment wants us here. Straggly Mustache hands me a set of keys and two sets of face towels. They are useful for drying off and not meant for covering up. The men around me stare, mirrors everywhere. Eyes follow me to an open courtyard behind the lockers; a modern Roman bath. But I don't head to the open showers first, I head over to the toilet stalls. In one, I get some reprieve from the gay gaze. They always want me. It's not arrogance, just observation. I douche with a hose and bidet. After I am all clear, I saunter into the shower. A smooth twink one rail away eyes me up. I turn my back to him using my hands to cup my ass cheeks, an invitation. He might have

1

been a few years older than me. He is as defined as I, with no softness in his abs. After drying off, he leads me up a flight of stairs next to the lockers. We ascend into the maze filled with cubicles.

I'm here every weekend. The darkness helps with the anonymity of it all, but I don't need that. My favorite spot on the cruising floor, the one I always return to, is an intersection of three dim bulbs. No uncles catch me off guard here. I work hard at the gym. I'm confident bathing in this scant light, having it hit all my body's definition. The men brush me with the points of contact ranging from my collarbone to my scrotum. All this while blasting remixes of Sia, Madonna, and Rihanna. Some have the gall to grab me by the wrist after I reject them. I tell them to fuck off. In the real world, they may be big shots whose cocks I have to suck, but in here, they are desperate, hungry for boys, the youth they've lost. The management of Bubbles knows this; it's why they let members under twenty-five come in for free on Fridays and the weekend.

A dud of a night. I'm about to head down to the steam room, but before I make it back to the staircase, I'm turned by the shoulder. The gall. I'm about to tell him to fuck off, but then the lithe silhouette plants his lips on mine. Soft lips, soft hands, and young skin. I run my hands down him; not as built as I am but toned. As he cups my ass and balls under my little towel, I bring a hand to his face. Thick spectacles. He pulls me, hand on my dick, into a cubicle and locks the door. He turns up the dimmer. He is lean and lithe, and any fat he has is concentrated in his ass. He leans on the latched door, running a hand through his platinum blond hair. For a moment, he looks confused; he furrows his threaded black brows, slick as sickles. He begins to grin. He's attractive, no doubt, but it's an appeal of difference, of pushing what a boy should look like. I don't know what to do with all this androgyny. Fuck. He's from the college. Was his name Noah? He looks different without clothes on. By the time he begins laughing, I lose all my confidence.

"Ashley? Is that you! You know, I always had a feeling." He embraces me like an old friend. The gall. It's fair to say that my face isn't the only place blood is draining from. "Well, isn't this fun?" he says.

I met Noah in a freshman class, *Myths and the Narrative.* Professor Cheong loves him, praising his deep engagement with the material. Noah references Vladimir Propp, saying that

2

all myths can be broken into constituent elements. The flood of his biblical namesake also appears in the Babylonian origin tale were studying, *The Epic of Gilgamesh*. As interesting as it all sounds, he goes on too long, likes the sound of his own voice too much, has too much presence.

In the cubicle, Noah snakes around me and climbs onto the foam mattress wrapped in faux leather that sits above a platform. On his elbows and knees, he looks at my reflection in a wall-length mirror in front of him. He grins again, arches his back, and lifts his ass up, spreading his cheeks. "You ready, handsome?" he says. I inch backward, the door rattles. Noah turns around. His upper lip curls.

"I'm sorry, is this weird for you, Ashley? I get it! It's weird seeing a classmate here, but it's not really, it's a small country."

"You know my name?"

"We're in the same intake, so why wouldn't I?"

Why waste your time putting names to faces when you have no real relations? What did he mean when he said he had a feeling? I don't go out of my way to look like a K-pop idol. Noah, he's the sort of person that expects you to know his name.

He pats the spot next to him. "Come on," he says, "I don't bite. Well, unless you're into that." He inches closer, slipping his right hand between my thigh and crotch. He nuzzles the nape of my neck. I get excited again. "Well, I'm glad the feeling is mutual," he says.

He's cocky. The difference between confidence and cocky lies in how much is said. He pushes me down and straddles me, barely giving me breathing room between kisses. He trails them from my neck to my pecs, then sucks on one of them like a baby. I moan as he switches over to the other side. The residual sensation of his wet tongue keeps the abandoned nipple rock hard. I think of him with his back arched.

"Wait," I say, "you've got the wrong idea."

"Wrut?" he says, still on my teat.

"I don't top. I'm a bottom too."

He dislodges, then shrugs. "Well, plenty of solutions to that." He flips around and wraps his lips around my dick. I cry out louder than I want to. Using his toes and thighs, he lifts his erection, piling it into my open mouth.

BUBBLES

Professor Cheong wraps up her lecture on Ovid's *Metamorphoses*. Narcissus became a flower after falling in love with his reflection. The ancient Greeks placed them around tombs, but this isn't the case for us Chinese. My Ah Ma buys them before Lunar New Year. The flower of vanity symbolizes rebirth; they grow as spring arrives. I bring this up in class, that myths are changeable. Professor Cheong is impressed. Noah rushes after me as I head toward the canteen.

"Ashley! Wait up."

"Yes?"

"Lunch? I wanted to talk about last Friday."

"We don't have to."

"But we could!"

"This isn't the time or place, Noah."

"Strange, you're so comfortable around the lightbulbs, but so weary in the daylight. There's nothing to be embarrassed about, you know."

No one needs to see me bared in the daylight. Why invite that judgment, when it does nothing good for you? At this point, I want to get out of sight from my other classmates before Noah gets more direct. So we queue up for Pasta Express. There is no red or white sauce left. The aunty asks us if we're okay with Aglio Olio. Noah says we'll have two and pays. The gall. Of course, he's a rich kid; only rich kids feel it's reasonable to pay for oil and noodles. He's opted for spaghetti; I hate twirling it on my fork.

"So that was fun. I was wondering if—"

"Look, I mean, I did enjoy myself, Noah, but we wouldn't work out."

"Youch. No, Ashley, not my thing."

"I'm not your thing?"

I am, objectively, every gay Singaporean's thing. It's all shallow optics in this country and I look like a dragonboat boy.

"Don't take it personally, buff boy," he says. "I'm not a boyfriend kind of guy."

Whatever. He's too flamboyant for me anyway: the way he dresses in Harajuku pastels, the way his voice goes up two octaves when he's excited; he even twirls his pasta with a limp wrist. Typical center of attention. It's not pride, it's arrogance.

"I don't want to force anything," he says, "but I was wondering if you'd like to go to Bubbles with me on the regular."

"But we're not compatible in that department either."

4

"Ashley, two bottoms can have plenty of fun!"

There are lines for every store in the canteen and the only thing keeping this place from feeling packed is it's ceiling being two stories from the ground. The space above us we can see but can't reach, it somehow makes us feel less cloistered. Crows and mynahs observe the human zoo from little gaps in the structural beams uncovered by bird spikes. Beeps from contactless payment terminals are pattering like raindrops.

"Not so loud," I say.

"It's peak hour, no one can hear us. Look, you want dick, I want dick, but it's nice having a fallback if we don't find anyone else we like, no?"

I only get a sense of myself when I gaze into a mirror like Narcissus. I only think of my body when I am forced to see it, otherwise it fades into the background. I build it up, other people feel it up. The midday sun streams in through the high ceiling, making Noah's hair sheen silver. He may be a wannabe K-pop idol, but he's practical, I suppose. I may not be his thing, but there's enough for him to like. I like him enough, I suppose.

"Sure," I say. "Fallbacks and no falling for. Easy enough."

Next Friday rolls around. After my *Survey of Literature* tutorial, Noah runs up to me across the quad. He's booked a Grab to Chinatown. Lorries and trucks full of industrial materials pass us on the PIE: concrete prefabs, steel beams, and suspended plexiglass. Noah smiles, admiring the canopy of raintrees lining the road. The way his upper lip curls when he is in deep thought is feline. I realize I know nothing about his inner life and might be a dick for that. I mean, Noah did eat me out for what felt like an hour the last time before deepthroating me, then swallowed every drop of my load without flinching. You'd think that would cultivate some familiarity, but sex is as easy as a handshake; it's entirely possible that there is no meaning in meetings. I'm surprised at how Noah's smile moves me to speak. Something in me wants him to feel familiar.

"Noah, you believe in anything?"

"Oh, plenty! But I suppose you mean a religion. No, I don't. What about you?"

BUBBLES

"I did. I was raised Catholic. I still pray to something, but she's not Mary anymore. Didn't like the idea of needing someone to intercede for me. Some mother in the sky to raise my complaints to."

"That's cool. You seem very independent, Ashley. Me, well, I guess we return to the void after all this."

The Grab drops us off. I'm about to walk into Bubbles, but Noah grabs me by the arm.

"It's so early. Aren't you hungry?"

"I don't eat dinner."

"Ugh, you're one of those boys. What was it? Intermittent fasting? Eat with me; I'm buying. I'm sure your next workout at the campus gym will cover the calories. How does frog leg porridge sound?"

We sit at a kopitiam on tall, stackable plastic stools in front of a foldable table. The frog aunty in knock-off Crocs waddles up to Noah to take his order. They talk in Teochew. It seems like he's a regular, so I let him do the talking.

"Wah! Boy! This one who? Boyfriend, is it?"

"No lah aunty, a friend from school."

"He going with you next door, is it? Aiyah! Going university also, handsome boy, try try lah!"

"Aiyah aunty, he's very handsome, but me, what kind of mother will want?"

"Don't say like that, hor. If you like girls, I already set you up with my daughter. I get your usual."

I find it strange that he can talk to older women like this. Maybe it's just Frog Aunty. They're not always so accepting. But surely, for every Frog Aunty, there is someone inhospitable, or worst, silently judging. I hate that it's so easy for Noah. He probably just strikes up a conversation whether he reads hostility or not. My mother, my two brothers and I live in a flat with two bedrooms. We don't talk; everyone is too tired. I do not get an allowance from my mother. I filed a special request to be able to work jobs on campus, a privilege usually denied to freshmen before their first set of grades come out. When I was an infantry officer during National Service, I helped pay the bills. I feel guilty now, getting an education. My mother tells me how proud she is that I got into university. She doesn't talk about the whole gay thing. The only thing my younger brothers ask me about is workout techniques. They probably know, but can't see me as anything but strong. Not the kind of strong that means anything, but the kind that gets you laid. I'm smarter than they think I am. It's better this way. When no one knows your capabilities, they ask you less questions. Albert and Aloysius go on about the girls they are dating; it forms their entire universe. I'm glad my mother can sleep easy at night knowing the two of them will be able to give her grandchildren.

Noah's talking to me, or at me, about how his TA for the survey class is super boring, takes everything too literally, doesn't have an imagination. As he goes into his little tirades, his arms and hands flail in wild gesticulations. Those soft hands sometimes land on me as he speaks, on my shoulders, my arms, and sometimes on my own hands, far rougher than his. I let them. He's touched me more intimately, but this feels more intimate.

Soon two large claypots arrive at the table with a ladle, two sets of bowls, chopsticks, and Chinese soup spoons. The porridge bubbles and steam wafts up, condensing on Noah's glasses. The other claypot is full of white frog legs dyed brown by soy sauce.

"You're very good with people," I say, "especially aunties."

"Oh, you understood!"

"My mother speaks Teochew."

"Ah, a Teochew boy then. She's a sweetie. The best frog leg porridge in Chinatown. There are better in Katong, but don't tell her I said that. Jiak jiak."

He ladles the porridge into my bowl, then tops it up with a helping of legs. I never got why this was a thing; it tastes like chicken and chicken's cheaper. "You're cute Ashy-boy," Noah says. "Do aunties make you shy? They're just regular people."

"The Singaporean aunty is the ultimate arbiter, the alpha and omega in all cultural standards. All aunties make me weary."

Noah giggles so much he hiccups. "Arbiter? Alpha and Omega? Well, aren't you full of surprises, buff boy?"

"I'm smarter than I look."

"Oh, honey, I never thought you were dumb! Just reserved."

His hands are on mine again, but this time they linger. As much as I would like to let them, I can't. I survey the kopitiam around me and, within the post-work, let's get a Tiger beer raucousness, I hear whispers. The other aunties in the crowd are breaking eye contact from their husbands or co-workers across them. Their eyes bore into me. My chest gets tight, but there's Noah, smiling. How? How is he this comfortable? It's infuriating.

"Ashley, you know, your Teochew momma's an aunty; it isn't that hard to talk with them when you think of them as mothers."

I pull my hands back and see him noticing something in me. He looks sorry, and I don't need his pity. I slurp my porridge and the tightness in my chest releases.

"My mother doesn't talk much."

Noah rests his chin on his palm and then uses his index finger to scratch the back of his ear. "They don't all talk, but I find, given enough grace, they can listen. Like, really hear you."

Wishful thinking. I just shrug, and it's not hard to change the topic, I just ask him about his TA again. He goes back to telling a story I can stomach, one without consequence. I keep slurping, occasionally chewing on earthy sinews of frog legs, it's chicken meeting catfish, I suppose. When we're done, Noah picks up his pride edition Kanken backpack and slings it over his shoulder. He leads us to Bubbles, telling me there's no need to keep my head down. "After dinner is the best time to enter the meat market," he declares triumphantly.

Straggly Mustache checks Noah and I in together, but says he can't give us lockers next to each other. Noah's already tucking his towels under his armpit and dashing into the sanctum. I take the time to collect myself and, in here, my chin isn't down. I see the gamut of naked men eyeing me, and all that's left is for me to get ready. We didn't really come up with a gameplan, but I suppose Noah will find me if he needs me.

A good diet incorporating a lot of fiber helps me to get ready, but no amount is full proof. Douching should be every bottom's responsibility. While the occasional accident may still happen, it's good to minimize the risk of that. I hate a top who doesn't understand why he needs to wait for me.

I find a salaryman in his thirties, who I can tell spends time on the bench press. After we're done, he talks to me about insurance schemes to avoid, gives me a kiss, unlatches the bolt, and says he hopes we run into each other again. In the blasting air conditioning, I imagine little changes I'd make to Bubbles if I ran the place. I'd put throw rugs in the cubicles, but that's another thing the attendants would have to clean up. I've seen some questionable residue. Bigger towels to cover us then, but no, we're supposed to be showing off as much skin as we can here. And no, turning down the air conditioning is a terrible idea; it would result in too many sweaty bodies.

Someone pushes the door open. I start. It's just Noah. He's not bothered wrapping his towel around his waist and has it slung over his shoulder.

"You done? Want to head off?"

"How did you know I was in here?"

"Saw you going in after I was done with my first. Just got done with my second."

"It's not a competition."

"I'm hungry. We can still get supper unless you're still *hungry?*"

I consider staying longer but that bowl of frog porridge has reminded me how good eating at night feels. Bodies are weird. Maybe God wanted me to be a top; I am more well-endowed than the insurance agent, more gifted than Noah in that sense too. But he has other assets, more pronounced if he bends down to soap his calves. As we shower, an uncle comes up to him, asking if he's just arrived. Noah's too polite, giving him the whole story, what time he got here, the guys he's been with. There's the same wild gesticulation, but I feel better that at least he isn't letting his hands land on the uncle, that despite both of them being completely nude, there is distance between them. The exchange is nauseating. The uncle is pushy, asking Noah to just try him. A cute boy like him can get whoever he wants, he says, but you cannot beat someone experienced. I turn and even though I'm already clean, I turn the valves clockwise again and start soaping up a second time; this exchange is making me feel grimy. Old, entitled fucks, the lot of them. No amount of experience is going to make anyone feel anything with that limp little dick, you old fuck. I stride towards the uncle, eyeing him up and down; he seems unaccustomed to outward displays of ire and he shrinks. I know I'm not Noah's, well, anything. So, I just turn to him and say "You done? Want to head off?" being fully prepared to leave alone. Noah's not exactly grateful but neither is he perturbed. He smiles at the uncle, thanking him for the compliments, which unfortunately buoys the old man up again. He walks me to my locker then heads to his. After getting dressed, we leave the sanctuary for the flooding lights of Chinatown.

Noah brings me to a rooftop bar, leaving a credit card for the tab. This generosity is starting to get uncomfortable. "You're too nice to the uncles," I say, sipping my daiquiri. "You don't have to be so…forthcoming."

"There's enough meanness in the world, no reason not to be civil."

Of course, he can say that; he has the luxury of letting them walk all over him. Out here, he can still go to rooftop bars and pay for ridiculously priced cocktails on a whim. Men in shirts and ties chat up women who are wearing dresses that could pay for my months' worth of meals. All this "industrial" furniture is a joke; people who come here know nothing of being stripped down. Poverty to them is an aesthetic.

I look up to the cloudless night sky. There's only one thing glowing in it, a great orb, white tonight. I think of my Ah Ma, tracing the outline of a rabbit across its surface, he's the companion to the goddess Chang'e, pounding ingredients for the elixir of life in a little mortar, which she also traces out. I know they're just craters, really. I wish there was more to see in the sky, but there's too much light pollution from the city for there to be any stars.

"You know, Noah," I say, "way back when, people thought that the moon did more than affect the tide. They thought it had the power to change people's moods."

"Your point being?"

"Lunacy is the word, Noah. Those men *can* change your mood. You'd be crazy to let them."

"Ashley, I'd rather be warm instead of only being capable of reflecting the light around me."

He wants to save them. In the *Epic of Gilgamesh*, there too is a story of a flood that destroys the world, but the Sumerian Noah is named Utnapishtim. The difference lies in the myth's outcome. For Noah, there is a covenant with God: a promise that world-destroying floods will never return. For Utnapishtim, it's being granted immortality by his pantheon. Changing one constituent element changes the story. I wonder what element I am and what Noah is. Are we the men surviving the flood? A pair of animals? Or the wicked men not on the ark?

Myths and the Narrative is coming to an end, and as I stare into Noah's backpack, bright red, he asks if we can head into a cubicle together from the get-go. If we can go to Bubbles, just together, with the intention to just be together, not as each other's fall backs. During our last class with Professor Cheong, he unzips his backpack sitting between us, revealing a big double-ended dildo. It's always a tossup, us sleeping together, but we seem to have become each other's lucky charm. We've gotten laid almost every night we went to Bubbles through the semester. Maybe the other patrons see us as social young men capable of forming relationships outside of the baths, maybe that turns them on, makes us more attractive. It's never a dud of a night when we just have each other though. When we do share a cubicle it's different, somehow less transactional, less procedural, less round peg into round hole. Noah and I do things that make us feel good: kiss, trace each other's curves, play with each other's sensitive spots. When we 69, he's warm, inviting, and, surprisingly, never gagging. We finger each other as we take each other in our mouths, and we know how we curve on the inside. He motions with his index and middle fingers, like he's saying come hither to me while he's in me, sending jolts through me. He loves sucking on my pecs, and when he does, part of me can imagine the milk of human kindness flowing out from them. It feels like we're taking our time, just to be, and I want during those nights for every bit of his skin to be on mine. I've come to enjoy the frog porridge, the suppers, and the intimacy we share. A covenant is broken with Noah's question, but I say yes, before hastily zipping up his backpack. Professor Cheong thanks all of us for the great semester, telling us, "Remember, myths tell us where we come from, so hold yours close and you'll know where you need to go."

Silicone never replaces a real dick, but it's not as weird of an experience as I imagine. Noah slips one end into him, then begins fingering me. When I'm ready, he slips the other end in. He places the soles of his feet onto my chest and grabs my wrists. Bending his knees, he begins pulling us closer, getting the toy deeper into each of us. After several pushes and pulls, I end up coming hands-free. Seeing this in the mirror, he grins. I pull my end of the dildo out of me and wrap my lips around his dick. I start rapidly thrusting the toy into him. He finishes in my mouth. I'm sure the uncles hear him. We stay in that cubicle. It's nice. He's the closest thing I'll have to a throw rug. We fall asleep in each other's arms. I know it's a mistake when we wake, but can't stop. I am his big spoon, tracing all his curves from the half spheres of his ankles, crescent of his ass, and eclipse of his open mouth as he sucks on my fingers. In the cubicle's mirror we are reflected as one body, celestial, held together by two gravities. Stillness is movement, ebbing and flowing. I've crossed the Rubicon from falling back to falling for and, somehow, my mouth is open, grasping for the openness of his. Somehow, I'm breathing under all this water.

When we shower, the same perverted uncle from a few weeks ago who couldn't take no for an answer is staring at Noah. Maybe he's just had too much experience hearing yes. I know that look—it's entitlement. He has the gall to grab Noah's ass this time. I lose it. I punch him square in the face. He falls on the wet floor, nose bleeding. Everyone on the veranda is staring at me, stark naked. It's not long before Straggly Mustache arrives on the scene.

We're still wet when we're outside. Noah is storming off. I rush after him. "Noah. Please stop."

"No!" he screams. I'm sure frog aunty can hear him from the coffeeshop. "I've never felt embarrassed in that place. I can't ever go back; do you know what you've taken from me?"

"He touched you without consent."

"It's a bathhouse! We touch each other; what's wrong with you? Why do you hate them so much?"

"You're worth more than that. You're worth respect!"

"I did the same thing to you the first time we met. Why don't I have a bloody nose, Ashley?"

I don't have an answer for him, but he's right, I do hate them. I hate all that I might become: entitled, distant, and hungry. I'm not Noah's anything and can't chart how that uncle's touch transformed me. When Noah was grabbed by him, I felt like I moved from not being an anything towards becoming nothing. I never wanted anyone to matter to me like this. I don't know how to love. I don't even know how to possess. Noah sighs. "You can't go on with these double standards. You're not better than them."

And he's right. As much as I can pull people in, I am also the lunatic pushing them away. I watch him hail a cab, disappearing into the night.

Despite Noah's hyperbole, nothing happens. The uncle doesn't press any charges. I face no reprimand. Straggly Mustache actually shrugs the next time I see him at the reception. These things happen, he says, but I should talk to my boyfriend about it and what kind of boundaries we want. I'm too embarrassed to correct him, so I just nod. Noah hasn't responded to my texts. Going to Bubbles without him, the maze seems darker, the cubicles colder, and the warm showers after, less invigorating. After men are done with me, I stay in the cubicle, bolting the door, trying to gather myself for the next fuck. I look at myself in the full-length mirrors but only see him. I replay all the reflections I saw of us. I've become as childish as my brothers. I've made him, if not my universe, a moon.

My mother, on one of her odd Fridays off, asks why I'm not going out. She's watching a re-run of Japan Hour on Channel News Asia, knowing that there isn't money to go on a holiday; there hasn't been since Dad passed. She smiles at the scenes of cherry blossoms, onigiri, and middle of nowhere train stations. Mom works as a Kopi aunty, but she doesn't own the store. She works so hard to put food on the table, long days on her feet, no benefits, and none of the profits. Noah would never understand—he feeds strangers on a whim. My brothers are out with their girlfriends, convent schoolgirls who swoon over their physiques. If I'm being honest, my brothers are also smarter than they look. We all are. It takes smarts to make it all balance out, to work with what we have. It takes discipline to not imagine that we need more. I sit by my mother on our sofa covered with a plastic sheet. It crinkles as I find my place.

"I'll bring you one day, Ma, to Japan."

She responds in Teochew. "Don't need to think of these things, Ashley, just focus on your studies. Have a little fun also.

You don't need to take your Pa's place."

"Good to have goals, right? Things to look forward to?"

"Just a night like this is fine. Lepak, watch TV, no need to be crazy. You really don't want to go out tonight?"

"You want to kick me out that bad?"

She hesitates before lowering the volume and turning to face me. I was careless with those words. She threatened it once. She's old, with more wrinkles than a woman her age should have. She places her hand on my knee and, when she does, I feel like my legs are skinny again. My body goes back to what it used to be before I started working out. As rough as my hands are, hers are rougher, speckled with red burn marks from the years of making hot drinks.

"I thought maybe you found a girl—sorry, someone special. I thought that's why you go out every Friday like your didis."

"You said I'd end up lonely, Ma."

"Aiyah, Ashley, Ma isn't very smart, you know that already. Ma was wrong to say those things. I still don't understand, but sometimes, I see boys like you—not like you, you look normal— but those boys, sometimes, they are together, sometimes, they look happy drinking Kopi. They don't kiss or anything, but I know they are together. Maybe that can be you also, maybe you can be happy."

There never was the space for happiness, and there is no hugging or crying after the exchange. Mom just turns the volume back up and gets back to her program. People like Noah, people who can afford, wouldn't understand how love grows in small spaces. How wanting is a luxury. There's only so much you can reimagine in a story. We don't skip meals because it's trendy, but out of necessity. There was a time where we didn't have to live like this, a time where we had more. I can't see that life reflected in me anymore.

LAST CALL FOR DON

Alfred P. Doblin

Don was dead. That was still a fact 17 months after, well, the fact. His picture was on the piano where the tip bowl usually was. Alan thought they should have kept the tip bowl there. Don would have liked that. But Don was dead and Don, Alan was sure, did not like being dead more than the placement of the tip bowl on the piano, so what did it matter about the tip bowl anyway?

Dead or not, Alan knew Don would like there to be a cake. A big cake. That was another issue with Don – one from a long, long list of real and imagined grievances with The Edwardian.

Over the years, Alan had heard them all. But the cake thing was a religion with Don. It was never big enough. Yeah, that sounds like a bad joke. Well, maybe it could be in another context, but the size of the birthday cake The Edwardian brought out on Don's birthday every year mattered more to Don than the size of a man's dick. A therapist would have something to say about that, for sure. Alan mused several shrinks probably did have something to say about that to Don, who had been in therapy for as long as Alan had known him. And that was a long time.

A two-man comedy routine began to play in Alan's head:

Man 1: "I want to break with my therapist."

Man 2: "Drop dead."

Man 1: "That was harsh. It was only a question. How do I break with my therapist?"

Man 2: "Your first statement was not a question. It was a statement."

Man 1: "You're missing the point. How do I break with my therapist?"

15

Man 2: "Like I said now – twice. Drop dead."

Man 1: "You're pissing me off."

Man 2: "I'm pissing you off? You asked, 'How do you break with a therapist?'"

Man 1: "Yes."

Man 2: "Drop dead."

It would go on like that for some time, Alan imagined, until finally Man 1 realized the only way to break with a therapist was to drop dead, which he would then do out of exasperation. Alan liked his comedy dark, and truth be told, not all that funny. Alan was a sucker for Chekov.

The room was empty. It was not yet 6 p.m., which was early for The Edwardian crowd, but nothing was the same anymore. Or least not yet, some 18 months after this second plague in Alan's lifetime had hit. It felt dangerous to be inside the bar without a mask, like being convinced by a very hot, muscular man to lay down on your stomach while he pounded you without a condom. There was PrEP now. And there were vaccines now. But did either come with a 100% guarantee? At least, the hot, muscular guy might get you off, while this new virus might still get you dead.

It was unavoidable, this thinking about death, about the 800-a-day-deaths in the beginning, back when Don died. He had played that last big weekend before everything shut down. Alan had stopped going out to places like The Edwardian a few weeks earlier. Alan was cautious by nature. That got him through the 80s and the 90s, so he could now be working his way through his 60s.

Not Don. There was irony for you. Don had lasted long enough to receive the magic drugs that saved him from death 20 years earlier. But the piper ultimately must be paid, like in those film franchises where a group of teens cheat death on a roller coaster or a plane only to fall victim to some other fatal occurrence.

Alan thought, although he did know that part of Don's history, that Don always had assumed he could dodge the bullets even back in the early 90s. But he couldn't then; that virus found him. So, it was no different in the spring of 2020. The new virus found him, and this one wouldn't take "no" for answer.

Alan looked at the text in his phone dated March 16, 2020:

"I'm okay. Already stir crazy though. Out of work for at least 8

weeks. Ugh! Hope you're holding up OK."

That was the last text. Five weeks later, Don was dead. Alan had texted him frequently after that first text during the beginning of lockdown. No response. The weeks passed, the sirens screamed through the streets, and the pots banged at dinner time. The pot-banging was more than a communal event to celebrate first responders and health care workers. It was also a loud reminder of where we all were and where we might end up: in a refrigerated truck in the back of a filled-up mortuary somewhere in a downtrodden part of Queens.

In New York City in the spring of 2020, Broadway theaters were empty, but funeral homes were SRO, horizontally speaking.

When Alan finally tried a landline number he had for Don five weeks into lockdown, he feared the worst. When a woman answered, he knew his fears were about to be confirmed. She was a friend of Don's who was staying in his apartment. Don was dead, dead that morning.

The months passed. Governor Cuomo gave daily televised updates. Trump told people to drink bleach, or something to that effect.

Fauci was glorified. Fauci was vilified.

Through my Fauci, through my Fauci, through my most grievous Fauci.

The dead piled up. Crime rose.

Shots in the arm.

Shots in the streets.

America had gone crazy and the only thing muted was your co-worker talking without sound on Zoom.

To Alan, now in September of 2021, standing with a drink in the backroom of The Edwardian, it seemed surreal, as if someone else had lived through it, a backstory in a novel about post-World War I New York City. But it was Alan's backstory to process. Don didn't have that burden. No backstory. Just dead.

The Edwardian was a sanctuary for Alan, for Don, and for the thousands of queer people who had moved through the three main-floor rooms of the old brownstone. The bar's name was a nod to its pretentions, and perhaps to the townhome's history. From its birth, The Edwardian lived in the past – a place somewhere between Miss Havisham's dining room and Belle Reve.

No one got that all in on their first visit or at least back when

LAST CALL FOR DON

Alan first came to The Edwardian nearly 30 years ago.

Before he moved to New York, Alan had been told about The Edwardian by his friends Robbie and Jim in Los Angeles. They said The Edwardian had his crowd – professional men mostly in suits, a good mix of ages – and there was a piano in the back. The Edwardian wasn't one of those cheesy Village piano bars where everyone was trying to be discovered singing the same goddamn songs from *Les Miz*, oblivious to the obvious fact that almost all the people in the bar were people like themselves: struggling actors with little money. The Guffmans they were waiting for would mostly be bridge-and-tunnel gays, singing out their Louise, or straight people from Ohio wanting to look at "the gays" in their natural habitat, which they had been told was a subterrain piano bar with little ventilation. The Edwardian was nothing like that.

Alan remembered walking east toward the bar that first night. He knew he was close because he saw a small cluster of suited men standing on the sidewalk smoking and talking. They glanced as he walked past toward the steps up into the bar. Alan was new meat.

The polished brass plaque announcing it was The Edwardian to the right of the door was unnecessary because the men on the street gave it away, just as the politically incorrect jockeys lining the wrought iron railings of the now-defunct 21 Club once had for that establishment. Up the stairs Alan went. A tall, bald man of color in an impeccable grey suit, white shirt, and bright red tie with a matching pocket square, stood sentry. He had a small clicker that counted the men one by one as each entered.

"Welcome to The Edwardian," the man said. He looked at his people counter and said almost inaudibly, "69."

"Thank you," Alan said. "I'm not sure I'm that flexible anymore."

One of the men on the street heard Alan and said, "I could fix that."

Alan knew that moment Robbie and Jim had been right; these were his people. He walked into the foyer. The air changed immediately from the coolness of late April to a sultry July. This was the 1990s and people still could smoke inside bars – and they did. A greyish fog was drawn into air filters in the ceiling that zapped and popped like insect traps consuming flies. Two men, around 40, were heading out as Alan was walking in. They brushed against him as they exited, both smelling of gin and cologne.

Alan didn't smoke, but he liked his gin almost as much as his men slightly scented, so he took in a deep breath and pressed further into the front bar. Men in suits everywhere. To his left a long bar coursed the length of the room. Men of various shapes and ages pressed against the men who had snagged coveted seats along the bar. Conversations were loud. Cosmos and martinis were the libations of choice. Lit cigarettes made the walk slightly dangerous as Alan moved through The Edwardian's first gauntlet. Men stood on his right against a half-wall that revealed a stairway downstairs.

He took in the faces as he walked: *Handsome. Average. Cute. Too old. Too drunk. Average, but not my type. My type, but unattainable. Crazy young. Crazy. I could marry him. Why is he fanning himself with a Madame Butterfly fan and where can I get one?* Alan had some unresolved issues.

As Alan moved onward toward the back of the bar, he could see there was a line down the stairs that was split with a long brass railing. Men going up on one side, men going down on the other; a metaphor for the mating rituals underway. He learned later there was a pay phone – it was still the 90s – and an ATM at the bottom of the stairs, in addition to a coat check. Alan pressed further in.

An anteroom opened-up with a small sofa and chairs to his right. The cigarette haze was heavier here, like a valley depression in Los Angeles where the air got stuck.

Three men were chatting and drinking on a sofa that could comfortably sit two. A young guy, maybe 24, tall, polished like a cubic zirconia, sat at one end of the sofa. He had longish black hair that fell onto the collar of a black and gold Versace shirt opened low, revealing a tanned chest covered in massive amounts of dark hair. He sat next to an older, balding man – older than Alan, at least – who was enjoying the view. The older man was suited in a dark pinstripe. His blue dress shirt was lightly splotched with sweat, his tie slightly askew, and his right hand that sported a large ruby on his ring finger stroked the Versace's upper thigh. To the older man's left sat another young guy, of similar age to the Versace, but less big, blond, and with light brown, four-day stubble. He was in Dolce & Gabbana, revealing a smooth chest adorned with too much jewelry.

The two young men stood out, not so much for their youth or even looks, but for their aggressiveness. Even their clothes shouted above the din of the bar. The Versace and Dolce & Gabbana pressed against the older, balding, pin-striped suited, slightly sweaty man in the center of the small couch like two sides of a panini press onto a caprese sandwich.

Several other men crammed into the anteroom, either seated on the two remaining chairs or standing along a wall that opened to a small hallway to Alan's left. The restrooms were there and the men standing nearest the restroom doors appeared to be awaiting their turn – their turn for what, Alan did not know, but he was no prude.

Boys will be boys. Men will be men. And gay men could be either depending on what the situation demanded. There were pheromones in the Marlboro-infused air and God-knows-what on the carpet. Alan pressed further still into the back room, a middle-aged Alice going down the rabbit hole.

The back room was large, with walls papered in a deep, red brocade matching the flushed faces of many of the patrons. The crown moldings were gold and the carpet, an explosion of floral, must have been brighter once but now showed the effects of time, feet, alcohol, and cigarettes. Yet there was something about the décor of the backroom of The Edwardian that made Alan feel there should be a casket somewhere.

A bar to his right ran the length of the room and it was as packed as the one in front, but the vibe was different. The front bar, by comparison, was subdued. The back room was more joyous. There was a good time to be had and it did not require the transactional currency demanded by the Versace and the Dolce & Gabbana. Alan looked at the faces and shapes of men. If life was indeed a banquet, as Auntie Mame would say, no gay man was starving to death here.

There was something for everyone at this buffet, but think twice about anything that looked like it had been sitting out too long without proper refrigeration, Alan thought to himself, chuckling at his own cleverness. Alan clutched his cleverness like some men clutch a string of pearls.

The bartenders were all busy, pouring drinks while chatting with the regulars, of which Alan quickly surmised were many, and of whose ranks Alan also quickly determined he would join. He could feel this was his place as clearly as he felt the occasionally stray hand grab at his ass as he pushed into the center of the back room.

Sofas lined the wall opposite the long bar to the right, and they were filled with characters yet to be defined. Straight ahead was an ornate, three-drawer chest and atop it, a large floral display that didn't know quite where to go. Alan felt the flowers were a metaphor for himself. Where should he go? It did not take long for Alan to figure that out.

The pulse of the room was to his left in the back corner. It was coming from the piano, a large ebony grand. Around the piano, men stood and sang. A very old man who resembled a diminutive Adolf Hitler – if Hitler had worn short-sleeved shirts and suspenders – cradled a Bud Light. A wide, tall man, early 60s in a blue suit, tapped coins on the Lucite cover over the piano top like Ann Miller dancing on a gigantic can of soup. A big, open-shirted man of about 48 in chest and age with a mustache wide enough to have its own zip code had his arm around a much smaller man who barely looked legal as they sang "Hello Dolly." Three 30-something men, who screamed Fire Island house share, belted, "I see the room swaying," as they sloshed cosmos, spilling on one another without concern. A cute, chorus-boy type nearing 30, with rolled up shirtsleeves that exposed muscular forearms, flashed a youthful grin that attracted the attention of the boys from The Pines and the ersatz führer sang with confidence. In all, nine men had secured spaces around the sides of the piano.

There was a second row behind them, which was notable because it included a man with a ventriloquist's dummy. Alan assumed at least one of them was gay.

At the center of this eclectic group was Don at the piano. It was Thursday night at The Edwardian, but it was like Saturday night anywhere else in the world. Alan had never experienced anything quite like this. There was incredible energy, and Don was the turbine generating the power. His hands flew up and down on the keyboard as if it was all random, but there was nothing random about it. The notes were spot on as Don flayed his arms and began to crouch lower and lower until only his head appeared above the keyboard. He was Liberace, Harpo Marx – he was 100% Don.

Of course, Alan didn't know any of that back then.

Don's face, while not exceptional, was expressive. It reacted to the good and poor singers who took turns at an open microphone at various intervals in Don's sets. Don wasn't rude to anyone that first night; really, never rude in all the years Alan would come to pass at The Edwardian. But Alan could see what

Don thought of someone killing – and not in a good way – a showtune. Don's face would contort in grimaces and smiles seemingly simultaneously.

Yet all appeared forgiven if the offensive singer dropped a dollar or two into the tip bowl. It wasn't the size of the tip – it was not like his birthday cakes – that mattered to Don, Alan would learn. A tip of any size showed respect.

That was key to understanding Don and then accepting him as a friend. You had to fully comprehend his infinite need to feel respected and appreciated. He was complicated and too often sad, but none of that was visible when he was behind the piano.

Don's face said, "Come on my ride. I'm not Mr. Toad and this isn't Disneyland. It's something better. It's a ride that lasts as long as I am playing and, on some nights, it will last longer when the guy who stood next to you at my piano, who loved the way you sang, 'Fifty Percent' from *Ballroom*, and began feeling you up by midnight, ended up in your bed. I can make that happen. I can make anything happen behind a piano."

And Don could make anything happen, except perhaps lasting happiness for himself.

Alan watched Don that first night from a distance. Weeks would pass before he moved through the ranks of the regulars and became a fixture himself, usually directly across from Hitler with the Bud Light and, if Alan was lucky, next to the almost 30-something guy whose name he would later learn was Sam. On this first night, Alan watched Don control the room.

Everyone in the back room seemed to be there for Don. That was the case 18 months ago, when the virus came to The Edwardian. And now Don was dead, and it was only his picture that was in the room on the piano where the tip bowl should be.

Alan looked around the back room. It was starting to fill up. He didn't recognize most of the faces. Where were the other regulars? The "Donettes," the quartet of silver-haired men from somewhere deep in Jersey who harmonized back-up to "Mr. Sandman"? Big Jim who sang "Rose's Turn" like the second coming of Ethel Merman in the middle of the backroom without a microphone or a sense of pitch? Or Little Jim who couldn't sing his way out of a brown paper bag and was once banned from The Edwardian for three months after telling a reporter doing a feature on the bar that it was a place for hustlers, which was neither true nor untrue, it just depended on your point of view on how many hustlers can fit on the head of a pin? And since Little Jim was not Jesuitical, Jellicle or evangelical, but rather just a little queer man with no talent, he found himself drinking at The Crow in the West Village from January through March of 2007.

And then there was the dummy with the ventriloquist. Where were they? Perhaps one of them had died?

That was the thing about now. Who died, who lived, and who got to take their spot around the piano? It wouldn't be the same without Don, and it was still hard to believe anything would be the same again. Alan remembered that was the way he thought back when AIDs was consuming his peers.

People either pass on or move on. If you did the latter, you could not look back.

The truth was, Alan hadn't been a regular at the piano for some time. He would still come to The Edwardian and would stop in the back to talk with Don, but the piano had lost its glow. It wasn't Don's fault. He was still Don. The crowd was changing. He and Don were changing. They were getting older and the crowd was getting younger – not young, but younger than them.

The Donettes hadn't been at the piano in years. They had a falling out with Don. Who hadn't at one time? Then they fell out with one another and when one or two of them came in without the others, they were adrift in the room, no longer tethered to one another and no longer able to stay afloat in a gay bar where the tides had shifted.

The smoke inside The Edwardian cleared thanks to Mayor Mike Bloomberg, and when the haze lifted, the suits started disappearing as well. It wasn't closing time for The Edwardian; it was closing time for Alan's generation. They could still come to The Edwardian, maybe hookup every now and then, but they were now looking for something else – someone else – and they were old enough to know they would not find it at The Edwardian.

Don and he talked about that a few months before the world ended. It was the Sunday after New Year's Day, 2020, and the bar was quiet.

"I like it this way," Don said. "It's family night," he added, smiling as he played some Henry Mancini. Don liked to play Mancini when the bar was not crowded.

"I guess," Alan answered. He was wistful. New Year's did that to Alan. It was a marker that another year had passed. "I guess it will be empty. People are still partied-out from Tuesday night. I stopped coming here on New Year's Eve at least a decade ago."

"I didn't have to play this year, because it was a Tuesday," Don said as he played "Moon River." "It's no fun. Amateur drinkers' night and no one tips well because they have a cover at the door. Like that makes me money," Don added with that my-birthday-cake-wasn't-big-enough face. "Do you want to sing tonight?" Don asked.

"Maybe. I don't enjoy singing that much anymore here. The crowd is different."

"I know, but you got to get your Dolly Levi going before the parade passes you by." Don effortlessly switched to the song from *Hello Dolly!* "Ephrem, show him a sign," Don added in a bad imitation of Carol Channing. Or it might have been a good imitation of Carol Channing from when she had become a caricature of herself.

"Maybe someone will paint the shutters forest green," Alan replied.

"They don't paint anything here that isn't red. Red and gold. Red and gold." Don moved on to "It Only Takes a Moment" from the same show. "I hear you. Most of these guys don't know the lyrics to anything anymore. They look at the words on their phone. It's like I'm not even here. We're invisible to this new crowd."

"I am invisible," Alan said. "You make the party happen."

"Vodka and pharmaceuticals make the party happen," Don replied as he segued into "Put on Your Sunday Clothes." "I keep the rhythm. I'm like a metronome."

"No one here knows what that is."

"You're probably right, but whether they know it or not, someone is always marking the tempo."

"That's kind of existential for The Edwardian. I never took you for a philosopher. A Philistine, maybe, but not a philosopher."

"I am a man of many talents. I am amphibious."

"Amphibious?"

"I was playing this audition once and the casting director asked the singer auditioning if he could move to left. The singer moved to the right so the director yelled out, 'Your other left,' to which the singer said, 'I get confused because I can use my right and left interchangeably. I am amphibious.'"

24

"You made that up. No one said that."

"If you have played for as many auditions as I have in New York City, you will have heard every permutation of English imaginable and then some. It's the only thing that makes the process entertaining."

"You should have your own bar, a place where people come to just sit and listen to you."

"I used to, you know."

"When? Where?"

"Back in the early 80s. I was the star on a cruise ship. There was a cocktail room on the ship and I played every evening. Very high end. Cole Porter-like space. It was heaven."

"What happened?"

"HIV. They tested everyone. I found out I was positive. They found out I was positive. And they fired me."

"Was that legal?"

"Most cruise ships don't sail under U.S. flags and I don't think it would have mattered if it was a U.S. ship. It was a hard time. I didn't know I had it… I didn't want to know if I had it because there was nothing to be done except to die. So, I found out I had it and got fired at the same time."

"That's just horrible."

"That was just how it was back then. You forget with time."

"Or with vodka and pharmaceuticals," Alan said surveying the room as he stood at the piano.

"It was a bad time. I was a pariah." Don quickly shifted to playing the song, "They Call Wind Maria" from *Go Paint Your Wagon*.

"That's a rather bitter musical switch," Alan said, noting the pun in titles.

"They call the infected 'pariah, pariah,'" Don sang off-mic. "Anyway, I was out of a job, I cried for about a month and then I pulled myself up by my jockstraps…"

"It's bootstraps," Alan corrected with a sour smile from the wordplay.

"I was never into cowboys and leather. It was jockstraps," Don added in a lighter tone. "I came to New York and here I am, the toast of Mayfair."

"You're going to switch to *Cabaret*, now, aren't you?"

"You know me too well."

"I don't know about that, Don. I don't think anyone really knows the real you. Maybe that is why we keep coming here.

25

We want to figure it out."

"Now who is being existential?"

"Do you ever think the end of *Cabaret* applies to us?"

"What in the ending?" Don was now fully committed to the Kander and Ebb musical on the keyboard.

"At the end, Cliff says, 'There was a cabaret and there was a master of ceremonies. And there was a city called Berlin, in a country called Germany. It was the end of the world, and I was dancing with Sally Bowles, and we were both fast asleep.' Maybe that's us here in our gay bars, dancing away the threats – the insanity outside these walls – believing that nothing can touch us here."

"Honey, I can touch you here and there," a stranger said, who had walked up to the piano and grabbed Alan's ass.

"Excuse me?" Alan said startled and annoyed. The stranger was unfazed.

"Showtime!" Don said loudly into the microphone and began to play the song "Cabaret." He winked at Alan, who moved away from the stranger, who immediately filled his spot at the piano. The contemplative moment had ended. Alan walked back to the front bar.

Alan must have spoken to Don after that night, but he could not recall when or what they might have said. That was their last substantial conversation before the lockdown, before the end of the world.

The back room was filling up now. It felt uncomfortably crowded and Alan wondered if this would turn out to be a superspreader event, an ironic outcome for a memorial for someone whose death was a result of a superspreader event. But Alan wasn't leaving yet. He needed to hear the tributes. He needed to hear the songs.

Someone Alan did not recognize came behind the piano. He said he knew Don well, but Alan could not recall ever seeing him in The Edwardian. Maybe it was before his time, Alan thought. The pianist began playing and, in between songs, people Alan did not recognize – most younger men – grabbed the microphone to say something neither meaningful nor insightful about Don. They had sung with him on some night or nights. They were the new generation. They were the generation that would become old long after Alan had become cold, like Don was now.

Then he would be fast asleep, indeed, Alan thought. He

wanted to leave but he wanted a sign. He wanted forest green shutters. "Ephraim give me a sign," Alan said out loud.

"I always thought you were a closet Dolly," said a familiar voice, coming behind Alan. It was Sam, the now-50-something younger man with still-great forearms.

"My God, I am so happy to see you," Alan said and gave Sam a big hug, which was out of character for Alan. He started to cry and was immediately embarrassed.

"It's okay," Sam said patting Alan's back as he released him from the hug. "That's what this is all about, you know?"

"I never cry."

"You never hugged me before."

"I'm sorry – a little emotional tonight. Are you here with someone? I haven't seen you in so long. I assumed you had a partner."

"I did. Not anymore. I used to be with Robert."

"Robert?"

"You know Robert." Sam mimicked the tapping of coins on the piano top.

"You were with that Robert?"

"Don't say it that way."

"It's just that…"

"Just that, what? You expected me to be with someone younger?"

"I don't know. Someone with less coinage."

They both laughed.

"He could do that with a credit card as well."

"I don't have a response," Alan said.

"It was fucking annoying, let me tell you," Sam said, laughing, ensuring that the moment stayed light. "He was a man of many talents, but tap was not one."

"Sorry."

"Don't be. We broke up before the pandemic. He moved to Wilton Manors outside Fort Lauderdale."

"Never been."

"It's not for everybody."

"It's not for me. Don, liked it, though. He had friends with a house down there and he would go down for a week in February. Some guys he met on a game night. *Settlers of Rattan.*"

"It's *Catan.*"

"Are you sure?"

"Yes, I am sure," Sam said laughing. "That was sacred to

Don."

"I guess that is why he never asked me back to game night. I thought it was about the people who built those woven inserts in furniture that always break through."

"Ha, ha, ha," Sam replied with a wry smile. "You didn't say that to Don, did you?"

"No, I did not. I still wanted to be able to sing at the piano."

"Smart man."

"I try," Alan said, beginning to wonder if he and Sam were having a moment. He shrugged it off. "So, is this sad or what?" He gestured around the room.

"I was thinking the same thing before I saw you," Sam said. "I know it's a memorial and it is supposed to be sad, but not this way. This is sad," he said, elongating the vowel clear down to 48th Street. "Don would not like this maudlin approach."

"And who are these people?"

"Exactly. I don't recognize most of them."

"They were latecomers to the party, I suppose."

"Or we left the party early."

"Maybe. Maybe. I didn't think I left the party, but I guess I have been pushed back from the action for some time. It took Don dying for me to notice that he might have been the only glue holding this place together for me."

"Okay," Sam said firmly. "You are sounding sad." He elongated the vowel again. "None of that. We survived."

"Yes, we survived. I survived two plagues."

"I wasn't old enough to be affected by the first one. It must be strange to be on the other side twice."

"That sounds like a war."

"Wasn't it?"

"Not a war. The plagues were not wars – struggles, I think. Forces of nature battling people. Like a Greek myth without a lot of shirtless Athenians and Spartans."

"Speak for yourself. I live in Astoria."

"Ha, ha, ha," Alan responded, mimicking Sam's earlier laugh. "Seriously, the only way to process what has happened now and then is to look to the Greeks. It's bigger than us. It's the gods versus mortals – something epic and tragic and, maybe some time far away from now, it will have a dignity and a beauty."

"You're a romantic, Alan."

"Maybe. Don wasn't, though."

"No, he wasn't," Sam agreed. "He wanted romance, but he didn't buy into the magic of it. He was always too cynical. Tragic. Something else for the Greeks."

"Are you selling real estate in Astoria?" Alan asked, trying to sound playful.

"I do sell real estate."

"I was making a joke."

"I know," Sam said. "We have known each other for, what? Decades? We have never talked about ourselves much."

"I guess not. You were 'All the Things You Are.'"

"And you were 'Trolley Song,'" Sam replied with a smile. "Don reduced us to our songs."

"He did," Alan said, also smiling. "Well, we were more than a signature song."

"We *are* more than our signature songs," Sam responded. "It was easier to know all of us by our songs – for him and for us."

"Easier, but maybe not smarter," Alan said. "Maybe there was something more to Little Jim than 'Send in the Clowns.'"

They both looked at each other and then started to laugh loudly.

"No, there wasn't," Sam said. "He was so *bad*." Sam stretched out the vowel like it was Gumby in the hands of an evil masseuse. "I wish this wasn't so wrong. I don't recognize anyone here, except you."

"Where's the guy with the bitchy puppet? Remember him?"

"Do I ever. He used to think I was his dummy and try to put his hand up my ass."

"You're kidding?"

"You don't make that up. After the third time he tried, I turned to him and said, 'You do that one more time, and I will shove that puppet of yours so far up your butt, it will be talking out of your ass for a week.'"

"What did he say to that?"

"Nothing," Sam replied and then paused with a broad smile and added, "but the puppet, Lord, what he said. What a mouth on him."

They both laughed loudly again. A stranger walked by them and said with concerted consternation, "It's a memorial. Show some respect."

Alan and Sam looked at each other and laughed again.

Alan spoke first, glancing at the offended stranger who was now at the bar, "Talk about a puppet up your ass."

"You are evil," Sam said, squeezing Alan's arm.

"I don't know about that," he said, finding himself increasingly attracted to this middle-aged version of his long-ago bar crush. "Why didn't we ever talk?"

"It used to be different here. I was different. And there was so little oxygen in the room when Don was playing. He was the center of everything."

"And now, he is where the tip bowl should be," Alan said, pointing to Don's picture on the piano.

"That is so wrong. Not even a good picture of Don. He looks so introspective – like he knows he's dead."

They both fell silent.

Alan spoke first. "Do you think before the pandemic, we were all dancing with someone and yet we were fast asleep?"

"You mean like in *Cabaret*?" Sam asked. "Dancing with Sally Bowles while the world turned black and Don was our emcee."

"Exactly," Alan said, impressed that Sam got the reference. "I was thinking about that earlier. That was my last real conversation with Don before everything changed."

"Here we are less than two years later back in the same place," Sam said looking around the back room. "I have spent so much time here. I met Robert here. I was young here."

"You're still young," Alan interrupted.

"Younger than you," Sam said with a smile as he squeezed Alan's arm to ensure that Alan understood that he meant it in caring way. "We both have grown older. To your point, we're always going to be dancing with someone while the world continues to move on in bad and good ways. We can't see all the evil out there and, even if we did, there are forces you cannot escape."

"Forces of nature, yes. Forces of men, I'm not so sure."

"We're not talking about the plague and Don anymore."

"We are. Don stayed here, inside this red and gold funeral home for like 30 years. He only left it because he died."

"A prisoner inside a funeral home freed by death. No wonder there is no cake," Sam said, trying to make a joke. "We do the best we can, Alan. It's like when we sing at the mic. We do our best in the moment at hand. Sometimes, that's all it comes down to. Don could have been more, could have been a contender," Sam said with a slight Brando inflection, "but Don was Don and, Jesus, Alan, he gave us a good time."

"Yes," Alan replied. They both fell silent again, now standing closer to one another, neither dancing nor fast asleep. More unfamiliar singers came up to the microphone. Then a silver-haired man moved past them toward the piano. "I recognize him," Sam said. "What's his name?" "I'm not sure," Alan said. "He looks familiar."

Another man of similar age soon followed, then another and another. At first, they did not hug or even touch, but they looked at each other with such intensity that both Alan and Sam were spellbound. The four silver-haired men stood silently by the piano one next to the other for what seemed an eternity and then, suddenly, the great chunk of ice melted and all that was left in its place were tears.

"It's the Donettes," Alan said. "They came back. They came back for Don."

"They haven't been here together in maybe a decade," Sam replied. "I used to love their choreography to 'Mr. Sandman.'"

"So did I," Alan said. "Do you think they will sing?"

"Does it matter? We don't sound the way we did 15 years ago. Better we hear them in memory."

"I am glad they are here," Alan replied. "I don't need the song."

"Don would be pleased."

"He would."

"But he would have liked them to have cake – a big cake," Sam added.

"I was thinking just that when I came in tonight. Don was all about the big birthday cake."

"It was never big enough," Sam said, and they both laughed. Sam locked eyes with Alan. "Alan, or Mr. Trolley Song, do want to go somewhere and have some cake?"

"Are you asking me out, Sam, or Mr. All Things You Are?"

"Yes, I am. Let's get out of here. Don would approve."

"Maybe he would. But I feel we haven't said goodbye."

"To a picture, Alan? He's in this room for as long as there is red wallpaper. Time to stop dancing and wake up. Let's go." Sam put his broad arms around Alan and they hugged.

The two left the backroom as someone started singing from *Hello Dolly!*. A new crowd of men had pushed against the piano, few probably knew who the man was in the picture atop the piano where the tip bowl should have been. But they sang. They sang.

Alan and Sam walked through the anteroom where three

men sat on the two-seat sofa, passed the bar in the front lined with men no longer fearful about the last virus. The room was not smoke-filled as it had been decades ago when Alan first came to The Edwardian so Alan could see clearly the faces of the men all looking for something and maybe some would find it. Maybe Don had been the magic or maybe The Edwardian gave him the magic. Time would tell. Time always would tell. It was many things, but Time was never silent.

As the two men approached the foyer, Sam felt something grab his butt. He turned around and it was the bitchy puppet. He had not aged, but the hand up his rear was different. It was a different man. The puppet winked at Sam knowingly.

"I guess nothing really changes inside The Edwardian," Sam said to Alan with a smile.

"Do you believe that?" Alan asked.

"I don't know," Sam said, squeezing Alan's arm as they moved outside. "It's time to see what's outside. That's our job. We're the survivors. Time to go outside. Let's get some cake."

"Yes," Alan said, looking back up the steps at the front entrance to The Edwardian with its familiar, polished brass plate to the right of the door. As they brushed past two men smoking on the sidewalk, Alan said, "Let's get a really big cake."

FRY SHACK

Meagan Perry

Josh checked his ponytail at the beginning and end of every smoke break at the Fry Shack in London, Ontario. The job and the gesture meant that, from grade ten on, a lingering canola odor was Josh's signature scent, and Matt never let him forget it. Matt and Josh had been friends since grade school, but Josh knew Matt would never work in a place like the Fry Shack. His family had money, and Matt knew how to make real money too. He had been selling pot and hash since junior high.

"Hey, greasy guy," Matt said over the counter. "How're things in Grillsville?"

"Bus to Detroit was packed today," said Josh.

"You could probably make fries there too and stay oily," said Matt. "Live off the tips."

Matt had a lot of free time to hang around outside the Fry Shack, teasing Josh about his big dreams, which were to get out of the Shack, travel to the nearest big city, and find another job with a boss who was not Doug.

"You know, you could get on one of those buses and head for the city." Matt spoke through a mouthful of potatoes and feta, the Fry Shack's signature Greek fries. "Come on, you know you want to."

Matt chewed his order, one eyebrow cocked at Josh. Josh kept his mouth shut. Doug was a boss with a knack for appearing the minute Josh got started about everything wrong with the Fry Shack and London, which led directly to Josh's plans to move to Toronto. Josh didn't want to hear Doug's opinion about his plans and what it would mean for him to move out on his mom. So, instead of letting loose, Josh looked past the metal counter at one bus pulling into the station and another starting off for Buffalo. The buses moving in and out of the depot reminded him of those desktop executive toys he saw in catalogues, a pendulum of hanging metal spheres that clicked against each other once they were set in motion, force moving back and forth between them. Josh tried one once at a science store. It started cool until the momentum ever so slowly drained out and the spheres slowed back to immobility.

Josh mentally tallied up his savings. If all went well, it was going to take him three more months to finish saving up for bus ticket money, and first and last month's rent.

Josh threw a basket of fries into the fryer to get ahead of the rush from the newly arrived bus, even though Doug was firm that nothing should be cooking until it had been ordered.

"Don't waste a fry, guy," he'd say. It was one of his classics.

Doug thought his rhymes were pretty funny. Josh used to think so too when he was a kid and Doug would come over for dinner with his mom, before they broke up and Doug gave him this job at the Fry Shack. Ever since, Doug's pearls of wisdom got served up as he counted the change from the register. He'd take a delicate sip of beer after finishing with the contents of each compartment, then move on to stacking the coins, tapping them into rolls and sealing them for the bank. When he wasn't sipping, Doug sent flirtatious glances at his beer. Josh thought maybe Doug had a drinking problem.

The early fries were just starting to sizzle when Doug rushed in, pointing at the fry basket. He slammed a six-pack down on the brushed steel countertop.

"What are you doing?"

"The bus just came in," said Josh. "You know they're coming."

Josh eyed the street, hoping to see a stream of hungry travelers, but there were only a couple of guys hefting their bags down the street.

"No eyes on the buyer, no fries in the fryer." Doug waggled a finger at Josh. He seemed very proud of this one.

"Too much drama, man," said Matt, looking directly at Doug.

"Get out of here," Doug said, and Matt stepped back, unapologetic.

A few passengers had finally veered off the sidewalk toward the Fry Shack. Although Matt had vacated the counter,

Josh could still see him. Matt was clowning a few feet out of the Fry Shack's light wearing the red baseball jacket he'd bought to stand out for his customers, laughing and pointing back and forth at him, then Doug, back at him, and then at Doug.

This scene or something like it played out most evenings, but Matt got more hyped up and glassy eyed as the months dragged on. Some nights, by the light of the Fry Shack, Matt's jacket shone like an alarm. His grin blazed, he shouted his orders, and he somehow convinced Josh to run him a tab. Doug deducted the money from Josh's pay checks.

Matt also developed the annoying habit of drumming on the counter while he waited for Josh to hand over his regular order, a large Greek fries and three cokes. He would shotgun the first cola and start in on the second before Josh had even started cooking the fries.

Josh was getting to his breaking point.

One night, when Matt ordered, Josh turned back to the cash register, trying to forestall the next stage of events: Matt asking if Josh could spot him.

Josh waited. Ten long seconds later, a pile of change rattled against the countertop.

"Thanks for nothing, man," grumbled Matt, stomping off into the dark. Josh sorted the dimes and quarters into small stacks, until the fryer let out another beep. He pulled the basket up and watched oil drain from Matt's abandoned fries.

"Old friend?" asked the next customer.

Josh nodded as he swept the coins off the grimy steel counter into his palm. He dropped the feta crumbs into the cash register along with the coins. Matt's handful of change hadn't even been close to the right amount, but when Josh got home at the end of his shift, there was Matt on the porch, like always, restlessly shifting around and tapping his toes.

"I thought that asshole would never let you out of the fry cage," said Matt, handing Josh a falafel sandwich, then holding out a joint. Josh nodded thanks and sucked a layer of sweet and sour smoke past the salt and grease he'd been breathing all night.

Josh, starting in on his falafel wrap, sat down beside Matt and dreamed of his departure. He had to admit that Doug was getting worse, threatening not to pay, yelling instead of rhyming. Matt broke the silence.

"I have a new deal," said Matt. "Supplier's from out of

town. You should get in on it."

"No, man, I'm almost saved up to leave," Josh lied. "I'll keep smoking your stash though."

Matt punched him in the arm, harder than usual.

"Gotta go. See ya, grease man."

Josh went to bed. When he woke, he had a big zit on his cheek that made it hard to shave.

Matt didn't show at the Fry Shack that night or the next. The third night, Josh sat on the porch, taking his time with a smoke, hoping Matt would show.

Day four, the customers were terrible: demanding, cursing about how slow the service was, angry at Josh for no reason.

"These fries are shit," was all Josh heard, and when he looked toward the window a cardboard container of fries was flying past the counter at him. A few fries sizzled against his cheek like hot shrapnel, a few splashed back home into the fryer oil, and the rest scattered across the floor of the Shack between Doug and Josh.

By the time the fries had all landed, Doug had his face out the service window and was shouting, "Fuck. HEY!" But the perp was out of range. Josh tentatively felt at his cheek, which stung where the fries had struck.

"Keep your head down to hide that frown," said Doug, swatting Josh on the arm. Then Doug bent to gather up the spilled fries onto a checked piece of parchment paper. His coordination was way off tonight – his hands were like mitts.

Josh kept serving, keeping his mouth shut. He was focused and sweating, doling out the orders, keeping tabs, remembering it was payday, wishing for the night to end.

At closing, Doug could barely hold the pen to write Josh's paycheck, and when he did, it was fifty bucks short.

"Here," said Doug. "Fix your attitude."

Josh stomped home to find Matt on the porch smoking like he had been there all night and looking terrible; the porch light glared off his sweaty face. He was eating a falafel as usual, but there wasn't one for Josh.

"Where you been?" asked Josh.

"I'm doing good," Matt replied. They sat, Matt eating and Josh smoking, until Matt's phone gave a squawk. He flipped it open and snapped it shut again.

"See ya."

He walked off at a clip.

Before bed, Josh signed his check and left it on the table for his mom. She'd hand him whatever cash was left over once she had paid the bills. He wasn't leaving this week.

It was the next payday before Josh saw Matt again, a chance meeting at the falafel shop just off campus.

"Hey, man, long time no see!" Matt gestured broadly at Josh for the benefit of a bunch of first years. Half of them had their mouths full, attentive to Matt as they glanced, uninterested, at Josh.

"See this guy? One of my oldest buds. Great guy. Makes a mean fry." It took Matt a second to realize his rhyme; when he did, he laughed too loudly and slapped his leg. "I'm Doug, man."

Josh nodded and walked over to the order counter. Matt kept up his dealer patter for the kids, dipping his hands into this pocket or that, then coming up empty with a grin, saying, "Four bucks." Matt must be selling pills now. The young customers conferred with each other. They startled as the shop's glass door slammed open. A guy sprinted at Matt. There was the sound of fist-to-face impact and, before anyone could react, the guy was out the door in a rush of grey and blue, leaving Matt curled on the tiled cement of the falafel shop doorway with his knees to his chest and his hands to his face. His customers stood like a herd of cows, the whites of their eyes showing as they glanced at each other. A couple of them swallowed what they were eating, but no one moved. There was blood, and Matt's eyes were already swelling.

Josh took Matt to emergency. Matt wouldn't answer any questions about what had happened, so Josh sat doodling spaceships on his cigarette pack with a hospital pen while Matt shifted around, picking at the lining in his jacket and checking all the pockets. A doctor eventually set Matt's nose and gave him one stitch. As the hospital door slid open to release them, Matt reached into his pocket, popped a pill, and marched off into the dark.

Weeks went by after that with no Matt, again. Doug was also missing a lot of nights at the Fry Shack, and Josh was taking all those shifts to save up extra money, so when the phone rang, Josh jumped for it without checking the number. But it wasn't Doug, it was Matt's mom.

"Matt hasn't been here in a while," she said. "But I thought maybe…is he staying with you?"

She sounded so hopeful that Josh lied and told her Matt had stopped by the Shack the night before.

A few Thursdays later, Josh was changing the fryer oil when her number showed up on his phone again, then she called a couple of times more. This seemed like a bad sign, so Josh turned off the ringer for the rest of his shift.

He checked his messages before lunch on Saturday; Matt had been arrested and taken to remand. Josh called in sick.

"Well, Lazy Daisy," said Doug. "I guess I'll work the night shift myself."

Josh hung up the phone, grabbed a clean shirt, and headed for Matt's subdivision. He felt guilty and wanted to see Matt's mom. Houses on the other side of town were big, with things like standalone freezers and extra cars. Matt's parents had all kinds of fancy stuff: frozen dinners, matching dishes, a fridge that made ice, and a Garburator.

As she opened the door, Josh thought Matt's mom looked weird: dried out, but with watery eyes.

"You want a coffee?" she asked, sounding like she didn't care if he had a coffee or not. "I've got some on – my sister is coming over."

Josh nodded and followed her through the living room to the kitchen.

She filled a cup for him, then took an apple out of a bowl on the counter, cut it, and arranged the slices on a plate like an after-school snack. She pushed the plate at Josh, who took a piece to be polite then went to sit at the table.

"Did you know?" asked Matt's mom, following him with the plate. "That he was dealing?"

Josh had never ratted on anything Matt did, so he said no.

Matt's mom bobbled her head up and down.

"You were his best friend, and you didn't know." Her voice rose. "Spare me."

She slammed the plate down, sending apple wedges bouncing from the dish to the tabletop, and strode to the front closet, where she dragged Matt's red jacket off the hanger. Josh thought maybe he should say something comforting, but his mind came up blank.

"Get out of this house, please," she said. "And take this fucking jacket with you."

She whipped the jacket at him. It carried the musty odor of weed, Speed Stick, and young man.

Josh caught the coat. He was somehow immobilized until Matt's mom opened the front door and gestured him out. Josh's hand trembled a little as he brushed at some dust on the jacket and left.

Not sure what to do with himself, Josh headed for work, where he found Doug unlocking the freezers.

"You said you weren't coming," Doug growled. "I would have stayed home tonight if I'd known you could work. Pain in my ass."

Doug flicked on the "Open" sign, then turned away to survey the bus station. Josh watched the waves of heat begin to move in the fryer tub, when Doug softened.

"Heard about your buddy."

Josh nodded, then hung up Matt's coat and started pulling fries out of the freezer compartment and moving them to the fridge beside the fryer.

"I'm going to get smokes," said Doug. "You want some?"

Josh nodded again. When Doug came back, Josh shoved the gift into his back pocket, but he didn't take any breaks that night because the Shack was so busy that even Doug threw on some fries a little early. It was a tough shift; Josh was distracted, and he messed up so many orders that Doug stopped being sympathetic. He got pissed off and sent Josh home.

"Mistakes lose money, and that ain't funny," he said, pointing Josh out of the truck.

Josh muttered that Doug should fuck right off and turned to leave, but Doug stopped him, pointing at Matt's jacket.

"Don't forget that."

Josh rammed his arms into the jacket and stomped out. Ten steps away from the Fry Shack, he pulled out a cigarette but couldn't find his lighter.

If you needed fire, Matt had always been the guy, so Josh felt around the jacket pockets until he located a Bic. When he pulled it out from the shoulder pocket, some twenties came with it. Josh lit his cigarette before he counted the cash – a hundred bucks.

At home, Josh huddled on the front step, looking out past the streetlights into the dark. It started to cool off, but he wasn't in the mood to sleep, so he shoved his hands deep into the front pockets of Matt's coat. Plastic crinkled somewhere in the jacket's lining and Josh dug for it, thinking it would be some dried-up weed, or just empty, but the bag was full of cash.

"Holy shit." He set his cigarette at the corner of his mouth to open the baggie with both hands. He counted the bills: two thousand dollars, in hundreds.

There was still one bus tonight. He scrawled a note to his mom saying he'd be back to clean out his room once he got a place and left $500 in Matt money on the table for her.

Josh walked back to the bus depot, trying to stay cool, hoping this cash wouldn't get him in trouble.

When he got close, Josh saw the bus station loom up behind the Fry Shack, where Doug was drinking and counting money on his own. Josh hadn't been on the ordering side of the Fry Shack for a long time. From here, it looked a lot cleaner than it was. Josh walked up to the window.

"Greek fries, please."

It seemed to take all of Doug's concentration to pile the fries into their cardboard container. Without looking up, he took Josh's hundred and handed back the change, bulldozing a path through old crumbs with the coins before he slid the service window shut. Doug never cared who the customers were as long as they handed over six bucks for 40 cents worth of fries and cheese.

Josh popped a fry into his mouth and turned toward the station. Once he got to the city, he'd call Doug and tell him to look for a new fry guy because Doug wouldn't remember if Josh told him now. As Josh began the march across the street, he heard the service window scratch open.

"See ya," called Doug. "Wouldn't wanna be ya."

WHEN HENRY BIT SHELBY

Izzy Beach

Henry had intended to stop seeing clients. She canceled all appointments with her regulars, referring them accordingly to friends and acquaintances looking for more human familiars. She already organized her estate as best and as discreetly as she could and canceling with her new clients was her final task.

Most of her possessions, cultivated over her hundreds of years, were already donated or sold to establishments Henry believed worth her time. The rest stayed at her apartment in the center of the city. The deed for which was ready to be given to Marguerite upon the moment of Henry's departure.

Henry had been avoiding Marguerite for the past few weeks. She was cowardly for it, she knew that, but Marguerite would have known what Henry was doing and tried to stop her. She was a lot younger than Henry, turned only thirty-six years ago by Henry herself. In the throes of her immortality, Marguerite spent her nights in the underground seducing humans and reveling in their lust. Henry couldn't blame her, she was the same in her youth, but she knew there would be no understanding from Marguerite, only anger.

Henry was prepared to spend her last week in solitude. Besides Marguerite, there was no one else she cared to be with. She had her books and her cat, Fuzz, for company. This, she convinced herself, was what she wanted.

Henry blamed the computer, as she often did.

It had dinged—Henry hated when it dinged. She was in the process of closing the tabs, her cursor hovering over the last one, when it happened. It was her professional email, her only email, the one she got client requests on. She knew she should have just deleted the account entirely, but if Henry was honest, she really didn't know how to do that.

She saw the name first, *Shelby Miller*. A normal name, pleasant and plain. It didn't look like a pseudonym but if it was, it was the most unassuming one she had ever seen—Henry was used to getting inquiries from "Scarlets" and "Ravens" and even a "Belladonna" once.

There was nothing particularly spectacular about Shelby Miller's email. Twenty-four years old, a secretary at a law firm downtown, just recently ended a six-year relationship, looking to practice dating before starting the real thing. There was nothing of the gothic, blood-filled fantasies Henry was used to. Which, Henry supposed, *was* spectacular in its own way.

Though, if Shelby Miller had found her way to Henry, there must be some semblance of blood-filled fantasies, else she wouldn't have offered up her neck to a vampire in exchange for a date.

There was no reason for Henry to answer the email. She had already stocked up on blood from the hospital for the remaining week and, though hospital blood had a tang to it that made Henry wonder what disinfectant tasted like, she didn't need a warm body to sate her hunger. She didn't need to, but perhaps she wanted to.

It was simple then, if you looked at it like that, why Henry agreed to meet Shelby for drinks that Friday. She wanted something fresh.

When the night arrived, Henry woke up just as the sun had finished setting and began her pre-date routine.

First, she brushed her teeth thoroughly. Using items often found in a dentist's office, Henry scraped, flossed and polished her teeth until they were the perfect glossy white of ivory. Then she showered. This was the shortest part of her routine even if she washed her hair—which she did that night. And finally, she had to pick out the right clothes. Henry had been in her work long enough to learn what her clients wanted based on the letters they sent her. Over the years, she had accumulated a wardrobe full of clothing that could accommodate a wide array of desires.

If her client liked *Twilight* and read popular Familiar blogs, Henry wore neutral clothes with more of a masculine edge. If her clients wanted a Carmilla or mentioned succubi, she donned a slinky black dress and heels. If they liked Stoker or asked what her favorite time period to live in was, she'd wear a frilly white Edwardian shirt and high-waisted slacks.

The clothes were important to Henry. She did not know what she looked like; when she looked in a mirror, it reflected back nothing, so she focused on the clothes. She could lay them out on her bed and inspect them as she might her own reflection. Things such as her face she did not touch; she never wore makeup as the precision of something like a cat eye was near impossible to do blind.

Henry did care about her hair, though. It was easier than makeup because she could feel the textures and manipulate accordingly. She kept it at a length that could be interpreted as feminine or masculine depending on how she styled it. Long enough for tousled curls and short enough to be slicked back.

Shelby had not given Henry any hint in her letter to what she would like to see when they met. Henry stood before her closet in her bathrobe, fresh from the shower and unusually stumped. She ran her hands over all the fabrics. Soft velvet; smooth satin; rough linen. They all swooshed past her swiftly moving fingers. In Shelby Miller's lack of instruction, she had given Henry a rare gift; a chance to wear what she wanted.

For the first time in a long time, Henry, without the pretense of another's desire, chose an outfit on her own.

Shelby never had the desire to be bitten by a vampire. She knew it was something people sought, and she could pretend to understand why, but she never saw that desire in herself. Brie said it was because she hadn't really talked to one and, once she did, she would understand the appeal. Shelby argued that sentiment—the guy that worked the night shift at her bodega was a vampire and they had spoken many times! Granted their conversations were limited to "Cash or card?" and "A pack of Marlboro Reds, please," but Brie didn't need to know that.

Despite Shelby's hesitation, Brie still managed to convince her to write up a profile on *Familiar with the Night*—an online matchmaking site dedicated to connecting humans to vampires for various reasons. For her part, Shelby thought it would at least help her get over Diane.

WHEN HENRY BIT SHELBY

Shelby had kept mostly to herself after Diane left for London. Giving a simple "I'm getting through it," when friends asked her how she was doing. She didn't want to be that lesbian that always talked about her ex. Luckily, most people seemed to believe her facade and, after three months, they stopped asking about it. But Brie was a different breed; she was nosy, and she knew Shelby too well.

Her friend had shown up unannounced at Shelby's studio a week ago. She arrived with take-out and a bottle of wine, claiming she was "just in the neighborhood." It was a planned attack, Shelby was convinced, a ploy to catch her in a weakened state. Which Brie surely did—when Brie pressed her buzzer, Shelby was curled up on the couch an hour into her third re-watch of *Bridget Jones's Diary*. There was no way she could clean up the pile of used tissue boxes and unwashed dishes on her coffee table in the five minutes it took her friend to ride the elevator. But the take-out was Shelby's favorite, so she couldn't stay mad when Brie pushed through her door and, upon viewing the state of Shelby's apartment, announced that this was an intervention.

Shelby supposed she should be grateful that Brie had arrived when she did. Shelby knew she was spiraling. Her days had become monotonous since Diane left. A cycle of work, getting stoned, scrolling through Diane's Instagram, and crying. Her face had begun to hurt from so much crying, her eyes perpetually red and puffy even when they were dry. She was a few weeks away from catatonic. Thankfully, Brie, as hectic and unreliable as she could be, had a way of getting things out of Shelby she didn't want to admit. Though Shelby knew if it weren't for the wine, she wouldn't have said as much as she did.

No, she had not gone on a date since the breakup. No, she hadn't had sex either. Masturbating? She tried, sure, but it just depressed her; she was never able to finish. It just wasn't the same as it was with Diane.

This last confession earned a reprimand from Brie.

"Uh-uhn! That bitch ate up all your sexual energy and then left you!" Brie exclaimed, making Shelby wince and take another gulp of wine. She turned on Shelby with a loving but stern expression. "You need to stop moping and do something about it."

That's when the topic of vampires came up. Brie had gone out with a few through *Familiar with the Night*, even had sex with some. Brie was lounging on the floor, take-out container on her lap as she told Shelby of her vampiric escapades. The comedic combination of a discussion on blood kinks and a mouthful of Pad Thai was enough to entrance Shelby. Though she did have her hesitations.

"You don't *have* to have sex with them," Brie explained, when Shelby asked, "but some of their clients do, consensually, of course. It's just an option. If you don't want to, that's okay." She paused, eyeing Shelby for a moment. "It's also okay if you *do* want to."

Shelby chose to ignore Brie's last comment, hiding her red cheeks with another sip of wine. She thought for a moment. She hated to admit it, but Brie's idea was a good one. A date with someone bound to be interesting, someone to get her out of her rut with no strings attached and no expectations. Well, except for one.

"So," Shelby began, "in exchange for going on a date with me, they get to... um..."

"Bite you? Shel, don't be a prude." Brie rolled her eyes, but she was smiling. "They won't *drain* you. That rarely happens these days anyway, thanks in part to communities like *Familiar!*"

"Won't it hurt?"

Brie shrugged, "A little, it kinda just feels like a hickey but better."

Shelby hadn't had a hickey since high school, even then it was a blip in her memory. She recalled a fumbling tryst in the back seat of her best friend's car the summer before they started college—they had the kind of friendship full of practice kisses for imaginary boyfriends that neither would end up having. The bites she was given and gave in that backseat were light and wet, fearful of leaving a mark. The next day there was no proof on her skin that she didn't imagine the whole thing—they never spoke of it again so, really, she may have.

Then Shelby met Diane on the second day of freshman orientation and forgot everyone else. They were together all four years and an extra year and a half after that just for good measure. Diane had a certain way she liked things, and, being the less experienced one, Shelby just let her take the lead. If it wasn't a part of Diane's desires, it wasn't a part of Shelby's.

So, Shelby never had the desire to be bitten by anyone, much less a vampire.

That is, until she met Henry.

WHEN HENRY BIT SHELBY

Henry arrived at the bar a few minutes early. This was what she usually did on dates.

The barkeep, Kathy, gave her a nod when she stepped inside. It was named *Laura's*. Opened by familiars in the late aughts, it was a place for humans and vampires to safely intermingle. Henry had been going there since it opened. The original owners were human friends of hers and even though they passed a few years ago, Henry still patronized it as often as she could—she had even left a small fortune for them in her will and hoped that it would help keep *Laura's* afloat for years to come.

Henry had called ahead and reserved a preferred booth in the back. That's where she waited for Shelby. She contemplated ordering a drink, but she didn't want to ruin her appetite. Shelby had written in a second email confirming their plans that her type was O- which happened to be Henry's favorite.

Though it was a Friday night, the bar was far from full. A handful of vampires and humans occupied the bar and a few couples huddled in the other booths. This was likely why Henry noticed when Shelby came through the door.

She was bundled in a coat and a red scarf wrapped over her mouth, shielding her from the snowfall outside. Henry had forgotten about the weather as she traveled underground to avoid humans and the risk of sunlight; she felt bad that Shelby had to travel in the snow.

Shelby unwrapped the scarf and looked around, the inquisitive but non-judgmental gaze of someone slightly out of their element. Her nose was pink from the cold and her round cheeks matched their hue.

Henry watched as Shelby removed her coat and shook out her light hair. The movement caused Henry to get a whiff of her shampoo—lavender, sweet. It must have been a popular brand because Henry recognized it from past clients. Under the coat, she wore a pair of brown slacks that hugged her round hips and a loose button-up shirt that revealed the pale expanse of skin on her chest, clavicle, and throat. Shelby was still glancing around when Henry raised her hand in greeting.

Everything about Shelby was round and supple like a ripened fruit. Her eyes were hazel and abnormally large, surrounded by long light lashes. Freckles dotted her face, some landing on her small pink mouth. When Shelby reached Henry she smiled, revealing a gap in her front teeth, and held out an ungloved hand.

"You must be Henry," she said breathlessly. "It's nice to meet you."

It wasn't that Henry was beautiful. Shelby had seen plenty of beautiful people in her life, kissed a few, fell in love with one. She even found herself beautiful at times. On those good days when her hair fell just right, and she momentarily forgot every skinny supermodel long enough to love her chubby tummy. No, Shelby could handle beautiful. Henry wasn't that.

The surface of her was easy to describe. Short dark hair, curly and messy, not in a fashionable way but in a way that said she really did just get out of bed; very pale skin, which Shelby expected; a mouth opened slightly in greeting; long nose, a little hooked and rounded at the tip; brows dark and creased, perpetual concern. But all of that Shelby bypassed quickly, as if her brain knew there was something more underneath.

Henry was otherworldly. The paleness of her skin was a distraction from the pearlescence of it. It was the fine hairs on her cheeks, Shelby realized, that caused the shimmer. Her partly open mouth was too soft-looking, too pink. It didn't match the pointed canines. At a glance, Shelby might not have noticed that they were slightly longer than a human's and as white as the falling snow outside. But Shelby was staring openly and saw everything. Henry's eyes were the last thing Shelby's gaze landed on, and she was glad for it because she realized she could not look away. They were a dark color that Shelby couldn't quite capture. In her seat, Shelby was sure they were brown, but as Henry stood to greet her, they were green, emerald and unreal.

"It is nice to meet you too, Shelby." Henry's voice was softer than Shelby would have thought. A little raspy at the corners but clear. The volume kept low enough to be heard by Shelby and no one else. Henry gave her a smile, half open but covering the fangs—Shelby wondered if that smile was practiced—and held out her hand.

The skin wasn't cold. It wasn't warm either. Not the clammy skin of a human on a first date—not like Shelby's skin. It was the same temperature as the air in the bar. Dry but soft. There were no calluses, no bumps from scars or scabs; the creases in the palm and finger joints seemed to be the only blemish Shelby could feel.

She let go and Henry gestured to the booth.

"Would you like to order a drink? I can get you a menu." Henry slid back into her seat. Shelby followed her, doing her best to avoid getting tangled in her scarf and coat.

"Oh, yes please!" The thought of something strong and alcoholic was very appealing to Shelby. She was nervous, though she hoped she didn't seem unusually nervous. Henry nodded and raised a hand towards the barkeep. In a matter of minutes, there was a menu in front of Shelby.

"I'll have a..." Shelby paused, her eyes glazing over the list of drinks, not wanting to pick something that sounded too juvenile, "a glass of Merlot, please." That was sophisticated enough. Though maybe *red* wine was a bit too stereotypical...

Before Shelby could spiral, the waitress nodded and returned to the bar with Shelby's order.

Shelby turned back to Henry, relieved that she would soon have something to do with her hands—they were currently under the table, her fingers tapping on her knee—and opened her mouth to say something. But all interesting questions, flirty banter, and frankly everything left Shelby's mind, because Henry's eyes were blue now, honest to God, Caribbean Ocean blue. Maybe she was hallucinating.

"I hope the weather wasn't too terrible for you," Henry said, watching as Shelby stared at her.

She never got used to it, seeing humans see her and never really knowing what they were looking at. There was one portrait of Henry that she kept. Painted as a wedding gift for her ex-fiancé a week before Henry was turned, it depicted a young woman in blue with long dark hair and a somber expression. Henry barely remembered sitting for the portrait, much less what she thought of it in comparison to her own human reflection after it was completed.

She supposed she could have gotten another painting done, but she liked seeing people see her and not knowing what it was they saw. It was like a game, a secret just for her. She couldn't see herself, but she saw them so clearly. She saw what they wanted. It was written all over their face, it was in their scent, the way their posture shifted. This was especially true with humans.

Henry always knew which humans were attracted to her, even if they didn't know it. She could smell it on them. It was musky and wet, like something unearthed. Long ago, Henry might have rolled her eyes at that human reaction, so base and so animal. Now she couldn't deny the appeal. Every vampire knew an aroused human tasted the best.

Shelby had that smell now, Henry noticed, barely hidden behind a floral perfume.

Henry leaned forward, smiling in a way that showed her teeth—she wanted to see what Shelby thought of them—and asked her how her day was.

Henry said something. Shelby tried her best to make her brain process the words, but Henry's eyes were back to brown again—this time they were more hazel, with lots of gold. Shelby thought that this color might be her favorite. Henry was smiling too, and her mouth was starting to look enticing. There were two indents on her bottom lip where the fangs, halfway hidden beneath a plump upper lip, pressed into the skin. It was cute, Shelby realized. At least to her.

"Sorry!" Shelby said, shaking her head. She wondered if Henry had some kind of hypnosis superpower, like Dracula. "Can you repeat that?"

Maybe that's why everything seemed to have vacated her brain and all she was left with was white noise. Or maybe she just had a crush. She couldn't remember what that was like. It had been so long.

Henry laughed. The noise seemed so normal, a little too snorty to be beautiful but sweet and soft. The widening of her mouth showed Shelby the full range of her teeth. The bottom canines were sharp too but not as long.

"You've never talked to a vampire, have you?" Henry asked, with a tilt of her head that told Shelby she already knew the answer.

"Not in length," Shelby admitted. She could feel the blood rush to her cheeks, and she was sure they were pink. "This is all new for me. I'm a little nervous."

"It's okay to be nervous." Henry leaned back, still smiling. "It's part of the experience, or fantasy, that little dose of fear." Henry paused, running a finger along a seam in the table before she met Shelby's eye again. "My clients, they like the threat of pain," she said, "the pleasure of longing. At least, that's what I hear."

Shelby wondered if that was why she let Brie sign her up for this. Maybe what she really wanted was pain. Maybe she was just punishing herself for everything that happened with Diane. Maybe she was going on a date with Henry because she knew it wasn't going anywhere and perpetual longing was the only thing Shelby was good for.

"Your other clients told you that?" Shelby asked as Kathy passed them, placing a teeming glass of wine in front of Shelby on her way. Shelby looked relieved and pulled her hands from under the table to take a sip. Henry hoped she didn't drink too much; intoxicated blood was not for her tastes.

"Some, though these are mostly my suspicions," Henry admitted. Candor with her clients was out of the ordinary, but tonight she let the words flow. "The danger of my kind appeals to their desires. I think that's why they come to me. I am the thing that goes bump in the night but they can touch me. There is something satisfactory about that." Henry watched as Shelby took another sip. "What about you? Is that why you came to me?"

Shelby spluttered a bit and Henry wondered if she was going to cough up some wine. Henry felt a little bad about teasing her, but it had been a while since she had such a novice client. Most of them knew a lot about her kind, or at least pretended they did. They must've thought their knowledge would impress Henry, but she found that familiarity a little tiresome after a while.

Shelby recovered as smoothly as she could and wiped her lips with the mini cocktail napkin before saying, "I don't really know."

She paused for a moment, seemed to be deep in thought, then spoke again. "I suppose I'm, well, lonely, I guess. Out of practice and in need of practice." Shelby shook her head, smiling, eyes turned down to the glass. "That probably sounds silly to you."

"No, it doesn't," Henry said. In fact, Shelby's honesty was endearing. None of her clients ever admitted they were lonely. Though, they never had to. Henry knew. She could taste it in their blood, see it in their eyes, their smiles, the characters they played. She saw the unnamed desire behind the fantasy: everyone wants to be wanted; everyone wants to be known.

Henry wasn't quite sure what she saw in Shelby yet; so, she watched and waited.

Shelby looked back, meeting Henry's eyes for a split second before she glanced down. But she spoke again, this time a little quieter.

"My last relationship," Shelby let out a short dry laugh, "I just went along with everything. I molded myself to be someone I thought she'd like. It worked for a while, she loved me, but after a time I just started to feel like *shit*. And I couldn't ignore it." Shelby paused, her fingers slowly twisting the stem of the wine glass, the contents sloshing.

"You ended it?" Henry prompted when the silence lingered.

"I wish I had the guts to do that." Shelby snorted. "No, she left me. Got offered a job in London and accepted it. Didn't even tell me until two weeks before she left." She sighed and sat back in the booth. "I was ruined. A total mess... still kinda am a total mess, if I'm honest." She paused to take a long sip of wine before continuing. "I know it's good that it ended, it needed to, it was time, but she's the only person I ever really wanted and now I don't know what to do with myself."

The last words came out slowly as if being pushed through a small hole. After she said it, Shelby looked up and met Henry's eyes. Henry held her gaze, those big hazel eyes seemed a bit dewy.

"So, I guess to answer your question," Shelby smiled sadly,

her gap tooth showing, "I'm here to see if I am truly dead inside or if I can want someone again," and a bit quieter, "if I can love someone again."

Henry laughed, she couldn't help it, there was something so sweet about Shelby's words. An innocence that Henry hadn't experienced since she was human herself. Henry knew Shelby could want again, wanting was easy—Shelby didn't know it but she was wanting right now; her want was pungent. Love on the other hand... Well, Henry wasn't there to love Shelby, but she didn't doubt Shelby would find what she was looking for again.

Henry leaned forward, calling forth the words she knew Shelby wanted to hear. "As someone who has lived hundreds of years and experienced so many heartbreaks, I can tell you, Shelby, you will love again. Even if you try not to, you will. Love is impossible to avoid."

It wasn't a lie, but it wasn't something Henry found soothing anymore. She remembered her loves. Only remembered; they were all lost to her now. The humans she'd watched grow blissfully old and die leaving her wrought with grief and envy. And the vampires... there had only been one she'd lost but one was enough. Henry watched her sire—a vampire who was only half a century older than Henry when he turned her— fold into his hunger, his age. She watched his mind crumble under the pressure of his years. She remembered his face the last time she saw him, the day he died. Sallow and grinning, his eyes red with hunger despite the blood that covered his mouth. That was the day she learned *forever* was nothing but a blackened eternity for the immortal to cower before.

As Henry watched Shelby from across the table, eyes wide and wet with unshed tears, she felt a pang of familiar jealousy. Shelby didn't know how lucky she was to have death always lingering in the distance. Heartbreak and all, Henry envied her more than she wanted to admit; she envied that promise of an end.

Shelby willed herself not to cry. Henry's face seemed so open, so genuine. Her words hammered into Shelby's heart. She suddenly had the urge to reach over and take Henry's hands in hers. The feeling was bubbling inside her, ready to burst but, luckily, the fear of embarrassment won out.

"Thank you," Shelby said, her voice a little watery but she covered it up with a delicate sip of wine. Then she laughed a little. "Sorry for being such a bummer."

"Well, that's the good thing about this little arrangement," Henry said, "you can be as much of a bummer as you want, and I'll still stay here and listen to it all."

For a price, Shelby thought. She glanced down at her glass; it was almost empty.

"I don't want to be a bummer anymore," Shelby said quietly, twisting the stem between her fingers.

"Then tell me," Henry leaned back, tilting her head to the side and Shelby saw that her eyes hadn't changed. They were still that lovely gold-brown Shelby liked. "Do you think you could want again?" Henry asked, and she smiled, grinning like a jack-o'-lantern.

It was the teeth, Shelby reasoned. Despite their sharpness, they were inviting, and Shelby found that her eyes were unable to leave Henry's mouth. The softness of her lips, the red of her gums, and the shock of white protruding from them. Shelby wondered if it was just the dry spell, or the wine, or her confession, but she realized she wanted Henry to bite her. Badly.

There was nothing more to say, so, when Henry stood, her hand outstretched, Shelby stood too.

There was a backstage to *Laura's*. Behind a heavy green curtain was a staircase leading down to a hallway lined with rooms. The floors were fine carpets, and the walls were covered in pale golden paper. The light fixtures were gloomy and romantic, made of shiny brass swirls. As Henry led her through, Shelby watched as the illumination shimmered over Henry's form. She seemed to wade through the light as if it were water.

They reached a door; there was a number on it, but Shelby barely noticed because she was holding Henry's hand. The skin had grown warmer under her touch, and she let herself be guided into the room. It was cozy and low lit like the hallway. There was an adjacent bathroom, the door slightly ajar, and a bed, with copious amounts of red velvet pillows adorning it, was set up in the corner of the room. The bed was placed in a way meant to be interpreted as unassuming, but its presence made Shelby slow down.

Henry released her hand and took a step, two steps, away from her.

"How does this work?" Shelby asked as she turned to drop her coat and purse on the plush chair next to the door.

When she looked back, Henry had her hands clasped behind her and she was watching Shelby intently.

"I bite you," she said simply. "It can be as intimate as sex, that's why the bed's there." She nodded to it, "Just in case that's how the familiar wants things to go."

"So, then," Shelby straightened her shirt, glad it was loose enough to allow space between the fabric and her damp skin. "It's up to me to decide how we do this?"

Henry nodded. She didn't move. She was so still that Shelby might've believed she was a statue if she were only walking by. There wasn't even the movement of breath.

"What about you?" Shelby asked. "What do you want?"

Henry laughed, the noise snaked down Shelby's chest and settled low in her stomach. "I only want one thing, Shelby, and you're here to give that to me."

Shelby shivered; she knew that. "But what if there's something you don't—?"

"Then I'll tell you," Henry cut in gently. Her body swayed forward a bit, as if she were about to take a step towards Shelby, but she didn't. Then she smiled again, showing her teeth. "Shelby, what do *you* want?"

Shelby looked at Henry. Let her eyes roam over her figure, the smooth lines of her body, the gentle curve of her hip and the jut of her shoulders. She imagined what it would feel like to tuck her fingers under Henry's collar and pull the garment—to the side; over her head; towards Shelby so she could catch her lips. She imagined putting her mouth on the soft skin under Henry's ear. She imagined what kind of noises Henry would make if she did that.

"Kiss me." Shelby's voice was so quiet she could barely register it. But Henry heard. She glided over, slid her hands up Shelby's neck to cup her face, and complied.

The heat was almost unbearable, and it was all from Shelby. She was radioactive, she was run through with electric currents, she was on fire. Shelby gripped Henry's forearms to steady herself. When Henry opened her mouth, so did she. The wet slide of Henry's tongue made Shelby's skin hum. Henry's hands moved to Shelby's waist and gripped tightly. Vaguely, Shelby recognized that was because her legs were losing feeling and she was growing limper and limper as the seconds passed. She raised her arms to wrap them around Henry's neck, whining into her mouth. After a time, Shelby's back met a wall, and she was sandwiched between it and Henry. Her hips rose of their own accord, trying to find something to land on. She moaned with relief when Henry's knee slid between her thighs.

Henry stopped kissing her. Shelby had to bite her lip to silence the sounds that bubbled up her throat. She was breathing heavily through her nose when she felt Henry's forehead press to hers. Shelby opened her eyes and was met with a glassy black gaze studying her. Henry was waiting for Shelby to tell her what to do.

With a shaking hand, Shelby reached up wordlessly and pressed a finger to Henry's bottom lip. Henry opened her mouth revealing those beautiful teeth. Shelby ran her finger along the point, letting it scratch the skin. Henry's tongue darted out to lick the mark and Shelby sighed as Henry pulled the rest of the finger into her mouth.

"Bite me. Please."

It was horribly embarrassing how hungry Henry had become. Shelby just fell right into Henry's hands, the perfect final meal. She responded tenfold to every practiced and perfected move Henry performed for her. In her ear, Henry could hear the thrum of blood coursing through Shelby's veins, the pulse of it beating under her burning skin. At Shelby's command, Henry bent down and sunk her teeth into the juncture between her neck and shoulder.

First was the salt, the sweat covered skin. The white flesh underneath. Then, the rush. It flooded her mouth and practically made Henry moan. Shelby had wrapped her fingers in the hair at the nape of Henry's neck and Henry let her even though it pulled uncomfortably. That musky scent of arousal wafted off Shelby in droves. She cried out and ground her hips into Henry's thigh when Henry began to suck.

The blood was sweet and hot. Henry closed her eyes and swallowed the first gulp. It ran down her throat and warmed her body. There was a burn to it, most likely from the wine, and Henry was surprised to find that she enjoyed the kick. She pressed her tongue over the wound made by her teeth and reveled in the new wave of blood that coursed from the opening.

Henry drank from Shelby for as long as she could without killing her. It should have been a herculean effort to pull away, but Henry did it with ease. She swallowed the left-over blood and licked the remnants from her own mouth before she straightened.

Shelby slumped against the wall, her eyelids half closed, and her chin tilted up. She was breathing heavily too, and Henry reached down to take her hands.

"You need to rest," she said as she guided Shelby to the bed. Shelby only nodded and yawned. She took to the bed easily, sinking into the plushness with a smile. Henry left her there for a moment to fill up a glass of water and rummage in the cabinet for a packaged cookie that Shelby could eat when she woke up.

By the time Henry came back Shelby was fast asleep and snoring. The wound on her neck was already closing and Henry knew by the next day it would only be four small scabs. Henry placed the water and cookie on the bedside table. She let her fingers linger on Shelby's cheek for a moment, feeling the flush return to her skin. Then she turned away, locking the door on the inside and closing it softly behind her.

Henry didn't pick favorites, but she was glad Shelby was her last.

She left *Laura's*—letting Kathy know Shelby was sleeping in room 13 and asking if she would check on her in a few hours—and walked home above ground.

This was a pleasure she didn't often allot herself, but she thought her last night should be special. The city around her was still alive despite the early hour. She watched the humans pass, clutching each other as they walked. The air they exhaled was sweet smoke and Henry, who didn't *need* to breathe, copied them anyway. She let her lungs fill and watched as her own air clouded before her face. As Henry walked, she found herself bumping against the crowd around her. She was drawn to them. They radiated heat; they were warm bodies wrapped around warm bodies seeking warmth. The tangle of them was beautiful and Henry felt that old twinge of longing to be enveloped too.

Her apartment was an old one overlooking the river. She had been in the city for so long sometimes her home felt like its birth point. The brick seemed to grow from the cobblestoned street like an ancient tree. Henry climbed the stairs, enjoying the wooden creaks, and bypassed her front door. She had already left enough cat food for Fuzz and opened all the curtains. The letter for Marguerite was propped up on her writing desk, ready to be opened the next night; there was no need for her to say goodbye again. Instead, she climbed further past the sixth, seventh, and eighth floors until she finally made it to the rooftop.

The snow had stopped hours ago, leaving a few inches of fluffy white in its place. Henry walked over it towards the concrete lip of the roof. She wondered if her footprints would make it through the day. Perhaps they would melt away in the sun, the last remnants of her gone. She reached the edge and surveyed the city.

In the apartments below her, people were waking up for their early morning shifts. Their lights switched on, casting warm glows through their windows over the snow-covered sidewalks. Henry listened to their bustle and watched the cars drive by the already plowed roads. She felt an overwhelming sense of peace drift over her. There was nothing more wonderful to listen to, she realized, than the world waking up.

It was still dark but, in the distance, there was a glimmer. Light reached up from beyond the horizon, stretching like the limbs of a drowsy child. The glow began to expand, red and purple rays slashed through the sky. The clouds tinged orange and pink and gold; brilliant, to match the incoming sun. Henry watched, entranced. She had not seen a sunrise since she was a human, and couldn't believe she had spent her immortal life in such darkness, without this simple beauty.

Henry supposed this was why she chose first light as her death. She wanted the last thing she saw to be beautiful.

TYPHOID HARRY

Lewis DeSimone

"I've been cooped up for one week too many," he says. "I really have to get out of Dodge." In the background of the call, I can hear the cacophonous banging of pots and pans. It's rush hour in New York, time to cheer on the essential workers. A thousand miles away, where I am, you can hardly tell anything unusual is going on. The streets in this town are no emptier than they were before all this started. That's why I moved here—to be in a place where nothing happens. I needed a whole lot of nothing.

I haven't heard Harry's voice in two years, since I got out of Dodge myself. Since then, our relationship has subsisted largely on shared memes on Facebook.

"I'm losing my mind, Jude." His studio apartment is starting to close in on him, he tells me, and the sirens are constant. I can't hear them at the moment, of course; the kitchen chorus is too loud. "I thought I'd take advantage of the situation and drive across the country, check one more thing off the bucket list."

"A road trip?" I ask. "I didn't even know you could drive." Harry's lived in New York his entire life and, as far as I know, has never even rented a car.

Of course he can drive, he assures me—unconvincingly. I decide to take his word for it, but I can't help picturing Diane Keaton behind the wheel of her VW, threatening to turn *Annie Hall* into *The French Connection*.

"So anyway," he says as the noise dies down (finally, he seems to be carrying the phone away from the window), "I was wondering if I could stay with you for a couple of days along the way."

The last few words seem to echo, and I imagine him now

58

sitting on the edge of the bathtub to get away from the pots and pans.

I'm not sure what to say. With things as they are, I have friends across the street I haven't seen in weeks except when we run into each other, mask-clad, at the grocery store. Now I'm going to welcome someone from ground zero into my house? A modern-day Typhoid Mary, shedding virus from coast to coast.

"I totally understand if you're uncomfortable," he says. Harry has mastered the art of the passive-aggressive, half-hearted request, the kind that comes with a don't-mind-me-I'll-sit-in-the-dark escape hatch. "But I've barely gone outside in weeks, so I'm sure I'm safe. And besides, we can keep our distance."

It doesn't take long to realize that my hesitation has less to do with the pandemic than with how we left things in New York. Or how *I* left things. It never occurred to me that those burnt bridges would ever be used again.

I'm still trying to make sense of the request when he launches into a story. Harry always has a story up his sleeve. "I'm not the only one losing his mind," he says. "A couple I know are having a relationship meltdown from being quarantined together. Too much of a good thing. Anyway, one of them has started confiding in me: it turns out their problems started long before COVID. For months, he's been suspicious his lover was having an affair, but now they're locked in together 24/7. Careful what you wish for."

Under the circumstances, the friend's only outlet is to call Harry and spill.

"Does it help?" I ask.

"I think so. It's helping *him*, anyway. And complicating things for me."

"For you? Why?"

"Oh, it's a long story. I'll tell you all about it when I get there."

And that's the hook. I've always been a sucker for Harry's stories. He fills them with tangents, backtracking again and again to delay the punch line and build suspense. You never know quite where Harry's stories are going, and that, I guess, is the point. As long as you're hooked, as long as he knows he's reeled you in, he's met his goal.

Back in New York, my ex, Peter, would regularly drag me out for drinks with his friends, and Harry would inevitably steal the floor with a long, convoluted story that kept everyone enthralled. It was less the plot that mattered than the style. I thought of him as the James Joyce of raconteurs: nothing he said made much sense, but the language itself was enough reason to stick around. He'd pepper each tale with jokes, highlighting the absurdities of the situation to make our laughter domino across the space, one person picking up a guffaw as someone else's was just slowing down.

Peter often laughed the loudest. He came to life on those nights, with those raucous people. I was content to sit at home watching old movies on TV, but Peter insisted on getting out of the house. He worked such long hours that there were many evenings when we didn't even have dinner together, but those nights with his friends were sacrosanct, and if I wanted more together time, I had no choice but to include everyone else.

Harry had a seemingly endless library of escapades and outrageous characters—I couldn't keep them straight, even when I'd heard the stories multiple times. Was it his mother who'd found a raccoon in her garbage can, or his aunt from Toledo? Was he at Grand Central or Penn Station when he was late for a train and ran headfirst into Harvey Fierstein? That was another thing: Harry's stories were pockmarked with celebrity sightings. But it was Manhattan; celebrities were as easy to find as Starbucks.

Once the laughter subsided and we all went our own ways, the mood faded. As we rode the subway home, Peter maintained an even keel. We might have been returning from a night at the opera instead of a bar. He would comment generally on how fun the evening had been, but seldom continued any particular shred of the conversation once we were alone. When the evening was done, he put it into a box. Alone, we shared a distinct experience, one that belonged solely to us as a couple.

It's images from those drunken evenings I have in mind— Harry hunkering down in a West Village bar, regaling us with the tale of his father's hernia operation over a vodka tonic— when he arrives on my doorstep about a week after that phone call. The midafternoon sun behind him on an empty suburban street, he seems completely out of place in black jeans and a rainbow t-shirt that strains across his belly. But he puts all confusion to rest with an enthusiastic greeting.

"Hey, Jude!" he sings out with a laugh. He still thinks it's funny, the 900th time he's said it. "Virtual hug," he adds, spreading his arms wide. I smile and back up to let him in.

As ambivalent as I was at first about this visit, I have to admit how glad I am to see him. He carries a trace of New York that puts me immediately at ease—chestnuts from midtown carts, yellow cabs slaloming up 8th Avenue, everything alive and racing against time. With his first words, I'm there again, in the city's crowded, darkened streets, even before I realize I've missed it.

The once-familiar Harry charm washes over me: The bright eyes that dance around the room in search of something to comment on. The lanky limbs that he seems not to know what to do with. A deceptive innocence designed to distract from the cogs turning methodically behind those same dancing eyes, so that when the inevitable joke or insight arrives, sheer unexpectedness will enhance the humor, drive home the absurdity.

I have bottles of Purell stationed throughout the house and, after closing the door behind him, bathe my hands in the sticky gel. "How's your trip been so far?"

And he's off. He tells me about an ex he stayed with outside Pittsburgh, an accountant who moved there because his husband got a job at a local law firm. "They seem like a strange fit," he says as I lead him out to the backyard. For safety's sake, this is where I entertain on the rare occasions when anyone comes over these days, hoping the sun will kill whatever speck of virus the wind doesn't blow away.

I've made a pitcher of lemonade and pour him a glass as we settle into patio chairs on opposite sides of a cast-iron table. "Why is that?" I ask.

"I don't know," he says. "Kenny used to be so much fun. Now he's just a homebody."

"It's Pittsburgh," I say. "What's he supposed to do, organize a drag ball?"

Harry's eyes widen, but they're still almost lost under his bushy eyebrows. His hair, still flaming red, is a mess, spilling every which way over his head after a couple of days on the road. He's one of the lucky ones, still blessed with a full head of hair well into his forties, but that's a curse during quarantine. Unable to get it cut for three months, he's starting to look like Little Orphan Annie.

Between that and the scruffy beard, I have to search his face for signs of the Harry I remember. What strikes me most is the weight gain. Harry catches me looking at his belly.

"The Covid fifteen," he says, patting the beach ball above his belt. "No gym, no walks around town except to buy too many groceries, which I eat like a fiend. Starve a cold, feed an anxiety."

I smile it away as best I can, but I can't help wondering: if fifteen of those new pounds are from the past couple of months, the other ten must just be the product of middle age. Instinctively, I look down at my own belly. It's only a matter of time.

Harry doesn't linger on the digression for long. Back to the ex-boyfriend. Or his dog, to be precise. This story is all about the dog.

"He's huge," he says, stretching his arms in an echo of the faux hug he greeted me with. "A Great Dane. The dumbest creature on earth, but that's his charm. So we're sitting by the pool, and the dog seems to get jealous because Kenny's paying too much attention to me. He comes up and nudges Kenny's elbow so he ends up knocking over his drink. And while Kenny's picking up the glass—I shit you not—the dog comes around and pushes my chair so I lose my balance and somersault into the pool. Ass over tea kettle, as my father used to say."

And he laughs. I've forgotten that Harry's stories always come with a built-in laugh track—as if he's signaling you when to join in. Or maybe it's just that he's his own best audience.

It's not just the weight gain. There's something incongruous about his being here. In my imagination, Harry doesn't fit anywhere outside of Manhattan, under artificial light. Here, with all the greenery of my garden behind him, he seems dangerously out of place, a motorboat making waves on a heretofore calm lake.

Even in the old days, when I saw him a couple of times a month, I would never have called Harry a friend. *Acquaintance* was a better word. We were at opposite ends of the social circle, me there because of Peter and Harry as a friend of Ron, the fulcrum of the group, the conductor who somehow managed to make a full range of voices sing in a kind of harmony. Whether he'd brought someone into the group himself or not, Ron assigned us all roles over time. I was the quiet nerd, the one he turned to for trivia questions, just to get the conversation started. A parlor trick. "Hey," he would ask me out of nowhere, "who won the Oscar for supporting actress in 1966?" And everyone would chuckle when I answered without a pause.

And Harry was the storyteller, the jokester. Unlike most of us, he seemed to welcome the role, Ron's pigeonholing. It occurs to me now, as he goes through this literally shaggy-dog story, that I have no memory of him having a one-on-one conversation with anyone in the group, or joining anyone as we broke off in pairs and trios at closing time and headed for the subway. I wonder now if anyone in our little klatch knew Harry any better than I did. Who was Harry's best friend? Who really understood Harry? Who laughed at his jokes genuinely and was eager to hear more? Thinking back, I remember how we would all take turns going to the bathroom—long breaks, far longer than anyone needed to dispose of a beer—and whenever you came back, Harry would still be talking. That was his charm, in a way. It was what we expected of him, and he played his part better than the rest of us.

No doubt I'm not remembering everything clearly. The gray cells start to kick off after a certain age. Maybe I'm being unfair, I think. Surely he's changed in the past couple of years. I know I have. Maybe that's all it is. We have to get to know each other again. Or for the first time.

Before Harry can start another story, I suggest a walk. Throughout my own time in New York, I missed the easy access to fields and forests I'd had in my childhood, not far from the town we're in now. Central Park never really did it for me. If you made your way into a grove of trees, you might be able to find an occasional point where, if you squinted, none of the surrounding buildings were visible—but you could never escape the noise. Despite the trees and the grass all around, you never forgot that you were in a city.

It's different here. Here, it's the town that rose out of nature, not the other way around. Lakes aren't so easy to pave over.

The lake is only a few blocks from the house, which is why it was so expensive by Minnesota standards, though I still have money left over from when we sold the condo in Chelsea. Location, location, location.

There are several people on the path, strolling alone or in pairs and, for the most part, keeping an appropriate distance. An older woman power-walks past us, face hidden behind a flowery mask she must have sewn from an old bedsheet. She swerves around a young couple walking in the other direction, holding hands, maskless. Most people forgo masks at the lake.

TYPHOID HARRY

It's safe outdoors, as long as you don't get too close.

"Everyone's so blond here," Harry says.

I laugh. "A lot of them, yes," I say. "This region was settled largely by Scandinavians."

"Doesn't that get boring?"

"Why would it get boring?" I try to stick to the six-feet rule, but whenever someone passes, Harry weaves uncomfortably close to me.

"I don't know," he says. "I like variety."

"There's plenty of variety," I tell him. "We have our issues, but I don't think the color of people's hair is the problem."

The George Floyd protests are raging across the country. I may be a bit defensive, since it all started here.

"No," he says, stopping for a breath as a bare-chested young man swaggers by. "I just meant, what if you feel like a brunet now and then?"

"I didn't move here to find a boyfriend," I say. I'm striving for humor, but it comes out snippy.

I'm an editor, I spend my life correcting other people's grammar, clarifying syntax, keeping a story moving. But an editor is only effective if his client pays attention. My remark is eaten by the wind as Harry keeps walking. And talking.

"Blonds are okay, I guess. For a change."

A tree branch is leaning over the path. I push it away and duck as we pass. In the interest of changing the subject, I decide to turn back to Harry's personal soap opera. "Speaking of blonds, tell me more about these friends of yours."

"Which friends?"

"You know," I say, "the guy who's having trouble with his lover?"

"He's not blond. Did I say he was blond?"

"No, I'm just…never mind. Tell me."

I'm beginning to feel like we're having parallel conversations. Discursive as they may be, Harry's stories always seem to proceed from a script. If you manage to break in, he has a tendency to answer the question he wants you to have asked rather than the one you actually posed.

"It's kind of sad, really. He just mopes around the house a lot."

"Who does?"

"My friend. But I think he's worried about nothing." He waves a dismissive hand in the air. "I can't buy that his lover's really having an affair. He's too nice for that. And besides, if it's with the guy I think it is, he's not his type."

My head's spinning to make sense of the romantic triangle Harry just dropped on me. "Do these people have names?" I ask.

He laughs, a blush coming sheepishly, incongruously to his cheek. "I've just become so paranoid about giving anything away—in case word gets out. Even in my own head, I find myself thinking of them as A, B, and C."

The excuse is absurd, possibly evasive, but I decide to let it go. We're all entitled to our little secrets, even the ones we keep from ourselves.

When he speaks of these mystery men—whom I may or may not know—it's with an uncharacteristic shyness, as if he weren't revealing things about them so much as himself. Harry's always been quick with a quip, finding lightness in everything, skimming the surface of events. Gossip is his forte; his own life, his inner life at least, seems always tucked away, hidden behind stories about others. In this way, Harry cultivates his own air of mystery—like a spy, I think, taking note of everything while keeping himself off limits.

A and B have been together for a couple of years. He won't get more specific than that. Nor will he tell me their ages or what they do for a living, anything that might individualize them. The object is to keep them generic, almost bland. Who they are isn't what the story is about.

"They're not fucking, that's the real problem. And apparently they used to go at it like bunnies, so he can't help thinking he's having an affair."

I feel like I'm having a conversation with Abbott and Costello. "Things slow down after you've been together a while," I say. In the beginning, Peter and I made love three or four times a week. We held hands on the street every time we went out. One day a few years in, not long after the wedding, I realized we hadn't held hands in ages, but I couldn't pinpoint when we had stopped or why.

I pull away from my memories to find that Harry's still talking. I've lost track of his thread.

"So we're on the phone almost constantly. He calls me every day, just for an update, even though there's hardly ever anything new to report. Mostly he's just stuck. Literally, like we all are these days. I don't know what to tell him anymore. He used to be such a fun guy. Now he's…well, not fun."

I find myself searching Harry's face for corroborating evidence. His extroversion has always felt to me like a cover for genuine emotion; when it comes right down to it, he's unreadable. But there's something telling in the "fun" remark. Fun is Harry's raison d'être. His eyes light up when he's telling a joke or one of his rambling stories. But when the tale turns more serious, like this one, all sign of emotion drains from his face, leaving something blank and inscrutable.

"Long story short," he says, though it's too late for that—we're already on the far side of the lake—"we've grown really close over the course of all this. I'm in love with him."

"In love?"

"Yeah. I don't know why I didn't see it earlier. I guess because his relationship seemed to be going so well. He was off limits. But now…"

I'm stunned. As far as I know, Harry's never had a relationship that lasted more than a month, and here he is suddenly talking about love.

He gestures toward the lake, where a few sailboats are struggling against the wind. "I always wanted to learn to sail," he says. "It looks like a lot of fun."

It's a standard feature of Harry's storytelling routine: start with something provocative and then veer off in a completely different direction. It keeps you interested longer, waiting for the return of the juicy part.

I sputter out a chuckle and ignore the non sequitur. "In love," I repeat. "Seriously?"

"Yeah," he says, still gazing out at the boats. "I can see myself settling down with him."

"Settling down? I thought you liked your freedom."

"I love my freedom. But when you know, you know."

I remember. I fantasized about marrying Peter after our second date. But at least he wasn't already taken.

"What is it about him?"

Harry purses his lips for a moment. "I always found him attractive. But it's not just about that now. Now I feel like I can see into his heart."

"And what do you find there?"

Harry looks flustered by the question and pulls at a chunk of hair. "He's a very wise man. And we don't just talk about his problems. He listens. He's a greater listener."

I look out at the lake. A canoe is passing by one of the sailboats, wobbling like it's about to flip over. At the moment, I'm a great listener, too. Not that there's any alternative.

"He really takes an interest, you know? Like in my work." He goes on about the mystery man's comments on his graphic design, how much he admired the font and color choices for a brochure Harry did for a downtown gallery.

The description goes on for a couple of minutes—the listening, the smiles, the ineffable sense of mutual attraction—and I'm still waiting to hear something concrete about this boyfriend twice removed. Does he have a limp? A favorite movie? A criminal record? So far he's just an abstraction, and I'm beginning to think that's the point.

I dodge a clump of goose shit on the path.

"Most of the guys I meet these days are looking for a daddy. They swarm around me, all these cute boys who were born during the Clinton administration. While all the guys our age are—"

"Married?" I fill it in for him, the word he hesitates to use. Probably because I'm the only person he knows who's already divorced.

"A lot, yeah."

I'm losing interest in the story. It's all too familiar, juvenile in its convolution as much as its romantic clichés. Love can be as simple as two plus two, and we'll still turn it into a differential equation. Harry may tell himself he's in love this time, I think, but nothing's really changed. He used to be motivated purely by sex; now it's some sort of romantic fantasy. He's changed the direction but not the speed, as if he had nothing but time.

I came here to escape romantic fantasies, the image of "the one" who would make me whole, and Harry's brought it all back. It was winter when I arrived in town, this lake frozen and covered in a smooth layer of pristine snow. I walked around the perimeter every day even then, even as the temperature dipped toward zero, simply to enjoy the silence. The silence became my refuge, the lack of distraction the source of the place's charm. And when the world suddenly shut down, I watched it on TV, but nothing really changed for me. I still didn't quite understand what all the fuss was about. Cabin fever has never been my disease.

TYPHOID HARRY

I put the coals on the hibachi when we get back and settle Harry at the table with a glass of Merlot. I've set up the guest room for him, but all he's done so far is drop his bag onto the bed.

As the burgers grill, he settles back and looks around the yard. "Do you ever hear from anybody in New York?"

"No," I tell him. I wonder if *anybody* means Peter. Regardless, *no* is the right response.

"I've had virtual happy hour with some of the gang," he says. "You should join us. I'm sure everyone would be jealous of your set-up here."

There's a reason I haven't talked to anyone, I should say, but I decide to let it go. I lost most of the gang in the divorce. Harry knows that. They're reminders I'd rather not have. Like Harry, they're relegated to Christmas cards and Facebook posts, and that's enough for me. The last thing I want is to watch those queens ask too many questions and get drunk in a *Hollywood Squares* arrangement on my laptop, with me a hapless Paul Lynde.

There were borders in Peter's life, clear lines to separate the worlds in which he traveled, the people in each one. As his husband, I was invited into the other worlds, my presence often demanded—whether to highlight our success for the sake of others, or to have a cover or ready escape valve when needed—but otherwise there was little interplay between work, family, and friends.

For a long time I admired Peter's ability to weave from one spot to another, to calibrate his behavior, even his personality, his projected self, to fit in with each group, to please, to meet expectations. That, I thought, was Peter's superpower; he could be whoever people wanted him to be, whoever he needed to be.

We change the subject over dinner. And change it again, more often than I can count. Each time Harry starts a new story, I pour another glass of wine. Somehow, despite seldom taking a pause, he manages to keep up with me. After bringing the plates into the kitchen, I grab another bottle on the way back out.

"Ooh," he says lubriciously, reading the label as I spin a foil cutter around the bottle, "Ménage à Trois."

"Maybe you should try it," I say as the foil slides off. "That would certainly solve your problem."

He laughs. "Sadly, I'm not attracted to his partner."

"It's just an everyday wine," I say. "The good stuff is in the cellar."

"The cellar," he says mockingly. "You always were a bit of a snob."

It's well past sunset and the garden is beginning to get lost in shade. With six feet of distance between us, I can just make out the expression on his face. He's not joking.

"That would not be far from the truth," I admit, trying to laugh it off. "The perks of a liberal arts education."

Now he's pushed one of my buttons. The first refuge of the ignorant is to call the knowledgeable a snob. It's the same instinct that gave rise to climate change deniers and antivaxxers, the same arrogance that leads people in a pandemic to pay less attention to epidemiologists than orange clowns.

The tension doesn't last long. Harry would never let a disagreement get in the way of a good story. He starts talking about the pandemic, the empty streets, a sense that life has shut down and will never wake up. "I miss *people*," he says. "No one in particular—just people, you know? New York without people in the streets and cars honking is not New York."

Maybe it's just the creeping twilight, the surprising softness in his voice, but I'm caught off guard by a sudden wave of sympathy. He seems to be talking about more than the pandemic. His need for connection is palpable. Maybe I was wrong about everything. Maybe Harry's assertive persona is just that, and always has been—a cover for something he doesn't want to show or even acknowledge, something the loneliness of the pandemic has forced him to look at. Despite the bluster, I suspect suddenly that he's acutely aware of his failings. He monopolizes conversations and cuts off the intrusion of other people's opinions because his own are so fragile. I'm picturing him now in the ABC absurdity, that string of nameless people, his personal three degrees of separation from imagined happiness. Having never known love before, he can't see beyond infatuation, the halo surrounding the handsome object who is not yet his. He thinks he's in love because he has no idea how love actually works.

I could tell him all about it, if he would only listen. I could explain how long it took to move from infatuation to love with

TYPHOID HARRY

Peter, the power of shared experience that goes so much further than right and left swipes on a cold screen. I fell in love with Peter quickly, but only months later did I realize that I truly loved him—when we were able to use shorthand to describe something we'd seen or done together, when we'd learned to appreciate our differences as much as our similarities. I had to know him in order to love him. And even that wasn't forever.

Harry finishes the latest story and remains silent for a long time—which, for him, is measured in seconds. I reach for the bottle and spill the last of its contents into my glass. No wonder the conversation is petering out.

I gaze off behind Harry's shoulder, toward the rosebush by the fence. It's just thorns right now. At the nursery, they told me it might take another season to bloom.

"So what do *you* want?" Harry's voice seems disembodied, the darkness swallowing him bit by bit.

I don't give myself time to think about the question. "Peace and quiet," I say.

He snorts dismissively. "Nobody wants that. You're a New Yorker."

"Does this look like New York to you?" Above our heads, the stars begin to peek out in the sky.

"Do you miss it?"

I sigh and wonder how I suddenly became the topic of conversation. Harry must have run out of stories.

"No," I say at last. "Shockingly, no."

Homesickness, I've learned, isn't about missing a place, but a time. I don't miss New York. I miss who I was in New York.

"I'd suffocate here," he says.

"Too much fresh air?"

"That, too."

"New Yorkers thrive on crisis," I tell him. "Drama comes with the territory."

"What comes with this territory?" he asks, gesturing. His pinky ring flashes, caught by the light from the kitchen window.

"It makes you think," I say. "When life slows down, you see the truth—without all that distraction. You see who you are."

"And who are you?" His voice seems gruffer now, impatient.

"I'm a coward."

I can hear crickets chirping. I've shocked him into silence.

"I know what I did to Peter. I know why he left me."

"Do you? Because I'm not sure you've learned anything."

He sighs heavily. "I was hoping you had. I was hoping to find some change in you on this trip. But you're still the same person, only the Zen version. All day I've felt your judgment. You sigh, you roll your eyes. All from the comfort of your boring little exile. You think this is real life out here, with your cozy little garden and fifty yards between you and the next blond-headed human?"

I have to take a breath. "Wow, where did that come from?"

"This is what Peter couldn't stand," he says. "The self-certainty, the control, the tightly wound character whose whole life is about these trappings, everything tidily in place, every *i* dotted, every *t* crossed."

I turn toward the six-foot-high fence, wondering if the neighbors can hear. From this angle, I can't even tell if their windows are open. The most I've ever heard from them is an awkward hammering at the piano, the 10-year-old pounding out a dirge-like approximation of *Clair de lune*.

"How do you know what Peter couldn't stand?"

"He told me."

"He talked to you about me? After we broke up?"

"And before. He needed someone to talk to."

I have trouble getting my head around Harry as a confidante, let alone Peter's.

"You told him to leave me."

He shakes his head. "I didn't have to. He knew he would never get what he needed from you."

And suddenly I see what's been going on all day. "Who's A?" I ask. "The mystery man you're in love with."

As the light dims, all I can see distinctly is his smile, hovering in the darkness like the Cheshire Cat's.

"Poor guy is going through it all over again. They say we're doomed to repeat our mistakes. Well, Peter replaced you with someone else who's breaking his heart."

"Who? Who's he with now?"

"You don't know him."

"How can I believe that, with all the other lies you've told today?"

"I haven't lied at all. I just changed a few names to protect the innocent, as they used to say."

"To toy with me."

The Cheshire Cat again.

"And I didn't break his heart."

71

TYPHOID HARRY

He lets out a huge sigh and leans back, as though to add distance between himself and the words. "What about Jack?"

"Jack?" Nobody knew about that. Only Peter and me, and I've spent the past two years trying to forget.

"You broke him," he says. He tosses his head, the red waves seeming to fire up the tree behind him. "He told me all about it. He was a mess after that."

"He told you about Jack?"

"Not that he had to. Jack wasn't the stranger you thought he was. I knew him. Hell, Jude, you should have known better. New York may be a big city, but some people know everybody. And I'm one of them."

Finally it all makes sense. I've never been able to figure it out before this moment. "You told him," I say.

It hits me suddenly that I've invited a stranger into my home. A Trojan horse, settling cozily in for the surprise attack.

"Like you know the first thing about love," I say. "Like you have any business butting into my relationship. You don't know what that was all about. And I don't need to defend myself to you of all people."

"I've struck a nerve," he says, his voice as dark as the night.

"What is this all about? You can't be serious about Peter. For Christ's sake, now, after all these years?"

"I've always wanted him," he says. "I just didn't know how much."

"Or maybe you just like them broken. Picking up the pieces is easier. What are you even here for? To throw this in my face?"

I finish the wine with one last gulp. It goes down painfully, as if I've hurt my throat with the words.

I'm used to silence. These days especially, I can spend hours with the clicking of my keyboard the only sound. There's a comfort in silence—peace, a chance to relax. And now, for the first time all day, the silence lasts for more than a minute. But something thrums beneath it—a thickness in the air, fear of what may come next.

When Harry finally speaks, his voice is hushed, cold. "You know, for all your embrace of this 'peace and quiet,' you resent it. You want it all back—Peter, New York. You can't let go, even though it's all gone."

For two years I've joked to myself about it—the increasing foreignness of New York, the past life that had once been mine. I've separated myself from it all, compartmentalized it as expertly as Peter compartmentalized his social circles. But in the back of my mind, I believed it was still accessible—frozen in time, ready to warm up at my touch.

The bitterness of Harry's tone reveals the illusion. New York has cut me off. My life has cut me off. From the start, the knife has been in my hand.

"Why are you here?" I ask. "Really."

"I just wanted to make sure it was completely over between you. I don't want to pursue Peter only to see him come running back to you. But I have nothing to worry about. There's nothing for him to run back to."

This is what it was all about, this bizarre road trip of his. He's come with the full intention of dropping his news on me like the Enola Gay.

As I stand up, the wine seems to slosh around in my head. I'm like one of those drinking bird toys from childhood, the red liquid rising with the heat up to the head until the bird tips over and dunks its beak in the water. Only I'm not sure I'll spring back up.

I stumble toward the door, the light from the kitchen blessedly piercing the darkness. My mind is awash in images—memories and dreadful fantasies alike. Peter with his head on my shoulder at Shakespeare in the Park. Peter lifting a brandy snifter in a toast before the fireplace, his face suffused in an orange glow.

I fear I won't make it to the door, to the light within. I take another step and *know* I won't. I stop, hand gripping the table beside Harry's chair. I feel my stomach churn and wonder if I'll throw up right here on the patio stones. I take in a deep breath to calm the feeling. And as I pass Harry, the tickle in my throat quavers and something else wells up inside. Beside him, inches from his body, I turn my head and—without thinking, without caring—boom out a loud, spittle-laden cough.

THOSE COYOTE TEETH

Charlie J. Stephens

Tonight Jada gets my attention when she shoots back a shot of mezcal and says to the crowd gathered at the gallery's bar that the best part of her last one-night stand was using a cucumber as a dildo.

Jada is married to a man named Jeffrey and their two-year-old son is also named Jeffrey. We've all met before at other art openings, the occasional party, and once chatted in the shade of a maple tree at the farmer's market, but never had more to say than the most basic of social niceties. *How's the baby doing?* And, *When is the next art opening?* that kind of thing. What I've noticed at these run-ins is that all three of them enjoy being the center of attention and that the Jeffreys often let their round, pale bellies poke out of their designer t-shirts. I assume Jada's one-night stand happened before the Jeffreys, but know it is better not to make such assumptions.

Only little Jeffrey accompanies Jada this evening. As I turn away from the bar, he yells out "Dildo!" from where he is perched on Jada's hip and everyone laughs. He beams out at us like a comedic savant and claps his hands together. His fat little baby legs remind me of the spicy Italian sausages I couldn't stop eating the last time I went to Sicily.

My girlfriend Claire comes over to find out what all the commotion is about. She is the university gallery's new director and spent months putting this show together. Claire is one of those extroverts who can remember names, faces, interesting anecdotes, and every tedious detail of what people like and dislike about a piece of art, which is how she landed this coveted gallery position. The art opening tonight is a series of paintings

74

from a Canadian artist who lives on Vancouver Island. They are huge, floor to ceiling, with a lot of rounded shapes and warm colors: oranges, browns, soft greens. Each one of them looks like a place I would like to climb into and have a good rest.

Claire kisses me on the cheek, squeezes my hand, and smiles at Jada and little Jeffrey before heading back to the main floor. She knows I'll probably go back to our apartment soon; we learned early on in our dating that we are perhaps not the most socially-compatible couple. I like going out, getting drinks, and dancing on occasion but am always ready to leave many hours before Claire. She prefers to be the last one standing at any given event and usually is.

Tonight when she comes home after closing up the gallery and getting one last drink with the artist and a few friends, she crawls into bed smelling of whiskey and asks, "Do you think it's weird that Jeffrey wasn't there tonight?"

"Not really. Guess he couldn't make it," I say.

I make my voice sound uninterested but when I roll over I can't sleep for another two hours after Claire passes out, wondering not why Jeffrey wasn't there, but why Claire noticed.

I stare at the ceiling and out of nowhere start thinking about how I came out at fourteen. My best friend Jenine stole Playgirl magazines from her aunt, and when I looked at page after page of penises, all I could think of were weasels, desperate for some weasel thing beyond my comprehension.

"People, like, want to touch these things?" I'd asked Jenine, who gave me a funny look before nodding. She said she thought it was pretty hot herself and told me that her cousin Sarah had even licked one once.

A few weeks later, as my mom drove me to the orthodontist to get my braces tightened, I fiddled with my seatbelt and blurted out, "I'm definitely GAY." It came out in a nervous rush, but I felt lighter immediately. My mom kept her hands on the wheel and her eyes on the road.

"Maxine, just please don't be the kind of homosexual that feels the need to be naked in a parade," she responded before turning into the parking lot and telling me to get an extra free toothbrush for her. "Your bare ass won't ever look as good in the hot sun as you think it will, trust me."

Sometimes I think Claire and I will be together forever, and sometimes I think it's a miracle we've lasted the past three years. We met at a bar, both there on other dates that weren't going great. I couldn't take my eyes off her—her sturdy frame, short messy hair, and a laugh that cut through everything—even from across the room. We exchanged numbers in the bathroom.

Up close she was even more attractive, with lines starting to emerge around her eyes from smiling, from sun, from life. That was kind of it—we broke things off with the people we had been seeing and went on our first date the next week.

We get along well, have enough varied interests that we usually have something compelling to talk about together, and our sex is satisfying if not the overwhelming gloriousness of those first two years. Everyone says we are great together and we've always agreed.

All this being true, more and more often these days I get lost in daydreams of spending the rest of my thirties alone in the Cascade Mountains somewhere, eating cans of cold refried beans and making all my clothing out of fern fronds, whereas Claire gets nervous if we are away from the city and her friends for more than a day.

This is not to say I'm anti-social. I think maybe I just read the Transcendentalists at too formative a moment—self-reliance and all that: Thoreau in the woods and Emerson seeing God in the leaves and branches. There are many humans I love to be around. Okay, maybe not *many*, but I think I'm pretty normal. I am decent at making conversation, have a couple close friends I've known for years, and I go out with my coworkers most Fridays after work—normal stuff.

Claire increasingly talks about wanting kids, but even just the idea of parenthood is an onslaught to my senses. Little Jeffrey is adorable but not adorable enough for me to go through with having one of my own. Even as a child, when I first learned where babies came from—and how they came out—I was certain that would not be something I'd be participating in. I love spending time with my friends' kids and I also really enjoy it when, at the end of our fun time together, they go back to their own house. I think of myself as more of a future honorary aunt/uncle; "Auncle Max" has a nice, unique ring to it.

Many years ago in college, my wildlife ecology professor who I met with regularly for office hours shared with me—in an ashamed, desperate whisper like she had just accidentally shat in the pool—that deciding to be a parent was her biggest regret. Since then, no one besides her has admitted it out loud, but when I look around, I see that my friends and acquaintances who once partook in relatively easy existences can now be found crying quietly in the bathroom with bloodshot eyes and goo on their shirts. They start fixating on the probability of terrible things happening and become prone to perseveration, worried for their wunderkind that at any moment in the near or distant future there could be bullying, drug issues, dismemberment, disease, and death. Even the emergence of a dumb, lazy or ill-tempered personality in their child would be its own kind of tragedy. Their beautiful baby could turn into a misogynist incel or a shut-in conspiracy theorist with a basement full of guns from Walmart. In the bright light of day, though, most people say becoming a parent is the best thing that ever happened to them. I just don't think I can do it.

If Claire decides parenthood is what she wants, that will most likely be the end of us.

This is probably the main source of my ambivalence about us, even when things are going well. She'll probably go on to marry some well-adjusted, esteemed, professional-type with inherited family money who really wants kids. She and I won't talk for years, but eventually we will make a kind of real peace and keep in touch with life's highlights. I'll become that estranged but friendly auncle who sends birthday cards with a crisp twenty-dollar bill from somewhere far away.

I'm a little surprised when Jada texts to see if I want to grab coffee over the weekend.

Claire drove up to Portland to attend a conference for the week and I'm shocked at how quickly I reverted to a kind of easy bachelorhood. There have been record-long showers, lazy mid-day masturbations, and eating cold pizza for dinner with a sense of profound contentment.

Jada and I decide to meet at The Filling Station, a cafe near the university filled with bright young adults who make me feel both geriatric and profoundly grateful to not still be in my early 20's. She gives me a big hug like we are old friends when I walk in but then suddenly seems nervous, twisting her hair around her finger while her eyes dart around. We talk about little Jeffrey's nap schedule, how she is getting back into making art while he sleeps. And she mentions Jeffrey Sr. being away a lot.

"The thing is," she tells me after an awkward silence, her face so lean and sad, "I just don't know how I ended up here, with this life. It feels very strange sometimes."

THOSE COYOTE TEETH

"Yeah, I get that," I respond, holding her gaze as my eyes well up, but not knowing what else to say.

I want to tell her the truth, that I don't know how I ended up here either. I worry about what that means for Claire and me when—until very recently—it's seemed as though we were so right together. I'm not ready for my recent worries to be laid on the table and spilled on by lukewarm cappuccinos, so I don't say anything.

"Do you and Claire want kids?" she asks, reading my mind.

I look at the wall behind Jada. There is a poster of Janis Joplin in tight bell bottoms, screaming into the microphone, all raw passion with her famous line printed across the middle: *Onstage I make love to 25,000 different people, then I go home alone.*

I think about how to answer Jada's question.

"Claire wants kids but I really don't. I like how my life is. Well, that might be stretching it a bit." We laugh more easily now. "I just don't think having a kid is a good idea for me. It sounds unbearably disruptive to the life I want to build. Sorry to say it. That's probably not very helpful."

"Actually it is helpful—it's very honest. You're not trying to convince me of anything. When people try to tell me all this is normal and these parental and relationship doubts will pass, I second-guess myself even more. I think I actually feel better right now than I have in a while."

We look at each other for a second too long. I want to ask her something but get distracted by her long eyelashes and the downy fuzz on her cheeks I've never noticed before.

I look down at the table and then back at her. "This is a weird question, but do you ever think of yourself as a portal? Like, really, isn't it so weird that a human can come out of another human? It's like all the special people with uteruses helped everyone who is here on Earth come through from the other side."

I look at her open face, suddenly desperate for her to explain this. I feel my cheeks reddening. "Sorry," I say in this new silence, "I guess I've just been thinking about portals lately."

She is looking at me so seriously but then she laughs, and that's when I first see her coyote teeth. She puts her hand over her mouth instinctively; I hope not from anything she saw in my reaction. It is alarming though, all those white, pointy knives, long and gleaming with gaps in between. Almost like normal teeth, but not. I wonder how I've never noticed before, because she laughs often, makes jokes. I remember that a few years ago, my mom told me that when I was born, she got a strange mole on her face, and also in that year the texture of her skin changed, her feet sloughing off layers of skin for no apparent reason. Apparently these types of unexpected changes are things that can happen as part of procreation. Maybe Jada's teeth were something like that.

"I can honestly say I've never thought of it like that before," she says, settling herself after my question. "I really don't know why I'm laughing," she says. "Maybe that explains everything: the truth is I was a portal and now I'm just very tired."

There's silence again but it's comfortable now. She looks at the clock and gives me a half-smile. She seems a little less sad.

"Thanks for meeting up with me, Max. I really needed this. You know, I've wanted to be friends with you for a while now."

I smile back, feeling better than I did earlier, but there's another feeling too that I can't place. We get up, hug goodbye. She walks back to her car and I watch her go—her lithe, canine body moving easily amongst the other, regular pedestrians. I feel both lightheaded and at a loss, and realize I just want to be outside, alone. This happens to me sometimes when I feel a rush of feeling, especially feeling I don't understand.

There's a place in the woods just outside of town I go to often. It's about a thirty-minute drive to the trailhead. The trail winds along a creek and down to a lake they stock with fish.

There's a rocky outcropping on the other side, far away from the little roped-off beach where people take their kids to splash around in the shallows. There's an unmarked, overgrown deer trail near there that leads to a cave if you know where to look.

Sometimes, like now, when I feel overwhelmed but don't know exactly why, I make my way there. It's a relief that close to downtown there's still real wilderness nearby. I have the sense that if I hid out there, it would take people days, maybe weeks, to find me. Sometimes if I'm having anxiety, I sit in the cave and feel worse, imagining a big earthquake finally hitting and dislodging hundreds of tons of dark rock on my body and the crushing and cracking and dust that would settle. But usually I feel better. I keep thinking about Jada's crazy teeth. I wonder if Claire has noticed them. I wonder if, when Jeffrey Jr. gets his adult teeth, they'll be all wild and pointy too. I wonder if her canine smile turns Jeffrey Sr. on, makes him even harder than that one-night stand cucumber. My mind sees Jenine's hand flip to a page in one of her magazines with an extra huge weasel penis, and I wonder what happened to her after high school.

I lay back on the rocks where there's an indentation that fits my body perfectly, stare at the dark, wet ceiling, and cry for no apparent reason, or for all the reasons, until I feel like myself again and head back towards home.

When Claire gets back from Portland, a day later than expected, something is off. I can't tell if it's her or if it's me. I let a couple more days go by, hoping it will pass. It doesn't.

"I have to tell you something," Claire says while I'm getting out the cream for our morning coffee. "I know you don't want kids, but I'm ready. I finally have the job I've been working towards for so long, and I feel excited for what's next. And I don't want to use a sperm bank; I want Jeffrey to be the sperm donor. I already asked him about it and he said yes."

"You talked to him before you talked to me?" I ask, setting my empty mug down on the counter and looking at her more carefully. "When did this happen?"

"We were both in Portland last week and met up," she says, avoiding eye contact.

"Does Jada know about this?" I ask.

"He's telling her this morning," Claire says. "I know this all probably sounds like it's out of nowhere and reckless, but it feels right to me."

"Wait," I say, figuring it out, "you guys...hooked up in Portland."

A nauseating wave churns in my stomach—what I imagine morning sickness must feel like.

For some reason I start thinking back to the wildlife ecology class I took from that one professor. She told our class about how coyotes are monogamous, but how well-adapted they are to change. I remember something about how they rarely make their own dens and instead just move into abandoned ones. I think about Jada and her coyote teeth, how razor-sharp they are, and imagine them tearing her house to unrecognizable shreds when she finds out about all this. I imagine Claire and Jeffrey in some fancy hotel room, and the thing is, it actually kind of makes sense. It dawns on me that I feel more relieved than angry, though I don't want Claire to know this yet. I give Claire my evilest eye, throw some stuff in a bag, and don't say another word.

It's a cold, foggy day so there are no swimmers at the lake.

The quiet hovers over the water like a blanket and back at the cave it is even quieter. I sit down in my usual spot, lean back and close my eyes, thinking about portals, and where this one might take me. The wind is picking up and rustling through the trees, a hawk lets out a piercing shriek over the water, and the sun is starting to burn through the fog high in the sky, illuminating everything. There are no long shadows yet.

I have the idea of asking Jada if she and little Jeffrey would want to come up to the lake to swim sometime when it's warmer, imagine the baby's sturdy legs kicking the water delightedly, and then inviting them to my cave—the three of us just lying there together in the dark quiet—not like in a coyote den, not forever. Just for a long, still moment, pretending we're home.

EZRA'S RED T-SHIRT

Tom Semmes

Arms crossed, Ezra glared at his parents, receiving tense smiles in return. His grandmother, investigating a beet speared on a fork at the other end of the table, was no help at all.

"But Janet," he protested, "what about the friendships I have developed?"

"You have...friends, dear?" his mother asked, not unkindly. "And, by the way, mother, maman, or mom is a more appropriate reference," she added, reminding him that using her given name was only necessary when she had clients in her home office.

It was true that it wasn't his schoolmates he would miss. Ezra had attended the Ida B. Wells Academy since kindergarten. But the school ended in sixth grade, and most classmates were transferring to a private school upstate. It was change, period. A new place, new people. Why couldn't he stay in one place forever? The roll he had just consumed sat heavy in his stomach.

"But is this really the best school for me...*mother*? Do I have other options?"

"When you pay your own tuition, you can choose any school you want. I am sure the local public school is fine."

"Damn philistines," his father muttered, taking a sip of Beaujolais and staring into space. No one asked for an explanation of this non sequitur because they all knew the reference: the local zoo board, ignorant of the historic use of elephant dung in Central African indigenous art, had rejected his submission for a mural. Unfortunately the loss of income had cut into family finances.

"Santy, let's not talk about this here. By the way, this roasted fennel is delicious."

Beatrice, with slow deliberation, finally began to chew. By this hour, her evening joint had begun to kick in.

That night, lying on his bed propped up with pillows, Ezra wrote in his journal:

Gerald Ford! What a stupid namesake for a school. I've seen where they're sending me. I first thought it was a prison; flat roof, lots of concrete, small windows. But Janet said, no, it's a school for kids. At the time I pitied them for being incarcerated there. And now I'll be entering it like any other common criminal. I doubt it's constructed on feng shui principles. That will hamper my education.

His fate sealed, a few weeks later Ezra found himself, at the ungodly hour of 7:10 a.m., trotting along a path through the protected forest land that surrounded his house, delaying as long as possible his arrival at school. After crossing a field (a depressing monoculture of identically severed grass blades gridded with white chalk), Ezra joined a noisy throng under a concrete portico. Adults stood on either side of glass double doors greeting "Welcome!" with wary smiles plastered on their faces. *Abandon hope, all ye who enter here* would be more appropriate, Ezra mused.

He found himself in a crowded auditorium and took a seat on one of hundreds of foldout chairs. Earlier that morning, he had carefully selected his outfit, rejecting choices like his army surplus fatigues or kimono, to adapt a camouflage the way an animal does to be invisible to its predators. But now that he looked around, perhaps wearing khakis and a short sleeve, light blue button-down shirt–looking like an easily-overlooked shop clerk–wouldn't help him blend in here at all. Most students were wearing colorful t-shirts or striped athletic wear. He pushed his round wire-rim glasses up his nose, let his straight brown hair fall over his eyes, and willed himself to disappear.

A heavy man in a suit and red tie ascended the stage. From the way the auditorium quieted suddenly, Ezra surmised it was someone of authority, most likely the principal. He winced at the tired cliché: "today is the first day of the rest of your life." It suggested that he would be trapped here forever, *like Sisyphus pushing his rock.*

The speech finally over, students were told to line up at tables to receive their school schedule.

"I'm sorry, I don't see your name here," a woman with white blouse and streaked blonde hair told Ezra. "Who was your advisor in sixth grade?"

"I…wasn't here in sixth. I was at another school." *A better school*, Ezra added silently. "You weren't here in sixth…" she repeated suspiciously. "He's a transfer. What do we do now?"

"You didn't tell anyone, honey?" a coworker with red glasses said. "You should have gone with the sixth graders for the school tour. Well, you'll figure it out." She slid him a hand-drawn map. "Put him in Schedule C. We're short in that group. Pass his data on to admin."

He followed the map to a long hallway and was assaulted by a cacophony of voices and slamming metal doors. He marveled at his locker's size and industrial impersonality, solved its combination, and pushed in his book bag, keeping a tight grip on the schedule. His survival depended on its grid of periods and breaks, calibrated to the minute.

There was little pedagogy that day. Bells rang, hallways filled and emptied. Teachers took rolls, handed out textbooks, led discussions about summer vacations. Finally, the last bell rang and school was over. He returned home the way he had come and was calmed by the forest's solitude and silence.

His mother greeted him as he walked in.

"So, how was it?" she asked with a nervous smile.

"Fine," he said, then walked straight to his bedroom, dropped his book bag, and shut the door. Sharing his feelings, or even witty insights, would only exacerbate his suffering and put his parents at ease. He was similarly quiet during dinner though his father had served apple crisp, clearly a bribe to get him to talk.

That night in bed he wrote:

So many rooms, so many corridors, like Dante's hell. An endless maze with no clear escape. I found the dining hall only by the smell of stale pizza which I was forced to consume. Note to self: Tell dad to pack me a lunch tomorrow. Anything would be better than the swill they serve there.

The next few days were no less chaotic, the schedule built on an asymmetrical plan where no one day was exactly the same as the next. But, inevitably, Friday afternoon arrived.

As he headed home, he noticed three boys leaning against the brick wall at the back of the school, eighth graders he assumed from their size. Their eyes fixed on him as he passed. Having hardly been noticed for the last few days, this made him uncomfortable. But this being a public space, he knew the rules on bodily autonomy. When they began to follow him, Ezra chose to think of it as an opportunity; his first encounter with natives of this strange new world.

"You new here? I've never seen you before," a husky boy with a buzz cut asked.

"Yes, I just transferred into seventh grade."

"So you don't know anyone here?"

"No, a brand new slate!" Ezra responded cheerfully, confused by the meaningful glances the boys shared.

They continued to follow him. Yes, he had seen the recent Star Wars movie and liked it very much. No, he couldn't comment on Mrs. Holmstrom's tits because he was in Advanced Placement English. Why were these questions so random and why were his responses followed by inappropriately loud guffaws? When he reached the path that led into the woods, Ezra wished them a good day.

They moved as one and blocked his path.

"Hey, did you bump into me?" another boy, thin as a scarecrow and with acne-pocked skin, said.

Ezra backed up a few steps but the third boy, pale and pudgy with small pig-like eyes, pulled in behind him, standing so close he could feel his breath on his neck.

"I...apologize if that is what you perceived," Ezra said, though in reality he hadn't bumped into anyone at all. "I would prefer if I could continue on my way."

The boys held their stance, smiling menacingly.

If not flight, then fight? That seemed pointless. In sheer pounds alone they outweighed him by a factor of almost five. Anyway, Ezra wasn't sure how the whole fighting thing worked.

Freeze, it would have to be. He waited to see what would happen.

What did happen Ezra would later realize had to have been planned beforehand. The speed was startling. Within moments he was flat on his back, his backpack opened and its contents spilled out, and his eyeglasses tossed in a bush.

"Be careful! Those are prescription!"

"C'mon, let's ditch this loser," Buzz Cut said heading back toward school. The others – Scarecrow and Pig Eyes as Ezra thought of them now – followed obediently.

Ezra waited until their retreating figures were swallowed by the forest. He collected his possessions, regretting textbooks that had been violated before they had hardly been opened. He found his glasses, brushed himself off, then headed home. Birds twittered in the trees unfazed by the human drama below.

At dinner his parents inevitably asked how school was going. He responded briefly, yet truthfully, "I am not sure yet. I am still collecting information." Maybe the fracas earlier that day was an outlier and there was no reason to involve anyone, or cause alarm, until he knew more.

An excerpt from that night's journal:

They showed us a movie about bullying in fourth grade, but I never thought it would happen to me! We were trained to use nonviolent communication; state our observations, express our feelings, voice our requests. I doubt that would have worked today. Their grasp of language or reason seems tenuous. Very Lord of the Flies. Maybe I'll be dead by next week and Janet will be sorry then!

Another week of school passed by: clanging bells, slamming lockers, and scraping chairs. The one saving grace was that the madness was at least more predictable. It was even possible that he actually enjoyed some of it. English class, for one, and the library was well-stocked, though his parents would never need to know that.

On his way home, Ezra's heart sank when he saw his harassers waiting for him at the forest's edge. At least they were consistent, as if they had penciled him in on their calendars for Friday afternoon.

"Come back for more?" Buzz Cut sneered.

"I am on my way home and prefer to pass unmolested," Ezra replied, voicing a preference he was sure would be ignored.

"Listen to him. 'I prefer to pass...'" Buzz Cut mimicked. "Talking so fancy."

"What a nerd!" Scarecrow snorted.

"So fancy," Pig Eyes repeated with a blank look in his eyes.

"I don't know why you bothered to transfer. You're never going to fit in here. No one likes your kind at our school."

"What...kind is that?" Ezra replied. He was confused that a public school might belong to some students and not others.

Buzz Cut ignored the question. "Grab him and get me some mud," he ordered. Scarecrow held Ezra's arms behind his backpack while Pig Eyes scooped some mud from a puddle left by last night's rain, holding his palms out like a holy offering. Buzz Cut marked Ezra's cheeks, nose, and forehead with slow deliberation as if performing some ancient rite of humiliation. He stood back with a discerning eye to admire his work; then, with sudden inspiration, pressed handprints on Ezra's shirt.

Pig Eyes grabbed leaves and sticks and rubbed them in Ezra's hair and was about to grab some more but stopped when Buzz Cut, wiping his hands on Scarecrow's back, gave him an angry glare. It was not a collaboration; this was his masterpiece. He motioned Scarecrow to let go.

"Faggot!" Buzz Cut yelled as Ezra hurried off.

Faggot. The word was swallowed quickly by the forest's silence but still echoed in Ezra's mind. At Ida B. Wells they had a policy that students signed entering fifth grade: "I promise not to use derogatory terms related to sex, gender expression, race, ethnicity, body type, or personal appearance." Breaking that rule could get you expelled. It was time for action now. Rules had been broken. It was time to talk to his parents.

Arriving home, his mother, in her office with the door open, looked up from her computer and noticed her son's muddied appearance.

"Hello, dear, have you taken up sports?"

"An unfortunate encounter, Janet."

"Oh. Shall we have a Royal Circle at dinner?" His mother had less understanding of school sports than Ezra did but as a therapist she was skilled in unearthing sources of human suffering.

Ezra nodded in agreement.

"Good. Ask Santiago if he wants to participate. He's in the kitchen. Oh, and clear it with Beatrice too. Wash up first, please."

Ezra walked into the kitchen and saw his father bent over a steaming pot on the stove, a spoon in his hand, conferring a time-tested recipe from a well-worn Julia Child cookbook.

"Hi, dad. What's cooking?" Unlike his mother, Santiago preferred the casual greeting for one's male parent.

"Ezra, sweetie, how are you? How was school?" He put down the spoon to greet his son, but stopped when he noticed Ezra's disarray. "Wow, I like your look. Very 'au naturel,'" he said, removing a stray twig from his son's hair then pulling him in for a hug.

"Thanks, dad. Are you okay with a Royal Circle tonight?" He wondered why his father wasn't more curious about his appearance but since he could have cleaned up by now maybe Santiago assumed it was an aesthetic choice on his part.

"Royal Circle? Sure. How about after the salad? Radicchio with orange vinaigrette."

"Thanks, dad. Where's Bea, by the way?" Ezra followed the direction of the pointed ladle.

Beatrice was tending the backyard garden in a muslin skirt and peasant blouse. In one hand, she held a green parasol while with the other she inspected her plants.

"Hi, Bea. Don't tell me. Monet's *Woman with a Parasol*?" Ezra asked. The scene did have a striking resemblance to that famous painting but in this version the face of the woman was lined and wrinkled.

"Aren't these babies beautiful?" his grandmother said, gently bending a red poppy toward Ezra. Then she looked up. "What the fuck happened to you?"

"I'll tell you at Royal Circle?"

"A Royal Circle? What mess are you in now?"

"That's a judgment-laden statement!"

"Okay, okay. Enough with the ethical communication crap. Did you get into a fight? Beat someone up?"

"Well…" Ezra hesitated, not surprised that his grandmother was the first to nearly guess what had happened.

At dinner, after his father had doled the sauce over the poached salmon and poured Chablis (half glass for Ezra), they took turns describing their week. Janet mentioned meeting Deepak Chopra at a recent conference. Santiago described a color palette for a new commission. Beatrice outlined her attempts to make a homegrown opium tincture.

When it was Ezra's turn everyone fell silent, curious why he had called a Royal Circle. They followed tradition, holding hands and calling upon the spirits and ancestors whose wisdom would guide them. Ezra, as "king" of this ceremony, lit a special candle that his dad had bought at the Renaissance Festival when Ezra was six.

"My Royal Council," Ezra began. "As some of you may have surmised, I have been a victim of bullying at school." He had washed his face but still had on the shirt marked by two handprints.

"Oh, of course!" his father said, realizing now that Ezra's appearance was not a matter of artistic expression.

His mother interrupted. "Excuse me, dear. 'Victim' is a charged word. Could you state clearly what happened without judgment? Let us come to our own conclusions."

"Oh, well then, I participated in an act of what is often referred to as bullying. Perhaps I could be referred to as the 'bullied'? I was smeared with mud and..."

Ezra's dad cut in, "Mud? Oh, you were down at that stream bed, weren't you? It has that earthy smell..."

"Santy, can you not interrupt?" Beatrice grabbed a home-baked baguette and waved it like a weapon. "Ezzie, pretend this is a talking stick. Whoever holds this...thing...has the floor. So what happened? What did you do? Fisticuffs? Challenge them to a duel? Defend your honor?" She handed Ezra the baguette.

"I am sorry to disappoint you, Bea, but I ran. An offensive position did not seem feasible. My question, my Royal Council, is how best to deal with this. Should I hope they get tired of it? Report them to the authorities? Study martial arts?"

Janet raised her hand and Ezra handed over the baguette.

"First, you need to understand what motivates your attackers. Typically one is aggressive because one is unable to express oneself otherwise. This could be due to childhood trauma or feelings of unworthiness, which are often correlated. I've dealt with cases of this. In teenagers, especially males, it is primarily about their psychosexual development. As the amygdala is not fully formed at this stage, their behaviors tend to foreground hierarchical displays of..."

Beatrice reached for the baguette and yanked it out of Janet's hands. "C'mon. It's because Ezra's the newbie. He needs friends, so they can help him beat the shit out of these assholes."

"Have you made any friends, Ezzie?" Santiago asked, grasping the baguette that Bea had shoved into his hand. "Maybe you should join the glee club. Or drama. The costume closet was a great place to hide when I was being bullied."

"You were...bullied in school, dad?"

"Yeah. A couple of times. Well, it might have been because I didn't pay the pot dealer. I can't remember."

"Ezra, dear," said Janet, reclaiming the "stick," "I think you need to communicate clearly that their behavior is inappropriate and draw some clear boundaries."

"Thank you, Janet. However they have only basic communication skills. Often they resort to one-word epithets like 'Loser' or 'Faggot.'"

Janet, flinching briefly, spoke carefully. "That...choice of insult is telling. Homophobic terms are often used to shield one from uncomfortable, suppressed same-sex desires of one's own, you know."

Ezra had not considered this. Actually he had never

considered anyone having desire for anyone before. Was he being bullied because he was "desired"? That didn't make sense.

Janet continued. "This acting out of stale stereotypes and toxic masculinity has to stop. If you fight back..."

Bea interrupted, "Fight. Fight. Fight."

Janet scowled at Bea and waved the baguette warningly. "If you fight back, you would be no better than a bully yourself."

"I know!" Santiago waved his hand for the baguette. "Ezra, how about if you lean into this! Be a mirror to their own sexual confusion." He took a bite out of the baguette and made a face. "This might have been underbaked."

"Oooh, I like this idea." Bea grabbed the baguette from Santiago and also took a bite, speaking with her mouth full. "Play the new guy, weird loner card, pull 'em in, and then beat the shit out of 'em." She finally swallowed. "S'okay" she said, affirming her son's baking skills, then forwarded the baguette to Janet.

Janet looked askance at its moist chewed end. "To make this work, one would have to temporarily trigger the frontal cortex so they become conscious of the absurdity of their actions. Then a conversation about boundaries may be possible."

"But how do I do that? Trigger them?"

"That...word...could be useful."

"You mean like wear a shirt that says 'I am a big fat faggot?'"

"You are hardly fat, Ezra. But that idea is worth considering..." Janet turned to her husband. "Santiago? What do you think?"

"Damn, I'd wish I thought of that," Santiago said. "Reverse their expectations of gender and power. Claim the tools of oppression." Stroking his goatee, Santiago looked dreamily at the ceiling. "I remember once when..."

"But wouldn't claiming the label be misleading? I'm not gay," Ezra blurted. Janet and Santiago briefly shared glances.

"Dear, you have all the time in the world to discover your identity," Janet said. "But this is only about taking ownership of a word. To claim its power for yourself so it can no longer be used against you. Also, this would be a powerful show of allyship with students who are...um...LGB...TQ!"

"You could make some new friends that way," his father added.

"Well then, it's settled." Janet leaned back, picked up her

glass of wine, and sipped it reflectively. She nodded to Ezra to blow out the candle.

Santiago, whistling, took to collecting dishes. "Just so you know, I did pay that guy for his weed," he said, walking into the kitchen.

Bea kissed Ezra on the forehead on the way out. "You da man," she said. Saturday's journal read:

Dad's excited to be working on my shirt. I picked out a bright red t-shirt at the mall, 100% cotton of course. Maybe it is a good time to change what I wear. My light blue button-down shirt was good at saying 'leave me alone' in a nice way but some students are starting to call me "Professor." Probably no one will notice what it says anyway. I question many of my classmates' literacy.

Monday arrived. Ezra donned the shirt, admiring the effect that his father had used to give a "ripped from the headlines" immediacy. He also wore a pair of jeans. T-shirt and jeans, he'd fit right in.

"Wow, you certainly subvert all patriarchal expectations wearing that," his father said when he entered the kitchen, serving Ezra's favorite: crepes with Nutella.

At school some students did notice the shirt, either laughing or frowning or pointing it out to their friends. But in the general chaos of unloading from buses and running for classrooms, he wasn't making a very big impression. Maybe it was just a word as his mother had said.

At Algebra, a boy sitting next to him, tall, freckled, with a head of curly red hair, took a long look at his t-shirt, made a disgusted sigh, and turned away. But class started as usual and Ezra thought perhaps his exercise of free speech had been accepted. He liked wearing the shirt; maybe red was his color.

A few minutes into class there was a brisk knock on the door and a woman with graying hair tied in a bun entered and whispered into the teacher's ear.

"Is there an Ezra here?" the teacher said, surveying the room. "The principal wants to see you."

Students oohed and one whispered, "Now he's in trouble." Ezra followed the school secretary into the hallway.

"Why does the principal want to see me?" Ezra asked as he hurried to keep up.

The lady lifted glasses that hung by a chain around her sagging neck, gave him a look-over and snapped, "I haven't the foggiest. Don't dawdle."

EZRA'S RED T-SHIRT

The principal's office was at the other end of the school and the procession caused a stir among students straggling to class. Entering the office, the principal, backlit by a row of windows with a view of a half empty parking lot, looked up with light gray eyes that almost disappeared in his florid, well-shaven face.

"So. You're Ezra…?" the principal said, referring to a paper on his desk

Ezra looked down at the nameplate that read: Curtis "Curt" McPherson. "Yes, I am…Curt."

The principal looked up sharply and indicated that Ezra sit in a hard plastic chair that faced his desk. "That would be Mr. McPherson."

The inquisition begins, Ezra thought as he plopped down. Wait, had he said that out loud?

For the principal's weary frown had suddenly turned into a scowl.

Mr. McPherson tore his eyes from Ezra's shirt and leaned back in his swivel chair, tugging his bottom lip and contemplating the ceiling as if seeking inspiration in its grid of fluorescent lights and acoustic tiles. Then he lunged forward, resting his elbows on the desk, held Ezra with a steady gaze and smiled. *Like a wolf grinning at trapped prey*, Ezra thought.

"Here at Ford, we pride ourselves on providing a safe environment for our students. We want everyone to have a voice and to be able to discuss in an open and frank manner the sensitive topics and challenging issues of our diverse society. You will find, Ezra, that we are a welcoming space." He paused for effect.

"Is this about my shirt?" Ezra asked.

The principal's shoulders sank and he sat back in his chair. "Yes, it's about the shirt. I am afraid that you can't wear that at this school."

"Why? Is there a dress code?"

"Offensive speech is not allowed in this school. Spoken or written."

"It's not written. It's airbrushed!" Ezra said, admiring his father's handiwork.

"I don't care if it's in braille or cuneiform!" The principal paused then continued in a softer tone. "Ezra, you're in a big fishpond here. We have people of faiths that might not approve of, well…and students that are…you know." The principal held out a hand with an obscure gesture that he quickly retracted. "Look, unlike the school you might have come from," he paused to refer to the sheet in front of him, "we don't march lockstep to liberal, leftist points of view."

"But I heard a kid say this on the playground," Ezra said, pointing to his t-shirt, "and the teacher didn't say anything."

"Look, we can't watch everything that goes on everywhere! You just cannot wear that," the principal said, exasperated. "Should I call your parents?"

"No! It's okay. I'll take it off!" Ezra started to remove the shirt, revealing a pale bony frame.

"What are you doing!" the principal hissed, taking a quick glance out the window then shooting across the room to shut the door.

"You said I can't wear it so I'm taking it off. Mr. McPherson. Sir."

"No, I meant...oh, here!" He fumbled in a cabinet and handed Ezra an extra-large tan polo shirt. "Put this on over that. Don't think you are the first to be so honored. Bring it back tomorrow."

Ezra considered the shapeless garment. It had a stain down the middle, probably from dribbled cafeteria food, and, regrettably, the fabric was 50% polyester. He pulled it over his offending shirt. He considered bowing Japanese style but, since the principal had returned his focus to papers on his desk, Ezra simply left.

Back in class, students stared at him as he found his seat. By his next class, English, word had already begun to spread. Though only a number of students had actually seen the original red t-shirt it seemed everyone knew about the tan polo. Groups of students whispered and giggled when he passed them in the hallway and he heard at least one student mention "the shirt of shame." Ezra had gone from being a stylish rebel to looking like he couldn't accurately put a fork to his mouth. It was embarrassing. Why had he ever abandoned his short sleeve, light blue button-down shirt?

And, inevitably, his three tormentors were waiting at his locker.

"So brave of him to raise our consciousness, isn't it, fellas?" Buzz Cut said with mock humility. He made a peace symbol then lowered all but the middle finger and poked it into Ezra's chest. Pig Eyes nodded his head rapidly like a bobble-head doll.

Buzz Cut then pushed Ezra hard into his locker and leaned in close. "Later," he hissed, blowing his fetid breath into Ezra's face.

They left, cackling among themselves. Scarecrow held out his palm to get a high five then dropped it when it was ignored, pretending to scratch an itch.

In the cafeteria, Ezra sat alone. Which wasn't unusual; most days, after practicing mindful eating, he read a book. But today his bubble of invisibility had burst and he sensed people looking at him, talking about him, yet also studiously avoiding eye contact. It was like being under a spotlight and in the shadows at the same time. He picked at the chicken salad croissant his father had prepared with little appetite.

From a table behind him he heard two boys talking. "Maybe, he just, you know, hates gay people or something?"

"I don't know, maybe?"

The hair on Ezra's back stood up and his pulse rate accelerated. Him, a homophobe? He'd read that book about Heather having two mothers in kindergarten! He'd been voted "most accepting" two years running at Wells! And he had gay friends, though their names eluded him at the moment. He wanted to swivel about in his bench to plead his innocence but held back. If he acted upset, wouldn't it look like the accusation was true? His head felt ready to explode.

Later at recess, offered twice a week as a substitute for gym, Ezra was usually content to sit on the grass and read. But today, discontentedly digging at the earth with a stick, he watched children play ball or draw on the asphalt. Why was he never asked to join? Would he want to if he was? Overwhelmed with conflicting emotions, he recalled a suggestion a therapist had once made and did a body scan. He noticed that his throat chakra was especially constricted as if stifling a scream or cry. But what did he have to cry about? It was his idea to wear the shirt in the first place. Did general crappiness count as a feeling?

Across the courtyard, Ezra saw three students standing in a tight circle, looking at him. One of them, a tall boy with curly red hair, suddenly broke away and headed to Ezra with eyes locked like a loaded gun. It was the boy from Algebra.

"Yes? Can I help you?" Ezra asked testily, abandoning any attempt to sound polite.

"You come to a new school and wanna start a movement?" the boy said, towering over Ezra.

The voice sounded familiar. Was this the boy who had sat behind him at lunch?

"Yes! I mean, no! Or I don't know…" Ezra trailed off. Why couldn't people just deal with his stupid shirt? "Why are you so triggered by this? Are you suppressing same-sex attractions of your own?" he countered, attempting to recall what his mother had said that had made sense at the time but seemed like meaningless jargon now.

The boy lunged at Ezra and yanked up the tan polo. "Yeah, sure, I'm queer and this…" he said, pointing at the red t-shirt's lettering, "really offends me. I don't need someone who doesn't know what their dick is for to lecture me about being a FAGGOT!" He pulled the polo over Ezra's head and pushed him to the ground. "How's that for triggering?"

Just that moment the school bell rang and teachers began calling everyone back to class.

Ezra pulled his polo back down, hoping no one had noticed.

Fortunately the rest of the school day passed without incident. Except for a few curious looks and whispers, students had moved on to other concerns. Ezra was returning to his invisible status and was glad of it.

As he walked home he looked both ways as he passed the rear of the school. The coast was clear. He removed the tan polo and stuffed it in his backpack. It was a warm day and the polyester fabric was so uncomfortable. He crossed the school field, entered the forest, and began to walk downhill.

His peace of mind was cut short when Buzz Cut leapt out from behind a tree.

"Oh, *Ezra*," he said, stretching out the name and holding out a limp wrist. "So nice to run into you again."

His followers appeared from behind other trees and stood off to one side, waiting. "It's…nice to see you too?"

Buzz Cut pointed to Ezra's red t-shirt. "Truth in advertising, isn't it, boys?" Then he turned to face Ezra. "What did we tell you about not liking your kind at our school?"

"B…but…." There was no logical answer to that question.

"Shut up!" he snarled, ripping off Ezra's backpack and pushing him into a tree's rough bark.

His eyes glowed with an inhuman anger. The others closed rank. Ezra was alone in the woods. No one could hear him scream. He imagined his rotting corpse found weeks later covered with leaves…his mother crying at the funeral. Tears of his own began to form. *I'm sorry, mom, I'm sorry. Dad, I love you.*

"Let go of him, Donnie!" a voice cried.

Donnie? Who was Donnie? As Buzz Cut's head swiveled to the direction of the voice, Ezra realized that Buzz Cut had an actual name. Was it short for Donald?

At the top of the hill was the boy from Algebra, his curly hair glowing in the sun.

"So who's going make me?" Donnie hissed.

"We are." Another boy appeared with fists planted on his hips, wearing a striped rugby shirt with a bright white collar that contrasted with his dark skin.

"Yeah. Lay off him. Or we'll tell your dad." A girl with blond ponytail and jean-jacket stood forward with her arms folded against her chest. Ezra recognized the three of them from the playground.

"Ah, so it's the pussy posse," Donnie said, snickering at his alliterative slur. "Of course you're all hanging out together. Fucking queers."

With the name Donnie, he looked more petulant than threatening to Ezra.

The boy with red hair approached, his lean frame towering over Donnie, who puffed out his chest but also backed up a few steps. "It's four against three. The math is against you."

Four? Oh, they're including me too. Ezra noticed Donnie was shorter than he remembered, no taller than he was.

The boy in the rugby shirt addressed Scarecrow. "Why do you hang around this psychopath, Sean?" He had a real name too.

"I don't get why you let Donnie push you around, Hughie. Have some self respect!" the blonde girl said. With an actual name, Pig Eyes seemed less pig-like and more…Hughie-like.

"C'mon. Let's lose these losers," Donnie blustered, then headed off into the woods. "Are you coming?" he called to Sean and Hughie over his shoulder.

Donnie's lackeys hesitated, looking first at him then at Ezra's protectors, eventually hurrying after their leader as he strode into the woods.

Ezra inhaled deeply then let out a big sigh. His chest and shoulders relaxed but his legs were still trembling.

"Thank you so much. I'm Ezra," he said breathlessly, holding out a shaking hand to the boy with curly hair.

"Yeah, we all know who you are. I'm Nate." He held out his

hand then, as Ezra reached to shake it, pulled it back laughing. "I'm just messing with you. Here." He held out a fist and Ezra, awkwardly executing his first fist bump, met Nate's gently.

"Jan," the girl said, her arms still folded but giving a thumbs up.

"And I'm Clifford. Nice to meet you." The boy in the rugby shirt held out his hand for a traditional handshake and Ezra returned it gratefully. "Your shirt is cool, by the way! I like the font. Where'd you get it?"

"My father made it for me."

"No way! Your dad? Wish I had a dad like that!"

Nate jumped in. "Hey, sorry about earlier but if I ever pulled a stunt like that, I wouldn't just get in trouble but I'd be disowned too. So it was kind of offensive self-defense?"

"Nice try, Nate," Jan said. "Don't we get pushed around enough already? No need for you to join in."

"Yeah, sorry. Truce?"

Ezra, warily, shook his hand.

"Okay. Thanks...yeah. My dad's...um...cool," Ezra replied, not sure who he was addressing. "Um...why are you here? I mean, I'm glad you showed up, but how did you know I was here?"

"I saw you walking this way," Nate said.

Jan interrupted. "I pointed you out first. 'Who's that guy going in the woods?' I said. It's a little weird. Mostly only stoners go in the woods."

"You were attracting a lot of attention today with that shirt, too. So I asked around who you were," Clifford added.

"And I knew those creeps would be looking for you," Nate said. "I mean, it's cool you can wear that but it kinda makes you a target."

Ezra could not deny the truth of that statement.

"Advice?" Jan spoke up. "If you want a place to hide, the costume closet in the drama room is a good place to chill."

"I do my homework there sometimes," Clifford said. "Guys like Donnie never go there. Teachers too. All the sequins scare them, I guess."

Nate broke in. "Hey guys, I gotta go. You coming, Ezra?"

"Coming? Oh...I guess it's not a good idea to go *that* way," Ezra said, pointing in the direction his bullies had departed. He began to giggle uncontrollably; the situation suddenly seemed so absurd.

"Yeah, I'd leave them alone for a while. Let them convince themselves that they won," Nate said with a wry smile, giving time for Ezra to pull himself together.

"Hey, maybe my mom can give you a ride? Where do you live?" Clifford asked.

"I live on Millerford Creek Road, if it isn't too out of the way," Ezra said, glad to be back on solid ground.

"Millerford! That's my street. Which house?" " Where it crosses the creek?"

"Wait, is that the house with all the weeds in front?" Clifford asked.

"Weeds? Oh, you mean the pollinator garden? My grandmother, you see, believes grass lawns are…"

"Oh, cool, whatever. Don't tell my mom that. And you might want to put that other shirt back on."

Ezra said goodbye to Nate and Jan and followed Clifford back to the pickup line in front of school. Clifford opened the rear door of a metallic brown station wagon.

"Hey, mom, is it okay if we give him a ride?" He jumped in, motioning Ezra to join him. A black woman with straightened hair and pearls turned around to give Ezra the once over.

"Thank you so much for the lift, ma'am. My name is Ezra."

Her shoulders relaxing but still smiling stiffly, she said, "Pleased to meet you, Ezra. I'm Mrs. Delacroix."

"Mom, Ezra's new at school. And he lives on our street."

"That's nice, dear. How are you liking school, Ezra?"

"I like it very much, thank you. The instruction is excellent and the students are very welcoming." *Sometimes a white lie is necessary to conform to social expectations,* he rationalized. He gave Clifford an embarrassed smile and got a wink in return.

"Hey, mom, do you think I can stay after school on Wednesday? Me and Ezra have a homework project we're working on."

"That's 'Ezra and I,' and we'll talk about it when we get home. I'll need to ask your father."

As the car left the parking lot and a momentary silence fell, Ezra looked thoughtfully out at the afternoon sun reflecting off passing traffic. He wasn't familiar with the assignment Clifford had mentioned but felt a warm glow thinking about it just the same. Did it really matter anyway? Wasn't life a little bit like a homework assignment? It is always more fun when you have someone to do it with. And a safe space like a costume closet to do it in. That was a deep thought that he would definitely enter in his journal that night.

And the red t-shirt? That deserved to be hung in a place of honor in his closet where he could admire it. But for now, he'd leave it off at school.

BEAVER MOON

Laura Corin

"Have you heard the queer wives' tale about the Beaver Moon?" the woman in a bright-orange beanie asked, the bonfire lighting up her face.

We had gathered in the valley on the property of one of my wife's friends to celebrate the autumn equinox and a blood moon, a total lunar eclipse. It was dark, the kind of dark we hadn't seen for months but that descended all of sudden when summer ended.

The party would have been better if I wasn't sober or if clouds didn't block the view of the moon or if I knew more people here. Really, it would have been better if I'd been home, under a blanket, drinking tea and reading a book, pregnant. Instead, I was here, cold, standing on dry, frosty grass, hoping.

"Tell it," an older butch woman who brought her own camp chair to the party shouted to the woman in the orange beanie.

I dug my cold hands into the pockets of my jacket, wishing I had brought gloves. There was something hard in one pocket. I pulled it out and looked at it by the light of the fire. When I saw what it was, I was so startled I almost dropped it.

"You okay, Olivia?" my wife Mari asked me from across the fire. With her black-knit cap, flannel jacket, and kissable neck, she looked like an androgynous model for some dyke outdoor wear.

I nodded at her, grinning. How did my wedding ring get in this jacket pocket? I had lost the ring last spring on a hike. We'd looked everywhere for it. I'd even gone back to the trail several times in the summer, just in case I'd find it after the snow had melted. When we couldn't find it, Mari got me a new one, which was lovely, an actual gem, not a crude small one like we could afford when we first got in engaged.

"Listen up, friends and foes—" Orange Beanie began in a dramatic, storyteller voice.

"Who you calling a foe?"

"I think she said 'hoes.'"

"Ah, yes, that we are."

The storyteller in the orange beanie cleared her throat. "The Beaver Moon is not to be trifled with."

I slipped the ring on. It was loose on my cold fingers. I must have taken the ring off during the hike and put it in this jacket for safekeeping, a jacket we didn't wear much. Too warm for summer, too cold for winter. A jacket for the in-between seasons.

"When there is a blood moon on the fall equinox, you can make a wish." The storyteller's voice carried across the party to the bare birch trees and tall spruce pines lining the edge of the property. My breath caught in my throat. "You can wish for anything you want." I swallowed, listening, as if the storyteller was speaking only to me. "Sacrifice something precious to the fire, and your wish will come true by the next full moon."

They told about how the legend came to be. I twisted the ring, no longer cold, on my finger, my heart picking up speed.

"I want a new job," Gina said, swaying, drunk, as usual. The last time I saw Gina, she puked in our car when I gave her a ride home from the bar. "I hate my job."

"You have to give up something dear," the storyteller reminded her.

"This beer is dear." Gina held it above the flames.

"Ah, but be careful. The fire takes more than was given."

"Don't let it take my beer too!" the grey-haired butch in the camp chair shouted.

"It's true. It really is," said Alexa, a tall woman with a gold nose ring and a short, purple-tinged fro. She dated my wife years ago, before I moved to Alaska. "We had a Beaver Moon when I was kid. My brother sacrificed his favorite sneakers for a new snowboard – and he got it. He won it in this contest. It was dope. But he broke his foot and didn't get to use it that winter. Too bad. I borrowed it, though. Sweet ride."

"Beaver Moon, red and full of glory, though I can't see you at the moment because of the damn clouds, get me a new job. As payment, I give you this beer – which I just opened and really want to drink." Gina poured the beer into the fire.

BEAVER MOON

The flames didn't dampen with the liquid or increase with the alcohol. Instead, a green glow flickered in the center of the fire. I approached the firepit to get a better look, but the fire popped and sparked. I jumped back. When I looked again, the green flames were gone.

"Did you see that?" I asked Mari, who was walking over to me. She had this confident swagger that I could watch all day.

"You almost caught my jacket on fire?" Mari stood behind me and put her arms around me, her head on my shoulder. She felt so good against me. I loved the weight of her pressing into my back. My body relaxed into her. A star peeked out from the clouds above.

My amazing wife. Smart and strong. Kind and funny. Sexy and patient.

She was almost enough.

But there was a hole in my heart, in my being. I wanted a child. I wanted to be a mother. I wanted it more than I'd ever wanted anything. We'd been trying for two years. Two years of frozen sperm shipped to Alaska. Two years of hormone injections and ultrasounds. Two years of Clomid migraines and heartbreak.

What would I give to have a child? Everything. Everything.

I closed my eyes, savoring Mari holding me. She never held me in public, never did any kind of PDA, only when we were near other queer people.

Maybe I should wish that she could be enough, that I could be satisfied with what I had.

She gave me another squeeze and went over to a friend to smoke a joint. She tried to hide her smoking from me, even though it was legal. She still saw a good girl when she looked at me and wanted me to see good when I looked at her. Not that I could see anything else. I still couldn't believe I'd gotten her to fall in love with me. I used all my good luck getting her. Worth it, sure, but if I were to have a baby, I'd need more than luck.

I fiddled with the rings on my finger. I had a new ring. Mari would never need to know I found the old one.

If only it were that simple. Toss in an object, watch it burn, make a wish, have a baby.

The need was so strong it pulsed in my whole body, creating an emptiness nothing else could fill. I wanted a baby. I wanted. I wanted. Dreams came true all the time. Why not mine?

It could happen. It could be happening now. I got my squirt

of sperm a few days ago. In two weeks, I could test. Two weeks of blessed, agonizing hope.

What if. What if. What if.

Before I let reason take over, I tossed my first wedding ring into the fire. "I want a baby," I whispered to the flames. "Please, help me get pregnant."

The green flames reappeared. The fire popped, sending a shower of sparks all around us.

We were out of bread.

I sighed as I stared at the sad, remaining, flat end piece, wondering if I had enough time at work today to go out for lunch since this wasn't going to make a very good sandwich. I checked the freezer drawer to see if we had any frozen loaves. Nope. I felt like I was going to cry. It wasn't about the bread, of course. It was hormones. I was as mercurial as a teenager. Tomorrow I would test to see if I was pregnant.

Mari popped in the kitchen to pour coffee into her thermos before biking to work.

"You seeing Gina anytime soon? We're out of bread." I hated the whining in my voice, the desperation. I sounded like a petulant child.

Gina worked as a driver for a bread company that supplied fresh loaves to the grocery stores in town. She gave us misshapen loaves, day-olds and extras they couldn't sell.

"Didn't you hear? She doesn't work there anymore." Mari added sugar to her thermos.

"What?" I had left social media months ago – everyone in my feed seemed to be having children or their children were experiencing all sorts of milestones, or it was about protests and war and how I should be doing more, which I should be but wasn't.

"Yeah, she got a DUI, and they fired her. She's working at Wolf Paw in the kitchen now, says she's going to get sober this time, for real."

I twirled my newer wedding ring around my finger. Gina had gotten a new job. The circumstances weren't ideal, but her Beaver Moon wish came true.

The fire takes more than was given. Would it take my other ring somehow? I didn't care. Take all the rings. Give me a baby.

"Do you miss it?"

"Hmm?" I blinked out of my daydreams of how my wish could come true.

"Your engagement ring. Do you miss it?"

I paused in my twirling of the ring and thought about telling her how I found the old one but threw it into a fire because of a queer wives' tale, but then I would feel compelled to joke about it and that might insult the magic. I shook my head. "I love my new ring. It's beautiful."

"You're beautiful." She drank in my face like I was a work of art. She was the sexy one that all the girls noticed, but she acted like I was a prize she had won.

Heat crept up my cheeks. I couldn't believe she still made me blush after all these years. "Do you miss it?" I asked her, worried now if I had given the wrong offering for my wish. She had picked the first ring out with a friend at antique store. I selected the new one in a jewelry store in the mall.

"I have you. That's what matters. I don't need no ring to know you're mine." The hunger in her eyes when she looked at me made me soft and eager. She hooked a finger through my belt loop and tugged me to her. "You wanna skip work today?"

I grabbed her short, black-brown hair and pulled her lips to mine. She could still light me up like a Christmas tree. "Get out of here. We'll both be late." I slapped her ass, shooing her out of the kitchen.

My period started between a budget meeting and a project meeting. I had felt the trickle while my coworkers talked numbers. I ignored it. I wished I believed in God enough to pray.

After the budget meeting, I dashed to the bathroom, the small, far one that no one liked to use. I didn't stop by my office to pick up supplies. I didn't want to jinx myself. But sure enough, blood streaked my underwear. Not light spotting that could happen when people got pregnant. A menstrual cycle.

I choked back a sob but let myself cry silently. I rested

my forehead on the cool stall door. I had to go. People would wonder where I was. I stayed a moment more, washed my face, squared my shoulders and pretended my heart wasn't broken.

No one at work knew I was trying to get pregnant. I didn't want to face their questions about logistics or their requests for status updates when the news wasn't good, and it was never good. "It would be nice someday," I would say when they asked if I ever thought about having kids, as if I could think of anything else. Thankfully no one had caught on despite all my doctor appointments and artificially enhanced hormonal surges.

I arrived late to the project meeting and without my notes. When my boss shared my idea as his own, an idea he had dismissed last week as unworkable, I didn't care.

Cameron, my best friend at the office, caught my eye from the other end of my table. "You okay?" he mouthed to me.

I shook my head and looked away. I wouldn't cry in this meeting. I would not.

When I got back to my desk, I texted Mari. "Period started. No go. L L" As if two emojis could illustrate the despair that sucked away at my being. I knew what would make me happy, but I had no idea if I would get it. It made sense that people could die of sadness.

She texted back right away. "I love you princesa. I'm sorry. Besos."

Mari wanted kids too, but she had no interest in being pregnant and didn't have that whole-body urge that I did. She would make a great mom, though, I knew she would.

I stared at my computer screen and tried to think about anything but the fact that I wasn't pregnant. Again.

Shards of what could have been scattered inside me, sharp and cutting. If I wasn't careful, the broken hope would be deadly, slicing out my will to live.

Sure, there was adoption and more attempts, fostering and aren't niblings great? Have you ever thought about getting a dog? But I wanted the package – the breastfeeding, the ultrasounds, the midnight cravings and recognizable features.

"Walk?" One of the tallest people in our office, Cameron was the only one who could actually lean over the cubicle walls. The fluorescent lights shined off his dark bald head.

I nodded, grateful. I had only dated a few men and the experience wasn't great, but the stirrings in me when I noticed how Cameron's muscular arms and chest pressed against his crisp work shirts made me think I wasn't 100% a lesbian.

"You want to talk about it?" Cameron asked after we'd gotten onto our regular loop, the sidewalk around the downtown city park.

"No." Yes. But how to bring up now? Cameron and his wife Amari were going through a divorce, and he wanted more custody of his daughter, an adorable kindergartener that I couldn't get enough of, so even though my heart was breaking, it seemed small in comparison. People who had kids never seemed to understand the awfulness of infertility.

"Would it help it I told you how shitty my life has been lately?" Cameron asked.

"Absolutely."

A broad dry leaf crunched under his shoe. "Amari is pregnant."

"Oh my god."

"I know, right?"

"Yours?"

"Yes, it was a moment – we're trying to – it doesn't matter. She won't keep it. Says it's already complicated enough."

I wanted to be supportive, I did. Cameron was a great father and wanted a big family like the one he'd grown up in, but all I could say was, "It isn't fair."

He paused. The sky was so blue, a baby blue. The breeze swept into my jacket, chilling me. I should have brought a hat to cover my ears. I told him how I wanted to be pregnant, how we'd been trying for two years, which was like five years for a heterosexual couple because of all the logistics, and how I thought this time was my chance but it wasn't.

He shook his head. "If I could take the baby from her and put it in you, I would."

We watched ravens fight over a half-eaten hamburger lying in the street.

In the beginning, I had actually considered asking Cameron to be a sperm donor, but Mari and I decided he was too close to be around but not the father. As if turned out, it was good. We had already gone through three sperm donors from the sperm bank. It would have been a nightmare to do all we needed to do with another party involved.

One raven took off with most of the remaining hamburger in its beak. The other stayed in the street, pecking at crumbs.

On the table when I got home was a bottle of my favorite red wine and a spread of soft cheeses, all of which I had been avoiding for the past two weeks in case the insemination had worked. I imagined Mari stuffing the wine into her backpack for the bike ride home.

Now, I could cry. Mari took me in her strong arms, smelling like her musky cologne and sweat from her bike ride. My snot and tears soaked her synthetic shirt until I had cried myself out. Still, she held me. Everything felt right in the world when I was in her arms.

"Sing me a song." My voice warbled from all the sobbing.

She pulled away and held my chin. She had been a favorite local drag king when we met and still performed sometimes. "You know I only lip sync, right? I can't actually sing."

"Sing for me. You know the one."

"I'll need to get my leather jacket and these pants won't do at all."

I sat at the table and poured myself a glass of wine. "I'll wait."

Several days later, Mari wasn't there when I got home from work. She got off work before me and usually arrived home before I did, even when I drove and she biked. I checked our shared calendar on the phone to see if she had something after work. Nothing was in there for today, but maybe she forgot to put it in. Or tell me.

Or maybe she had told me and I forgot. I had started the process over for this cycle, ordering the sperm and hormones, arranging the ultrasounds to check my ovaries and the blood draws. I was still upset I threw my engagement ring into the fire last month for a wish that didn't come true. What had I been thinking?

I texted my wife, checking in. Just in case. No reply.

It was getting late. She should have called by now. I was getting hungry. I didn't want to be that needy wife. The hormones sometimes made me paranoid. Still, I looked up the location of her phone.

It was at the hospital.

My body went cold. There were tons of reasons she would be at the hospital and not texting me.

Right?

Someone would have called if it was bad.

Right?

I didn't have time to think more. I grabbed an apple for me and an energy bar for her and raced out the door.

The next week blurred together, a river of anxiety and hesitant relief. Mari was alive, that was what I clung to. A car had run a red light and hit her as she biked home. Somehow, the bike, miraculously undamaged, made it back to our house. Somehow, I changed clothes and ate food. Somehow, I notified work. Somehow, I didn't stalk the driver and add another patient to the intensive care unit.

Mari woke up in moments between surgeries, high on painkillers and anesthesia. The bruises on her face and arms looked worse each day. The swelling around her eyes increased.

The doctors and nurses told me she was lucky to be alive. They were glad they didn't have to fly her to Seattle. They listed off the surgeries and the this and the that. Though I was the type to remember all the medical terms, I couldn't recall what they said other than there were things they still worried about, elements that made the furrow never leave their brows as they spoke to me, reasons she had to stay in the hospital.

Mari's mom came up from Idaho, smelling like clean laundry and faith, making the trip in flash like she couldn't do for our wedding when we had months of planning. We took shifts sitting by Mari's bed in the hospital. She didn't annoy me as much as usual. In fact, I was grateful for her prayers. We needed all the help we could get.

It was the afternoon but felt like morning when Cameron and his daughter Jayla stopped by for a visit. They brought a bright blue stuffed stegosaurus. We all used to have dinner together at each other's houses before his divorce. Jayla always got along best with Mari. They raced cars around the living room and made slime with shaving cream. Of course, Mari got along with everyone so I shouldn't have been surprised.

I ran my fingers down the spikes of the dinosaur. "Is this for Mari?"

Jayla nodded. The beads at the end of her braids clicked together. "And you. His name is Samilicious."

"No. They get to decide the name, remember?" Cameron told his daughter. "It's their dinosaur."

Jayla stuck her lower lip out, clearly not happy with that idea.

"I think Samilicious is the perfect name. Thank you very much." I hugged the dinosaur. "Welcome to Room 2254, Samilicious. I can't wait to take you home." I went to put the dinosaur on the small shelf with the other cards, but I couldn't bring myself to let go of its soft body.

Jayla hugged me too. I couldn't seem to let go of her either. Her hair smelled like spring flowers, such sweetness among the sterile cleaners of the hospital.

Cameron stood over us, seeming taller than ever. "You want to hear all the gossip at work? We could take a walk."

I didn't give a damn about work. The machines beeped. Mari should be cracking jokes, not lying there with too many tubes in her, the stitches on her shoulder held together with what looked like clear tape, but it was a relief to see Cameron. I hadn't realized how much I missed him.

"Do they have ice cream in the hospital restaurant?" Jayla asked.

"Good food first," her dad reminded her.

"Go eat. I am with Marisol," Mari's mom said. She never liked me, and I didn't think that changed any this week, but we had found our rhythm.

I brought Samilicious the Dinosaur with us on our walk to the cafeteria. Jayla did all the talking for us. Instead of the gossip at work, I learned about who had thrown up in her kindergarten class this year and where. Her high voice had its own melody, like a song I could always listen to.

Cameron met my eyes over her head and raised his eyebrows with a you-still-want-kids? expression.

I shook my head. He didn't understand. This moment was exactly what I wanted.

It was snowing lightly outside. We paused by a big window

in the corridor and watched the flakes fall. Jayla described the Halloween costume that she was hoping her dad would make. I'd heard he was pretty handy around the house, but a fairy shark robot seemed different than building a coffee table, especially since Halloween was next week. She took my hand without prompting. My other arm cradled the soft blue dinosaur. Her little fingers were warm.

The nurses on break and other stressed family members in the cafeteria reminded me why I was at the hospital. My gut twisted, heavy and thick, despite my hunger. The harsh lights and too many bad food choices overwhelmed me. When the clerk told me the lollipop was for my daughter, I just stared at him.

He wiggled the lollipop out to me and gestured to Cameron and Jayla who went to find us a table. "For her, if that's alright with you and your husband." The cafeteria clerk smiled a kind smile that reached his bushy, white and grey eyebrows. He was someone who had seen a lot of distracted people at their worst. "You have a beautiful family."

"Thank you," I said, mouth dry, not having the energy to explain. I took the lollipop and made my way to the table.

Jayla took the lollipop from my hand without pausing her story about the Tricycle Incident, as if the candy could only have been meant for her. She was light-skinned like her mother. I could see, looking at me and Cameron, how she could seem like a blend of us, like she was ours. I sat with Samilicious on my lap, as if I were holding it for my daughter, not for my wife, not for me.

I was about to nod off in the uncomfortable chair, Mari's mom dozing in the makeshift bed, when I saw the ugliest card on the table next to Jayla and Cameron's homemade one.

It was not even a get-well card but a raunchy birthday card about beer goggles. Someone crossed out Happy Birthday and wrote, "Can't wait to laugh about this at your next birthday. -Peace, Gina."

Gina. Goodness. Seven years I'd been with Mari, and I still didn't get why she was friends with that loud, obnoxious person. I wondered if we'd connect better now that Gina had a new job and a new relationship with sobriety.

And she got her wish and I didn't. And Alexa's brother had gotten his Beaver Moon wish all those years ago. I had paused the sperm and hormone shipments and my appointments during the last few days. I wouldn't try again this cycle, not until Mari was out of this mess. And the moon was almost full again.

I wrapped my arms around Samilicious and hugged the dinosaur tight, mourning my wife's health and my chance this cycle for a baby. Cameron's ex-wife probably had had her abortion by now. He said she wasn't his first lover to do so. His girlfriend in high school wasn't ready to parent and neither was he. He said he felt like he could get a girl pregnant just by looking at her. Except me, of course.

The sinking feeling in my gut charged up to my throat until I felt like I was choking. I tried to swallow. I tried to breathe. Mari's mom stirred in her light sleep, rosary beads clutched in her hand. Mari was so still but not at peace. Some cuts had already started to scar.

If I lost Mari, Cameron would comfort me, as he did. And in that easy way we had with each other, I would find my way to his bed. He would get me pregnant. The Beaver Moon had laid it all out. I'd be a mother. I would get my wish.

The fire takes more than is given.

I cried out loud enough to wake up Mari's mom. "What happened?" she asked in a sleep-filled voice, her accent thicker than normal, not awake enough to hide it.

"I have to go. I'll be back," I promised.

The snow had stopped as I drove out of Anchorage to the valley, a dusting of white on everything. The hour drive took forever and passed in a minute at the same time. The moon was so big and yellow and almost full. Was it full? What day was it? It couldn't be full yet. It couldn't. I did the math as I drove over an icy bridge. Tonight was the full moon.

I couldn't remember where the party was. Mari had driven us there and guided me on the drive home. Everything looked different with the snow.

After twisting through this street and that, I pulled over and hit the steering wheel over and over. I screamed until my throat hurt. Panting, I saw the street sign ahead. Finger Lake, that was right. We had laughed about the name.

I swallowed. I got back on the narrow road and drove. It was quiet out here, far from the city. Full of bare birch trees and skinny spruce pines. No cars on the road. Snow muting everything. I drove to the end where the pavement crumbled into frozen mud. Lights were on in the small, still-being-built house. Tyvek siding covered part of one wall. The house sat on an acre or so of property, owned by a lesbian couple I'd met a few times. Lots of cars were here a month ago. It felt so empty now.

At first, I crept along the woods to get to the firepit, but then I didn't care if they saw me. I didn't care if they thought I was crazy. I ran to the firepit and swept off the snow, thicker here than in town. I pulled out wood turned to charcoal and coal gone cold. I dug my fingers in the ashes for my ring. It had to be here, melted and ruined perhaps, but here, here. I clawed in the ashes.

"I take it back! I take it back!"

I clawed and dug under the watchful full moon, clawed and dug.

THE HUNDRED YEAR MAN

J. Duncan Davidson

With Jake's afternoon plans canceled, and since DB never seemed to have anywhere to go, they'd gotten lazy and fallen asleep listening to the street noise coming in through the open window.

Later when Jake woke, it was nearly 5:00. He peed, drank water from the tap. The flushing toilet roused DB as well, who was propped up on a pillow when Jake looked in on him. Instead of returning to bed, he pivoted towards the kitchen to make a call he knew would be overheard.

"Lara..."

Usually when DB came by, he didn't stay long. In five minutes, he'd dressed and was at the door trying not to interrupt and giving Jake a nod before disappearing. Watching him go, Jake thought to himself how easy it was with him, that nothing more was ever expected.

Lara had been explaining, "I'm at Emm's house now. He didn't have a key, so I looked and found a spare on top of the window." Her tone had grown cold since morning. A sadness had crept in that Jake figured he should've seen coming. She went on. "This place is a time capsule." She paused. "Jake. I know I told you not to bother coming, but there's something here you need to see." Her voice trailed off, tired.

The house was the last holdout on a street now full of orderly townhomes and a reminder of how different the neighborhood had once been. Its shabby state mimicked its owner's decline. It was where Emm had lived his entire adult life and where his wife, Beth, had died some years earlier. As far as anyone knew, there'd never been any children.

In contrast to the property's general decay, a bed of roses near the front door looked vigorous and well-tended. They summed up the amount of gardening Emm could still manage and were the reason Lara knew him at all. They shared a sidewalk, and they talked occasionally when he was outside and she walked by. She called him "Emm" out of affection anyway. Emm for Emmet. Her daughter called him "Rabbit," partly because "Rabbit" sounded an awful lot like Emmet to an eight-year-old's ears, but more because she liked how he peeked out from behind the bushes like a timid bunny.

The morning when Emm was found collapsed in his yard, Lara had been out front walking home when the ambulance arrived. Seeing how scared he looked on the stretcher, she'd promised without hesitating to go with him to the hospital so he wouldn't be alone. It was only later after the emergency was over that she'd stopped to think about where that impulse to help had come from. It was with surprise she realized it was because of the way Emm had looked at her from the ground, so frail, before he'd squinted his eyes tightly shut, reminding her too much of her own grandfather...who'd got sick, grown emaciated, lingered for weeks, then passed in agony with no one beside him.

The next day, Lara told Jake the full story about how Emm had fallen down a flight of stairs then laid on the kitchen floor until finding the strength to crawl outside. "His shoulder is fractured badly. The doctors say his bones are like sawdust, so the surgeons won't operate. There's nothing to be done." She'd stopped talking, wondering what it would be like in Emm's shoes to hear that kind of news. "It's bad." Then to make the point: "he's really old."

For Lara, being in Emm's house felt disorienting like she was a child again visiting her grandfather's home and waiting to be scolded for touching things. It made her remember how his need to have everything a certain way hadn't changed when she was older and, needing a place to live, he'd taken her in.

She was sitting on the couch when Jake entered without knocking. Seeing the expression on her face he sat down beside her and asked, "Hey, you okay?"

To which she replied, "Of course."

The room was tidy, unexceptional. There was one framed print on each wall and an assortment of decorative objects suggesting an older generation's middle-class ambitions. It seemed nothing had been changed or added in decades, like Emm at some point had stopped living. Looking around, Jake said, "I see what you mean."

Lara grabbed a photograph of a young woman off a side table, likely Emm's deceased wife. She waved it at the room. "Someone's going to have to get rid of all this stuff." She left the thought hanging that Emm wasn't coming back again, ever.

To satisfy their curiosity they walked through the kitchen, opening drawers and cupboards, then poked their heads into the bedrooms. "There's nothing much here," Lara said, and Jake agreed. The entire place was somehow empty, not of things but of human spirit. He wondered how that was even possible. When he mentioned his thoughts, all Lara said was, "Wait. You'll see." She then took him to a doorway that opened onto a steep flight of stairs leading up to what Jake assumed would be the attic. The bottom steps were still wet where she'd sponged off Emm's dried blood. She pointed up. "This is what I wanted to show you," she said, then waved for Jake to follow.

At the top of the stairs they entered a large yet surprisingly cozy room that got its odd shape by following the configuration of the roof. A small dormer window let in a delicate evening light. In contrast to the ground floor this room felt crowded, disorderly, with a jumble of furniture squeezed in. There were dressers, bookshelves, antique chests, and a desk pushed up against the opposite wall. The best part was, to Jake anyway, how every surface, every square inch of tabletop and wall, was covered with objects and pictures that spoke of years of passionate collecting. The air smelled faintly stale and sweet at the same time, of acid damaged books, motor oil, dried flowers, and mildew. "Emm's private room," he thought. Lara turned on a table lamp, causing a smile to creep over Jake's face.

Everywhere his eyes settled there was more to look at. Emm had nailed pictures to the underside of the rafters so close together that the frames touched creating the effect of two tapestries running up the underside of the roof to meet at the ridge line, reminding Jake of the inside fabric of a pup tent. The pictures were of different sizes and styles and didn't appear to have anything in common, some of landscapes, some of animals, some just playful scenes of people. The largest was a poster of a college rower in a racing shell, a young man with a muscled back pulling hard on the oars. It was next to a sepia toned painting of a lone farmer plowing a field with a horse.

There were prints of such things as a stone barn, old cars, a house being built. Mixed in were a handful of Vietnam-war era snapshots of men in stained uniforms hamming for the camera. As Lara pointed out, "Heroes not heart throbs," fit men, but with pear shaped bodies. They grinned broadly with American smiles, smoking American cigarettes.

What stood out amongst all the clutter by the way they were lined up and given extra space on the wall were five photographs set on a chair-rail running behind the desk. They seemed to be an odd mix of subjects until Jake noticed the figures in each one of them were all men...men at work, men sleeping, men caught in moments when they didn't know or care they were being watched.

"There's something else," Lara said. "Look." And she pointed at an upholstered chair set in the corner. Carefully draped across its back was an orange and gray plaid shirt, ironed flat, with its sleeves arranged along the chair's arms. Lined up on the seat beneath it were a pair of jeans that were well-worn to a rich chamois texture but still a comforting indigo. The pant legs hung down to the floor where a pair of workmen's boots had been placed with one boot aligned with each leg. A wide leather belt ran through the pant loops, and on the adjacent table lay a baseball cap, a watch, and a pack of gum that, by the look of the brand, would be at least fifty years old. It was the idea of a man seemingly caught in a moment of repose, carefully arranged, without the animal parts of blood and bone.

Jake just stared. "Well, I didn't see that coming."

"It's why I needed you here. To make sure I wasn't going crazy."

From that moment on Jake's mood changed and he hesitated to touch anything. The contents of the room had suddenly become personal, as if the man in the chair could somehow stretch out and claim everything within reach. He left drawers unopened and cupboards closed. Lara went to stand by the window. "All this stuff..." It weighted on her, too, and suddenly she wanted to get away from the house. "We're here for those photos anyway," she said pointing at the five above the desk. "Emm made me promise to bring them next time I visit."

Before heading back downstairs Lara took another look at the chair. Then on the way out, she said what they both were thinking, "Looks like Emm has a surprise or two left in him." Which she followed with, "As if it matters now." To which Jake silently disagreed. With Emm dying, it was exactly the right time for such things to matter.

It surprised Lara just how much the attic had got under her skin. So much so, before leaving she'd asked Jake to hold on to the photographs, which meant he had them with him later that night. The contents of the room had affected Jake deeply as well, but had less haunted than thrilled him. Being surrounded by Emm's stuff was like finding a private diary that he wanted badly to read. On reflection, there was something comfortingly familiar about the room's contents also, and he sensed a kinship with Emm that he was pretty sure Lara didn't share. He couldn't decide if it was wrong to pry, but he knew he had to work out what the room meant to Emm, and especially to the man Emm became when he thought no one was watching. He sensed the photographs could offer important clues in that effort, so the first thing he did when he got home was to lay them out across a table to examine each more closely.

He proceeded methodically. The photos were all old black and whites, as best he could tell, spanning most of the twentieth century. Each was about 7"x10" in size and mounted on cardboard. The oldest, dated 1915 on the back in pencil, showed a scene at an old-fashioned shingle mill with a row of men lined up in front of an open building full of machinery. Their ages range from mid-teens to early fifties. The ones in their thirties wear the big mustaches popular ten years earlier, while those younger and older are clean shaven. Their faces tell the hard luck story of itinerant workers with low expectations used to long hours of dangerous work. But one stands out. He has swagger. He's young and well-formed, confident. There's something modern about him, like he's part of a future the others can't quite grasp yet. He reclines with his legs splayed in casual invitation. He'll be the one telling stories at night about the women he beds, while the others listen greedily.

A younger man sits beside him, curled up like a pet. Lacking all swagger, he's simply a boy trying to make his way in the world of men, not knowing its rules yet, wearing a plaid coat and work pants not unsimilar to the clothes draped over the chair. He looks at the reclining man with something near whole-bodied admiration. There's timidness in his gaze, too, and also something close to desire, which the older man responds to with the friendly gesture of laying his arm over the boy's shoulders.

Jake tried to imagine what their lives would've been like. In the quiet of his apartment, he lets his thoughts wander, projecting himself back in time. He drifts into the scene, settling in amongst the men posing for the camera. He feels the sun in his eyes, the damp lumber soaking through his work clothes. It's morning. He wakes before first light to start a day of hard labor. He watches his workmates milling around the machines, imagining their habits and the body fatigue that can't be shaken off, the complex smell on their clothes of wood smoke, pitch, and sweat.

He thumbed through the other photos in no particular order. In broad terms, they showed two men in front of a house, a cigarette being lit, a war time combat scene, men sleeping on a subway train. He followed the subject's eyes. He went back to the first image again and smiled. It suddenly occurred to him that the photos do have something in common. In each, there are men interacting, but what jumps out after seeing the five photos together is that, in each image, there are two men completely absorbed in one another, as though in the instant the photograph was taken, no one else mattered. They show moments of unexpected intimacy, whether tender or desperate.

There's a background slow-burn eroticism that can't go unnoticed either, and for Jake, the overtones confirm the simple truth that Emm desires men. Even Lara had sensed it in the attic and had rolled her eyes at its undeveloped, boyish expression. Jake thought about calling her, but figured it was too late.

It made him rethink what he'd seen in the house. The contrasting conventionality of the downstairs rooms suggested they might've once been the wife's domain, and the attic the one place Emm had made his own and felt at ease. Jake saw Emm sitting at his desk there, late at night, the rest of the world walled out, while his wife...anyone who kept an ordered house like that would've known what happened under its roof...left him alone. Jake imagined that before she died, Emm would come home from work to begin an evening routine with a woman he'd made an understanding with. They'd cook, eat, clean up. She'd watch TV while he disappeared upstairs with the door left ajar so she didn't feel shut out completely. They got by.

Lara had no idea what kind of work Emm had done for a living, but it was easy for Jake to assume there'd been a string of bosses who required conformity. In his time, Emm would've become good at hiding what he felt. He'd never give a reason to excite or disappoint. Jake saw it all in the photographs. He speculated that when Emm was young, occasionally he might've stumbled through sex with another man, although likely never had a proper affair and never known real intimacy with a man. Lara would've chalked that up to the behavior of a different generation. Seeing the photos, Jake realized the intimacy Emm craved was in them.

He looked more closely at a second photo taken much later around the year 1970, a stark nighttime scene of two men standing in a city alley. There are streetlights reflecting off puddles in the asphalt. One man lights the other's cigarette. They lean in towards the flame, each face half lit. They inhabit a world of their own making, one that grows, solidifies, then collapses in the seconds a match is struck, flares, burns down, then dies. Their eyes tell the story. Locked together there's nothing except each other, nothing else in time or space that matters.

At that moment, DB called up from the street. "Hey, forgot my backpack. Is now okay?"

Jake let him into the building and, seconds later, DB was standing beside him looking at the photos laid out on the desk. He stood close enough for his thigh to press up against Jake's shoulder. He ran his hands down Jake's arm. "Any interest in round two?" He asked with a spark in his voice. Jake wondered how DB was always ready for more sex.

Instead, he handed him the photo of the alley scene and asked, "What do you see?"

Without thinking, DB replied, "Really?" Then he went quiet and studied the image more closely, trying to tease out every nuanced detail like he'd found a photo of a forgotten brother. His tone became serious. "Yup. I see hope. This tells me there'll be a tomorrow."

The following day, Lara urged Jake to come with her to the hospital to personally give Emm the photos. "Something tells me he'll be happier if they come from you." In the car ride over, Jake asked how Emm was doing, to which she replied, "Look. He's in pain, scared, and won't get better. Remember. He's smart enough to know where he's going to die."

Emm had been moved from the ICU to a private room. When they arrived, he was sitting in a chair and didn't recognize Lara at first. His mouth hung open. His fingers twitched. The TV was on. It was always left on for company. The IV pole next to him pumped antibiotics and morphine. He coughed. The doctors had already warned Lara it would be pneumonia that killed him. Still, he looked at Jake and tried to push through his confusion. "Do I know you?"

"Emm, this is a friend," Lara said.

"Hello." Jake tried to make the word sound familiar, as though in a parallel universe, they'd already shared a long history.

They talked about old movies and dead actors, Emm explaining how Heston and Connery had "grit." For someone who'd lived through the entire era of modern film, he only really cared about spy thrillers. Lara sat back, trying not to act bored. When a pause in conversation finally came, she cuts in.

"Emm, that thing we talked about. You asked for the photos. We've got them here."

Jake handed over the package he'd been carrying, expecting Emm to open it right away. Instead, he clutched it in his lap. "Appreciate it," was all he said.

Lara changed the subject before Jake could begin asking questions. "Emm, I've something to discuss. It's about the house. Before you get back home, we'll need to make things ready. No more stairs for you."

It was the worst thing she could have said, being cold and dishonest, pretending Emm would go home. Emm looked around the room with a sense of panic in his eyes, real dread. Jake sat back watching, knowing there was nothing he could say or do to make it okay. Emm began muttering something about how Beth wouldn't have it. "Nope, she just won't have it." Then he looked right at Lara surprised at finding a middle-aged woman standing in front of him. "The house?" He half remembered the question. "I don't care about it. Just don't take my David from me."

And there it was. The name of the imagined man whose shirt and pants were laid out on the attic chair. Lara glanced at Jake with a this-just-got-more-interesting look. Then Emm stared right at her, said plainly, "He's all I got."

Lara stood, thinking how her own grandfather had deteriorated and become quarrelsome with dementia, how he'd reverted to treating her like a child. The forced standoff that followed had only made her more selfish and so she'd walked out on him, so she wasn't with him when he died. She then said to the room, "I'm off to find coffee. Jake, you want one?"

And she was out the door, leaving Jake alone to pick up the pieces. In the hospital silence that followed, Jake tensely wondered who'd speak first. He gave in. "She's only trying to help. You know that, right?"

Emm almost said something. Paused. "You know, Beth wanted a daughter. Real bad." He shut up. He paused again. "The house...I've tried to keep it the way she liked. For her sake. She would've wanted that."

Jake looked at the man. He seemed so small, lost in the padding of the chair, cocooned in bandages and the sling supporting his right shoulder, childlike yet incredibly old, made twice as old by the process of dying. There was resignation in his voice. Jake began to realize even though Beth was gone some thirty years, she still held him in her grip.

What Emm wasn't saying was gnawing on Jake. He was so used to everything being out in the open. He wanted to say, "I've seen your attic. I know what you are. You're just like me." But he said instead, "We'll make sure to take good care of David."

Emm simply looked overwhelmed, ready to break into tears. It was too late for him. He'd sorted his way through a long life, and it was too late to rearrange the scaffolding holding the bits in place. After a minute, he said, "I've changed my mind." He held out the bundle of photos. "You take them. I don't want them anymore."

It was the moment he gave up. After that, Emm tried to become invisible. A fragile man, he pulled the blanket bunched in his lap up around his chin and closed his eyes, giving the clear message it was time for Jake to go.

On the way back to the car, Lara talked about one of her daughter's upcoming school events as if she'd already put Emm out of her mind. Jake had been part of Alissa's life since birth, and while he wanted to listen, he couldn't stop thinking about one of the photos held snugly under his arm. It was of a World War II battle scene with a medic hunched over a badly wounded soldier surrounded by exhausted men taking refuge from the onslaught, each one of them scared, dirty, amazed at still being alive, the medic and the warrior bound together in a look that reverberated back and forth across time. "This is happening. Stay with me. This is happening." An interaction exactly opposite of what Jake had experienced with Emm.

When he got back home, Jake placed that one photo at the center of his desk to study it better. The medic was about twenty-five years old, just half Jake's age, yet still their arms had similar shapes as he could tell because the medic's sleeve was rolled up to keep them out of the way. Jake rolled his sleeve to match and realized he was proud of how the cuff framed his bicep.

Slowly, ever so slowly, he let himself be drawn into the scene. He became the wounded man, began to feel his fear of never being whole again, his pain. He could hear the artillery fire and gunshots, men yelling. He could smell the sulfur laden atmosphere and bombed raw earth. He let himself believe the smallest amount of hope that the stained hands touching him would save him. The medic looked in the soldier's eyes, somehow trying to reduce his pain by shear will power alone, two souls connected in the instant the shutter released, miles away from the carnage surrounding them.

For some reason Jake pulled up his pants and synched his belt tight to show off a high waist, something like how one of the soldiers caught in the image wore his pants. He then began limping around the apartment with fatigue. He felt the stirrings of panic-stained exhaustion, the soldier's dilemma of being part of something vital yet hopeless. He took a picture of himself and texted it to Lara, who responded with a set of question marks, not for a second noticing the reference to one of Emm's photos.

Over the following week, the doctors kept Lara informed of Emm's deterioration. Pneumonia had established in both lungs and he was on constant oxygen. Lara told Jake about Emm's decline as if reporting on the weather. For distraction, they agreed to meet out for a late lunch, with Lara suggesting that her husband, Harold, and Alissa join as well.

An hour before taking off for the restaurant, Jake pulled aside another of Emm's photographs, this one showing two men asleep on a graffitied subway train. In the image, the first man reclines in his seat while the second nestles up close against him for warmth and comfort, his head cushioned on the first man's breast. They appear gaunt, sexless, with strained faces acquired from addiction and destitute living. From the style of clothes, the photo would've been taken around 1995. There's an ambiguity to how they've ended up on the train. The only thing that seems to matter is they've found refuge together in sleep. The image was shot by a photographer who knew how to turn spiraling self-destruction into glamor, and it felt relevant, partly because Emm was emaciated and on morphine, but also because over the previous week, DB had been spending more time at Jake's apartment and Jake had begun to see in him hints of the same ability to find comfort in a bad situation. Then, of course, for Jake, it triggered the memory of his own past.

To get ready, Jake threw on a pair of black jeans and t-shirt. Because he knew it would get a reaction, he brushed on dark eye shadow to cover both eye sockets and topped off the effect with liner and accent to suggest a string of sleepless nights. He knew he was being an idiot, but it didn't matter.

Half an hour later Jake met Lara on the sidewalk outside the café where Harold had already gone in with Alissa to find a table. It was rare for the four of them to get together. About once a month he and Lara went for cocktails to blow off steam, but it was unusual for Harold to join and, of course, Alissa never did on those days. For Jake, it always felt good to see Lara's husband. One of his better qualities was he never seemed threatened by his wife's friendship with him.

When they were all seated, Harold showed nothing more than vague curiosity at seeing Jake's makeup, knowing the effect was done for Lara's sake and not his. It simply reminded him that Jake and his wife had once been inseparable, that there'd been a time when they'd lived impulsively and made bad decisions, especially Lara who was more headstrong and more of the leader. He knew that watching Emm die made them both relive those days, because how could it not? It had been the time Lara was the most out of control, after her parents had already shut her out, and there was only her grandfather left to make sure she knew she had family who still cared. Then he got sick. The only way she'd pulled out of her steep decline, or so Lara claimed, was that the week after her grandfather passed, in a pragmatic moment, she'd asked Harold to marry her. "Boring Harold," she called him. And to his face. It was part of their love talk and okay since he felt pride in his steadfastness, and knew that, when she did so it was because she recognized in him the anchor that saved her.

The first thing Lara did after sitting down was to draw a finger through Jake's makeup, then pull back fast like she'd been burned. "Shit!" She laughed shaking her hand, dusting her finger off, her eyes twinkling. All Jake could think about was how beautiful she looked in that moment. Really beautiful. Naturally beautiful. In years past, she'd been taken advantage of because of it. If anything, she tried to hide it to stop the attention she didn't want.

"I know. It's silly."

It was inevitable they'd talk about Emm, but he came up only once when Lara mentioned that a hospital administrator had pulled her aside to discuss estate recovery. The table had gone silent. What was left to say? Emm would die, and that was that.

"You know he desires men."

"Of course."

"And he won't talk about it."

"I know."

She'd once been a person who tried to "fix" people and probably, in the past, would've confronted Emm on this, but that impulse had faded when Alissa was born. No matter how much she did or did not want to help, she kept telling herself Emm was not her responsibility, that she owed him nothing, that she could walk away from him if she wanted because Emm in all respects was an outsider. Indeed, after taking one look at his attic, it was clear he'd cut himself off intentionally. Of course, Lara wasn't about to let him die alone.

Alissa sat by quietly drinking a lemonade, acting bored but secretly thrilled at being included in the adult conversation. In general she liked "Uncle Jake's" unpredictability. Harold made a point of never talking badly about people in front of her, but sometimes it sneaked out.

"Not all lives get a happy ending. Some..." he looked right at

Lara knowing what she'd gone through and feeling protective, "...can't be saved." In Emm, Harold knew a drowned man when he saw one. Or so he thought.

Jake, in the meantime, had become distracted by a table of four men: young, toned, handsome. In conversation they played with verbal spars and jabs, followed by hooks and uppercuts. They used the tricks of youth without fully understanding the tools they had. Not yet. They showed off confidence in careful grooming, with trimmed beards, aggressive mustaches, and well-styled hair. In his mind's eye he watched the decades fly by. The clothing would change, the body language, too. It was all done to be noticed, which was why he couldn't stop watching them. Jake wondered how Emm saw David. Was he masculine, slight, or something else? Were his features delicate or broad and husky? He wondered how David, in Emm's imagination, wore his hair. It seemed unlikely he'd be anchored to the styles of any one particular decade.

He told Lara matter-of-factly, "You know, Emm was in love with the man in the chair."

To which she replied with a laugh, "Well, you're the expert on men." Which made Jake laugh, too, because he had no idea what that meant. How could anyone know for certain what made a person desire another? What did Emm want? All he could imagine was he'd somehow found what he needed in the photos...in different men in different pursuits at different times and places. It seemed Emm, in his own way, had created a private, universal man...a man he'd made up out of character traits spanning the decades, a man who thereby didn't exist and couldn't exist in any one time. And Emm would be at his side.

They chatted for a while longer, then the meal ended and Jake was back on the street. He texted DB, who responded immediately saying he'd be in Jake's neighborhood later that evening to meet friends, and could stop by beforehand to kill an hour, if it was okay.

At around 8:00, there was a knock on the door. To shake things up, Jake asked DB if he wanted a beer, but the offer was declined. For the first time, they didn't have sex and talked instead about anything besides the photos or Emm. Then DB was out of time and Jake was all set to be left alone again when DB asked, "Any interest in coming along?" To which Jake nodded, yes.

There was some unformed thought pressing on the back of Jake's mind. Before they headed out, he asked a question. "How do you do it? How do you make it all seem so easy?"

DB just looked at him, hand on the doorknob, trying to figure out what was really being asked. He finally said, "The only thing that comes easy for me…I care about the person I'm with."

And there it was.

In each of Emm's photos the figures are grounded in the decade the photograph was taken, but the expression on each man's face is outside of time…"Just you and me. There's nothing else." It's what makes each man the same man across time, across a span of a hundred years. It's what makes David, given form by clothes and pulled from captured moments of real men's lives. It made Jake wonder what it would be like to talk with such a person. He'd be someone who showed no outward sign of a particular fetish or type, someone who drifted down the sidewalk with a vague outside shell, not hinting at who he was inside, someone with ambiguous race, neutral style, nothing that suggested background, education or work. For some reason it occurred to Jake that DB was just that sort of person. He thought about how he himself had worn so many different faces over the years and he couldn't possibly say for sure what it was that made him him.

The last photo is the one that brings a real sense of peace to Jake. It's of two men dressed in Sunday-best standing in front of a farmhouse sometime around the year 1935. The Depression is in full swing. Nothing in the photo is remarkable; the house being plain, the landscape uninteresting, nothing else in the photo matters except there's pride registered on both men's faces. They stare at the camera, smiling for each other. Both about age thirty, they've made a life together. They stand side-by-side with arms hanging down so their hands disappear into the tall grass. It was impossible to see if their fingers touched, but it was what Jake wanted to believe more than anything.

He imagines Emm sitting in his attic chair. It's late at night. The man is tired. He craves the warm feeling of company but has none. His wife has died. All he has left are the men in the photos. When he needs a savior, he pulls out the battle scene and becomes the wounded soldier. When he wants connection, he finds it in the cigarette being lit. He finds guidance with the sawyers, peace with the boys sleeping on the train, love with the farmers.

When the last photo was taken, Emm would've been around sixty years old, his body changed, grown weaker, less desirable. He'd still be working, finding the night hours the only time he can let his guard down, when he'd gather strength for the coming morning when he'd go back to work and bluster with the men and be gentlemanly with the ladies, a pattern he'd learned over time would stop anyone from getting too close.

Jake knows what he has to do.

The next day he goes to Emm's house without telling Lara. He'll explain afterwards when it's done. Something has stuck in his mind...Lara teasing Harold at the café, with a smile on both of their faces, Lara knowing at some point she'll finally forgive herself, saying, "There's always one more chance to be saved." On the trim above the window he finds the house key.

He goes up to the attic room where the late afternoon sun angles in through the window cutting a hard geometry across the floor and up one wall. It's the cigarette being lit, and the objects on the shelves are caught in the bubble of light...the baseball mitt once held in a boy's hand, a comb, a hockey trophy, a pewter plate the color of smoke. There's a canoe paddle leaning against the wall next to fishing poles. The list goes on, each item once important to someone. Their stories, real or imagined and collected over the years, are safely stored away in Emm's head, but not for much longer.

Jake opens a drawer. More photos. More histories. The room is one memory trove, a repository of men who've come and gone. And in the corner is the chair with plaid shirt and pants laid out, where Emm had made a man for himself that distilled down all the others. When Jake looked at the chair what came to mind was DB's smiling face.

He goes downstairs to the bathroom and rummages through the cabinet until he finds electric clippers. In front of the mirror he buzz-cuts his hair off into the sink to erase whatever style it had before. Same with his beard. Then stripped naked he stands in front of the mirror again, a man without visible connection to time. His thoughts drift and for a minute he tries to decide if there's one figure in the photos he wants most to be, then gives up and heads back upstairs to the attic.

David's clothes lay on the chair exactly how he'd first seen them. He picks up the pants and tests their size against his bare legs, puts them on. Loose and slightly too long. Same with the shirt. The boots fit snugly. He places the watch on his wrist and the gum in his pocket. From a large bowl he picks out a chrome lighter, a blue pen, old French coins. They get tucked into his pockets as well. A chain with crucifix goes around his neck. With belt and cap he's ready.

Dressed as David he looks around the room one last time. Up high on the wall is a small photo he hadn't paid attention to before. It's of a street kid in some city looking straight at the camera with a complex mix of disgust, envy and opportunity on his face...emotions targeting the photographer. There's also fear and exhaustion mixed in from being abandoned. He nudges it aside and there's a second photo paper-clipped behind it. It's a self-portrait of Emm staged to appear in all ways the same, right down to the expression. Jake pulls them down and put them in his pocket, too.

It's late evening when Jake arrives at the hospital. He navigates the corridors and elevators that leave him disoriented before being escorted back to Emm's room by a tired nurse who states proudly, "He's been no trouble at all," which Jake takes as proof that Emm has been put at the end of the corridor where he's easier to ignore.

He enters the room with the nurse staying back at the open door. Emm is in bed, a frail, white sheath of wrinkled skin. He's been dozing, but half wakes in his morphine stupor. Jake sees the eyelids rise. The eyes still have life in them. Jake sees the change as they register the plaid shirt and cap, the living body of his David. They seem to glisten. There's only the sound of an IV pump as Jake walks up to the bed, bends down and kisses Emm on the mouth, like he's been wanting to do for a hundred years.

MARTINI (HOW I ENDED UP SLEEPING WITH MY FRIEND ALEX AND THEIR EX)

Marcy Rae Henry

Okay, so I'm drinking. Red. From Spain. It's called *Museum* and, even though it sounds like the type of bottle set out next to a dozen of the same at a gallery event with little seedy crackers and warm cheese, it's decent.

It's also awful considering I haven't, in total, drank for seven years. Seven years is a long time. People say your hormones, your taste buds and various aspects of your physicality alter greatly every seven years. I don't know if that's true, at least in a seven-year cycle, but what I do know is that it's been a long time since I embraced the urge to drink a decent red from Spain.

Why I'm drinking is and isn't dependent upon what's been going on in my life. Sometimes I simply can't think of a particular reason to stay sober. Other times, I can't think of a reason not to. Also, I miss Primavera and that doesn't make anything any easier. She died nearly three years ago. How many ticks is that on the clock? How many beats of a heart? How can I have lived and showered, made coffee, and wandered museums alone for that long?

I don't know why, when I start out talking about sex, I end up talking about her. I always end up talking about her. That's why, when people ask me for everything from crown to shoestrings, pulling primarily at the strings around my heart, they realize it's not available. It's not in stock. It's been discontinued.

Primavera haunts me.

Simply said, I loved her. And she loved me. We were in love.

129

MARTINI

What this meant was that she wanted to live here, with me, and I wanted to relive my life with her. Take her to Egypt and discuss the conundrum of the Sphinx, of life, death and falafels. Take her to Spain, show her where I went to school, review flamenco, drink wine that turns to blood and back again. Travel to Morocco, watch people fingering triangular lutes, singing in Arabic. Finger Primavera meaningfully. Smoke hashish and howl at the crescent. Make a home somewhere, plant dark tulips, watch movies, and, finally, die of age.

Even if I didn't one hundred percent believe we'd stay together to the end, which I mostly did, I still imagined a million scenarios for us—and some for her alone—but none of them included her being dead. Now, she'll never be in my present. Here in Chicago, where trees are starting to fill in the windows and the windows reflect my 34-year-old face, reddened from the bottle of red. Here where I listen to Afro-Celt Sound System sing *Eistigh liomsa sealad* — "Listen to me." The bagpipes make me watery and for some reason I wonder if I ever loved the long-term boyfriend because I can't recall crying over him. When we parted I felt hurt, sad, perhaps. But not devastated. The love I had for him had no room for "forever." A Buddhist would laugh at me. Were I Buddhist, I'd laugh at myself. Instead, the red helps me consider the forever loss of Primavera and, as the bagpipes loosen my pipes, something I haven't thought about in a long time floats to the surface.

After watching a particularly moving film, Primavera and I began critiquing the actors' performances. We traded places with them. Placed them into our lives and watched them move around. Put ourselves right onto the screen, pressing up against the glass and peering at our lives being acted out by others. We rode up the rising action and, at the climax of the story, very unoriginally asked each other, "Okay, here you need to weep your eyes out, ugly-style, no faking. Snot running from your nose. How will you do it? What will you think of?"

And we both admitted nothing real or fictitious could make us cry like each other. The things we'd done to each other. What we neglected to do. The times we were ready to walk away. Somehow, after all that upchucking, we ended up in bed clawing at each other, calling out each other's names. Then she pulled out a surprise. Purple straps and purple attachment, as she called it. We'd never talked about it, but I'd always wanted to try. She didn't like penetration, so I knew the roles we'd play.

She slipped it through the hole and stepped into the straps, tightening them over hips and thighs. Stroked the purply appendage, joking, *If you get pregnant it's your problem, not mine.* Whispered, *Gonna come inside you.* She pushed me onto the bed, checked to see if I was ready.

"Ready?"

"Yes."

"Sure?"

"Yes."

And she slid it in and it was harder than the real thing. I clutched her back and she pumped away the way others have pumped away above me, only I loved her, so it felt not exactly better, but more meaningful. She came right away. A small one. *Huh huh huh* in my ear. Didn't pause, just kept going. Until I came, clamped onto her shoulders. She waited until I was completely done, then tore the whole apparatus off and rode me into a crescendo and came hard this time. Loud, guttural sounds.

Next time I asked her to put it, on she rolled her eyes. I didn't get it and said, "Thought you liked it."

"Thought you didn't like penetration."

"I like it with you."

Suddenly, she was a sugar cube melting on my tongue. She told me she'd do whatever I wanted.

She put it on again reluctantly and, after that, never again.

To keep coming with Primavera, I would have sold my sticky soul and sworn allegiance to a god by any name. And after I found out she died, I haven't been able to sleep with anyone else. The longer it goes on, the more entrenched celibacy gets.

When my friend Alex found out about the state of my crotch, they booked a flight to Chicago to "help out with things." I start drinking to prepare for what might happen. Then I stop drinking so I can stop crying and go meet Alex.

On the way to the train station, I go into Get Baked to get a cappuccino, but don't really want to sober up, so I walk out with a tiny piece of coffee cake. I try not to let it crumble all over the dirty train. When I step out of the station, I spot Alex next to a girl with a buzzcut and a tight green jacket. The ex. Alex was trying to get her to meet us in Chicago while she was back in the States on leave. Alex can be very convincing. They run over, pick me up and spin me around.

"You're red-faced," they say, putting me down.

"Been drinking red. You're skinny." I squeeze their waist.

"It's the T." They Vogue a bit. "Gives different angles to my face."

"And your voice."

"Yeah, I should've warned you about that."

"No worries, you still sound like you, only deeper."

"This is June." Alex gestures towards her.

June steps up to shake my hand and I go in for a hug. "Glad you made it to Chicago."

She hugs me back shyly. "Same. I have one night and wanted to see this one."

Alex smiles beautifully and drapes her arm over June's shoulder. The three of us walk over to the Brew and View for the matinee showing of Dot the i. I warn them, "The screen is in poor shape and the projector slightly off, so drink up."

"That makes it better?" June asks.

"Makes it not matter."

We order a round of beer.

"When was the last time you drank?" Alex asks.

"Seven years ago. When was the last time you two saw each other?"

They share a look.

"This is the first time since Alex left the Navy," June says.

"Since June shattered my heart," Alex adds.

"What's that? Five years?"

"Six."

"Six and a half."

I laugh. "Okay, so why am I here? To make sure things don't get out of hand?"

"To ensure that they do." Alex holds up a stein and we all toast.

I've seen the film before and don't feel bad getting up to pee three times during it. Each time I come back to my seat, Alex and June are a bit cozier. Holding hands, head on a chest. The protagonist is badass. We think she's piping hot, and I also think the boy is beautiful. Alex says, "Sure. He looks like a girl."

When the film ends, it's only six. The time when nothing

really happens. The time when people return from work and decide what they're gonna eat. What they'll do for the night. If it's a weekend, which it is, the time to start getting ready to go to dinner. Choosing clothes and underwear for the night. If there's a chance anyone may be slipping off the latter, choosing wisely. "What to do with the six o'clock hour?" I ask. "You don't even know where to put it. Is it evening? When does evening separate from night?"

"I'll tell you about six," Alex says. "It's not the time to start philosophizing. Let's switch venues. Isn't the Kit Kat Lounge up the street?"

"Twenty-minute walk to Boystown." I point the way.

Alex and June, hand in hand. The spring has a chill, but the chilly air with a hint of spring is hopeful. We pass the place where Primavera and I had our engagement party. A small, elegant venue just outside the gay area.

"Isn't that...?" Alex asks.

"Yup." I nod.

"Sorry to bring it up, but...have you heard anything?"

"My ex died three years ago," I tell June. "I still don't know the circumstances. Five years together and I never made any friends through her. Never kept in touch with anyone connected to her. There were rumors: suicide, overdose, murder, natural causes. I was out of my mind from not knowing. So, I got ahold of her sister..."

"She talk to you?" Alex asks.

"You sure you want to hear all this now?"

"Of course, of course," Alex says, impatient. June holds onto them and nods.

"When the ex, Primavera, moved out for the last time, after leaving who knows how many times before, I said: Leave now and never come back. I'll change the locks. Go on with my life. Over. Finito. She said: Good. You'll never see me again. Change the locks, fuck a fleet of sailors, drink yourself to death. I don't give three, two or one shit!"

"She really make the sailor comment?" June wants to know, smiling.

"And then some." Alex and I nod at each other. "The day she left I gave her some space. Went and bought chocolate, frozen pizza and new locks. When I returned to a big damn mess, I popped the pizza into the shitty oven, knowing half would still be frozen while the other half burnt, and went about changing the locks. I cleaned up for a couple of hours, threw the pizza in the trash, then went out to buy a burrito. Turns out Primavera's flight was canceled and she tried going back to what was then *my place* and couldn't get in. The neighbors said she made a fucking racket. She left a lovely note, promising to come back and shit out a hemorrhoid on the threshold and, I guess, went and got a hotel room. I tried calling her—no answer—so I tried her sister, who berated me for locking someone out of their own home and fuck-your-hole and blah-blah-blah fuck-you. Flash forward to the day I call the sister and beg her to tell me how Primavera died. Lame insults: I don't deserve to know that sort of personal shit, who did I think I was demanding anything after all this time? But she doesn't hang up, so I insist. Then I guess: Suicide? *No way.* Foul play? *Also no. It was an accident.* Accident. Okay. What kind? Mix of chemicals, car crash, dropped something in the tub, slip and fall, anaphylaxis, wrong-place, wrong-time, snake bite...? She finally jumps in, *Call it a prescription accident. And don't call me again.* That was it. All I got."

"Jesus and his mom." Alex shakes their head. "That's awful. She OD'd?"

"Pills on accident or pills on purpose. Strange. She wasn't a popper. Could barely gag down a Tylenol. It's just another one of those things I'll never have an answer for, never understand, unless and until I make it to a heavenly realm to inquire."

"You can start repenting in middle age." Alex touches my shoulder.

"Maybe. Anyway, I started writing stories of each possible scenario."

"Good. With each one, a bit relief?" they ask.

"Don't know about that. Perhaps they're just keeping me from losing it altogether."

"But they're keeping you from getting laid!" Alex punctuates the air with both hands.

The Kit Kat Lounge, never to be confused with Klub, I tell June, is monochrome with black and white films projected onto bare walls. People who star in them look like stars. Hair slicked back or pin-curled perfectly into place. Pre-body positivity.

The sun is still around and the films look faded, but Kit Kat is candlelit and has potential. Few people, but we sit at the bar. At the end, a petite girl next to her gay boyfriend. They've gone shopping. Bags piled bag-like below their feet. They talk to the top of each other's heads. Looking around desperately to see if anyone is looking at them, which I am, but not in the way they'd like. It's a martini bar and the choices are grand. Crème brûlée, chocolate cream pie, peach cobbler, apple crisp. I order a banana split. Alex and June get tiramisu. They're thick and creamy and damned if mine doesn't taste just like a banana split and I'm splitting in two before I'm a third of the way through it.

Alex and June have gotten past the surprise of seeing each other and the you-look-great pleasantries and when they start talking about their breakup I ask, "Shall I go find a friend?"

A bachelorette party just walked through the door in ridiculous regalia and Alex says, "Slim pickings here. Besides you've heard it before."

"Alex's version, at least." June winks. With the buzzcut, it comes across as charming.

"Okay, then," I take a sip and vow to slow down a bit. "Do you think if you guys were able to be out, you could've stayed together?"

"Can of worms," Alex says, licking the rim of their glass. "I think that, when I put in for a transfer to Japan and June claimed she did the same, we would've stayed together if that turned out to be true."

June looks like a puppy who's been shouted at.

"Did you have much of a say?" I ask her.

"Not as much as Alex's thinks. We ultimately get sent where top brass decides."

"But you asked to go to Italy!"

"I preferred Europe to Asia." June shrugs.

"So why not just tell me?"

"I didn't want to ruin the time we had left together and, honestly, Alex, I thought we'd hook up again after that tour."

"We've gone over all this a million times, and I still don't think you understand how I shattered into a million pieces in Japan."

June grabs Alex's hand. "Sorry—I truly am. I was hoping a change of scenery would make it easier. And that it would be temporary."

They both look at me. I shrug. "How to run from love? The

bitch finds you and does exactly what she wants with you."

June stands on tips of her toes and kisses Alex on the nose. Says, "Seems to me what love wanted was for you to have a bunch of affairs with people who were ass over teacups for you."

Did Alex tell her about the lesbian mountain parties where women roamed the woods and kissed and licked and sucked and enjoyed being women? Did they tell her about the one-night stands with married Japanese women who wanted to be spanked and tied up and experiment with anal plugs?

"It was never more than scratching an occasional itch." Alex laughs.

"Hope you saw a medic for that..." I add and, despite the resolve to slow down, tip back the remaining contents from my triangular glass. The bridal party loudly toasts the bride with her little fake veil. They look to be late-twenties and from the same sorority.

"See anything you like?" June asks.

"Just the images on the wall," I say. "Know this one?" Edward G. Robinson, aka Chris Cross, is painting Joan Bennett's toenails. "It was banned in some U.S. cities for being so dark."

"Looks like *The Woman in the Window*."

"Yeah, yeah, same actors."

She and Alex look at each other. It's obvious they never stopped thinking about each other. But there was no plan. For meeting, for getting back together, for staying together. There were empty promises. Pain. Distance. I know how much June hurt Alex, but she has something childlike about her that makes it impossible not to like her.

When she heads to the bathroom, Alex asks, "What do you think?"

"About June? I was expecting someone who wanted to crush you into little Alex-bits. Sweep them up and hold them close while telling you everything is cool until you believe her. Because you so badly want for everything to be cool and because you're broken and wanting the pieces to somehow become whole again."

"Talking about me or you?"

"Talking about June. Kinda shy for a military girl with a buzzcut. Hard to imagine her holding onto your ankles."

"Like to?"

"Watch? Maybe."

"No, join us."

"I'll drink about it."

The first time I slept with a woman, I got nice and toasted and, after an awkward dental dam and tongue piercing, was sure everyone could tell. I felt guilty about drinking so much.

June returns and orders us another round: pomegranate, watermelon and cantaloupe. "From now on, drinks are on me."

We protest.

"Really. I just got a big bonus and, you know, I live in military housing and don't have much to spend my money on."

"Well, alright." Alex removes their thick leather jacket and drapes it on the chair. They reach for June and kiss her mouth; they twist their necks and kiss again. Alex puts a hand on my cheek and kisses the other. Then June kisses my check before kissing Alex with an open mouth.

Alex looks carefree, not like they usually do with the city dangling all around. There were twisted times before leaving Chicago. Throwing silverware at the wall. A cat who ignored them for days because Alex told it, "I think about other cats when I'm petting you." In the mountains, they stopped looking over their shoulder and forgot about the stun-gun in their pocket. I'm sure it's in the leather jacket. Alex never travels without it if they can help it.

We all taste each other's drinks and, when they start making out with each other, it gives me the opportunity to check out June more closely. A lovely Italian blouse with fake rhinestones. Baggy, olive-colored men's pants with a black leather belt around her waist. She resembles the protagonist in *Dot the i*. Deep set eyes, wide sensuous mouth. I'm still suspicious, as I would like Alex to be. Sociopaths can be charming—Primavera charmed the pants and panties off me the first time we met. It took months before I saw signs of impulsivity and lack of remorse. While it's hard to hate June, she lied to Alex like a politician and fucked off. But she's generous and well-traveled. And Alex is into her. And when they kiss, it stirs something in me.

The bachelorette party witnesses and whoops. They pretend to kiss and smack each other's asses. Sorority girls acting like frat boys. The bartender goes over and asks if everything is okay. "More alcohol," they chant.

Bartender looks back at June and Alex, entwined, and come over to ask us, "What are you celebrating?"

It parts the two. Annoying. Why not just ask if we need something?

Alex says, "We're all in the same city at the same time."

"Splendid." He brings us another drink. Doesn't add it to our tab. It's more delicious that way. He's clearly "family," as we used to say in the 90s. In fact, the whole wait staff looks queer. And they're happy that way.

Before going back to the corner to cuddle with June, Alex gives me a short back rub. I didn't feel like a third wheel before and feel even less like one after. We're all buzzing like a live wire and the sun is sinking melancholically. Other folks come in.

"They want to feel what we feel," I say and raise my glass, "because we look good feeling it." We toast to us.

Another bachelorette party, more heavily made up than the first. They've all gotten their hair done. Probably from the same stylist. They're white as paper. Straight as an arrow. All the clichés. A couple give us a dirty look. Maybe just June and Alex. Alex laughs and lifts their glass to them. Then they kiss June. Say, "Come here."

And I do and they kiss me. They're soft and careful. June grabs my hand, kisses my fingertips. It gets the second bachelorette group talking. The three of us exchange kisses. They don't kiss me as passionately as they kiss each other, which is fine by me.

June kisses my neck, says, "You smell amazing."

"Everywhere," I admit.

"I'd love to find out." She stares at my chest, then lower.

"Put it on the books," I say and Alex grins so much, it's almost audible.

The two girl groups find their way to each other and congratulate each other. A few look over at us. We're a topic of conversation.

"Do the bachelorettes know they're in Boystown?" I ask.

"There are rainbow flags everywhere," Alex answers.

"They might not know what they mean."

"Everyone knows what they mean."

"Should I go over and ask if they know about the drag show?"

"Yeah," says June, "ask if they're gonna be in it."

When the show starts, there isn't a queen under six-foot five. Layers of makeup over day- faces. Overexaggerated mouths, gestures. They swish and swirl their way toward us. Lip-syncing, giving us pharaoh eyes. All eyes on their hot high asses. The mics are turned on between songs so the queens can ask the crowd about their night, what they're celebrating. Bachelorettes #1 inform the crowd this will be their friend's second marriage. One queen says, "Do it 'til you get it right. Or enough money."

Bachelorettes #2 all try to talk at once. Drunken, obnoxious. They don't need a mic, but one grabs it from the queen and says her friend will be the sexiest bride and they will be the sexiest bridesmaids in the history of weddings. No one has or will ever be more fuckable than them. The brown queen says, "Then I hope you have dresses other than those, mamita."

"Hey, what's wrong with our dresses?"

"Bueno, they're not old maid dresses…they're old ho dresses. Like, hang it up! Grow up!"

Everyone in the place is cracking up. The girls aren't having it. They start cussing at the queens and insulting the wait staff. "We're paying your wages. How you gonna let them treat us like this?"

Someone turns the music back on and two performers belt out Chaka Khan, sing-shouting into a turned-off mic. They walk around flirting with everyone. June tips them accordingly. Everyone does, except the fuming #2s.

The sun has slid all the way down. We're in it for the long haul. Too many drinks in to turn back now. June signals to the waiter.

"What can I get you, sweetheart?" he yells.

"Champagne, please," she shouts. "The most expensive bottle you carry."

He goes to check it out. Comes back and we huddle together to hear. He says they sold the most expensive the night before but can give us the next best and we want that. And he's happy to get it for us. We see this and invite him for a drink. He says he has to refuse. But tells us he would like to, very much.

As we down the now most expensive bottle in the house, Alex runs their finger down my back. My back shivers. I put my hand on their thigh. June puts her hand on the other thigh. The music is turned up a notch. My clothes thump against my body. Though no one can hear, I sip and burp as politely as possible. June says the cheaper the champagne, the worse the hangover, but I can't tell the difference between a $100 or a $200 bottle of bubbly.

When the show is over, we've half the bottle left. Ambient music plays at a low volume. Whitish noise within whitish walls. I ask June and Alex where they used to get it on when they were on the ship and they say, "Oh, there are places. Especially when someone is on night duty."

"Dirty bitches. The thrill of getting caught."

"One time we were in the supply area and I had my hands down this one's pants." Alex points to what's in June's pants. "One of my roommates came around the corner and scared the hell out of us."

"Jesus, Alex, how'd you know you could trust her?" I ask.

"She was cool. Never held it over me, just made us promise to be careful."

When June and Alex kiss again, I realize I've never seen Alex kiss anyone else this way. I don't really know June, but I haven't seen her kiss this way either. Being that I've kissed many in my life, I can say, you don't kiss everyone this way. Not even close. Despite years, oceans and lies, here they are. And I'm vibing on what they feel for each other.

Suddenly, the dude who must be the manager comes over to tell them to knock it off. "Knock it off," he says. "The other patrons..." he tosses a thumb at the #2s.

"The others what?" Alex asks.

"Someone complained."

"So?" Alex again. "Other patrons lay down $260 for one bottle?"

Abundantly wrecked, I think: Well, we haven't paid yet. You can run a tab and run away. Cancel your card. June will never be in this club again. Not in five years. Certainly not in the time it takes for the entire wait staff to change. The bar to change names. The films to slide off the walls.

She's talking with manager-dude, keeping her cool. "We're in a gay neighborhood. We're not hitting on their mothers..."

Ambient music goes on. Bachelorette parties go on. People say things they mean. Perhaps something they'll regret. I can't hear what else June and Manager discuss, but they seem to have come to an understanding. He leaves. I stare at the bridesmaids, trying to finger the culprit.

The second Alex and June cuddle up again, Manager stomps over to them butt-clenched. The wait staff look horrified. Our waiter rolls his eyes. "I thought you got it." Manager is more

aggressive this time. "Other customers don't want to see that."
"Then they shouldn't watch," Alex says. "Would you tell
straight people not to kiss?"
"If someone complained…"
"Have you had someone complain about breeders kissing?"
"Do you have to use that word?"
"*Kissing*?"
June tries to make some conciliatory remarks and, suddenly,
I want to hear the Dead Milkmen. Jump up on the table and
shout out, "Anarchy!" Instead, I gulp what I know is my last
drink at this joint. The table next to us stares like we're an
eclipse. I want to say fuck-you with my finger. Exasperated,
June throws down near $400. I can't see myself dropping half
the rent in a chic bar. Not even to support the gay area. But it
ain't feeling like that. June tells the manager she's tipping the
server directly and walks over to do so. Alex tells him they're
never stepping back in as long as the manager is there. They
kiss all the way to the door.
He follows us. "No more."
"We heard you the first four times." Alex says. "Now *you*
knock it off!"
Alex is five inches taller and leans over him. He puffs up
and steps closer. I've still got my glass in hand and say, "Step
back, Jack. You're too close for comfort."
"What are you gonna…?"
"I'm serious, step away from us."
He doesn't move.
"You're afraid of people looking at us? Well, they're looking
now." I hold the glass up and simply let go. It shatters all around
his feet on the floor. A few people cheer.
As I walk out, feeling for whoever will have to clean it up,
I see our server pump his fist in the air. Alex and June walk out
behind me.

Back at my house we sit on the large striped rug in the living
room. I light a candle that scents the room with sage and put on
some 80s tunes. Alex gets up and strips down to "The Killing
Moon." The heavy leather jacket, folded nicely on a chair. The

purple button up. Jeans with a thick belt. Multi-colored socks. They dance in a thin black t-shirt and black boy shorts. June and I look up admiringly. Alex's long as hell legs look different. Less round, more muscular. They reach out and pull June to her feet. June grabs my hand, but I say no, not yet. She and Alex kiss. Long and lingering, hands on asses; the kind that *should* get you kicked out of a bar.

When the song ends June pulls two cigars out of her bag. I open a window. She lights one and hands it to me. Lights another for her and Alex and we smoke out the second-story window. Alex starts feeling up June, blowing smoke over her shoulder. With the trees filling in, I doubt anyone across the street can see a white hand freeing a breast from a Rhinestoney Italian blouse. Alex turns June around and puts their knee between June's legs. June moans softly, moves against the knee. Alex runs their hands over the buzzcut. Unbuttons the olive-colored pants. Soft Cell through the speakers.

Alex puts out the cigar on the concrete window ledge. Places it on the coffee table, next to a metal water bottle. Tilts their head at June and says *come here* with one finger. They strip June naked and get on their knees. My cigar glows red, my apartment yellow with the candle and faint light coming in from streetlamps and city. I smoke that damn cigar as I watch Alex slowly knee- walk June over to the wall and go down on her. Maybe better to say: go up on her. It's on.

I stay in the audience. June runs her hands through Alex's short dark hair. I watch her hips move against Alex's mouth. I watch Alex's bony beautiful fingers on June's ass. Slip some fingers in. They look into each other's eyes before June flattens palms against the wall and rides it out. Alex works their mouth. Uses mouth, fingers. Plants long fingers on June's thighs and June sighs. More deeply each time. Then her breath speeds up and she sounds labored, laboring. It's work to come. Hard work. And she does and her voice goes up about two octaves. It's the most femme sound she's made all night. Alex stays down but June pushes them away. I know that feeling—when it's too much. Too sensitive. It almost hurts.

Alex stands and cracks their neck. Drinks from the water bottle. Hands it to June. She sips and says, "Got anything stronger?"

I go to the kitchen and return with the remaining bottle of red, *Museum*. And, like the protagonist in *Dot the i*, coffee mugs.

I pour one mug, then two, and June grabs the bottle by the neck and drinks from it. I set the bottle on the coffee table and she presses up against my back, naked, hands moving lightly over me. Alex grabs a mug. Drinks. Wipes the corner of their mouth with their thumb and hooks both thumbs into my jeans and pulls me close. A hand on either side of me. Their tongue between my teeth. Second-hand cigar taste. Reminds me of making out with guys in high school. The thrill of tongues tasting of an immature amount alcohol and cigarettes. Rubbing up against each other madly in someone's sibling's room. Feeling hardness against softness through the clothes condom. A hint of what is yet to come.

Alex's hand slips between my legs. My hands are on their chest, which they then move to their shoulders. They unclip my belt and push me gently into the vintage thrift store chair. Crushed midnight blue velvet. Wooden arms with the stain wearing off. June is pulling my pants slowly from my body, holding one foot and then the other. I lean back in crushed blue velvet. June stands behind me, kissing me upside down, while Alex puts their mouth in the right place.

Rest my feet on the short table, slip, try to find balance. Three fingers, one too many. Throw my legs over shoulders. We stay that way for some time. I squeeze and lift until I can no longer kiss. Close my eyes. I'm angry. Angry at the night, the manager, the bachelorettes who couldn't mind their fuckin' business. I'm mad at Primavera. It's been building for a long time and I haven't had an outlet. So, I'm angrily fucking and Alex digs it. They have a spell on me, control over me. On me, on top of me. In control. I think of Primavera. Who did she think of while fucking me? I think of Alex. Then I let go. The spell is broken. Just like that. I reach it and almost buck them off me.

When I fold myself down on the floor again, we're all at each other's mouths. Kiss, hum and buzz until the alcohol evaporates. We finish the bottle of red. We all finish in one way or another. June and Alex lock hips and June rides until they both reach it one more time. I start and end watching.

We lie around, looking at each other, laughing, touching hands. It's nearing one in the morning. The time to make a decision. Do we call it a night or are in we in for the long haul? We could go up to Clark for some greasy food. There's Saint Seb's, I tell them, the lesbian bar a few blocks up, named after the gay icon. They've re-done the walls and the exposed brick

MARTINI

is nice, but the drinks are in plastic cups and after midnight there's a sense of desperation.

"We could get a drink. Top off the night."

"We could go to the booze store on Foster."

"They have chips?"

"And ice cream."

"We could order pizza."

"We could do that. We sure could."

EPICENTER

Miah Jeffra

The earthquake begins with that uncertain hiccup and roll, what could be mistaken for a wave of nausea, but then made clear that it indeed resides outside the body, one moment past itself and then another. The world trying to walk on a waterbed.

My phone goes off simultaneously with the nasal alarm usually reserved for Amber Alerts. The screen says *Critical* in red, followed by *Earthquake—Drop, Cover, Hold On. Shaking... Sonoma County, CA, USA.* I wonder what the inclusion of Shaking was particularly meant to inform us of. As opposed to, what? I pull the glass of wine already in my hand to my lips, swig. Sigh.

I say, "Fun."

This isn't my first time. But it is the first in my cabin. My cabin in the redwoods. *My* cabin, I think. It is now all mine. Not ours. And *he* is in San Francisco. *His* apartment in San Francisco, no longer ours. Shaking. It figures, I think, the first week alone in this house and there's a natural disaster.

I look out the living room window, out past the Japanese-style garden, the koi pond with the waterfall feature, across the narrow pine-needled road and behind the high-stilted house that gives me a great view of the river between its skinny legs. The remains of the sunset are glinting off the sliver of water—a bit of light flushing the brush on the banks—that dribbles through the thirsty canyon. Yeah, I'm performing environmental meditation during an earthquake, so what? It's the Californian way.

There isn't much action at first. The koi pond ripples, like it is shivering from some sudden cold. Everything else beyond the

145

window looks the same—muted and calm—while the window-frame wiggles. The redwoods surrounding the house appear to be nonplussed. They peer down at the wobbling house. *Newbies*, they think: me, this house, all the things humans built, arrogant concrete, prideful beams, hubris asphalt.

The Japanese garden was my idea. All of those years researching Zen art practice for my dissertation. Meditative aesthetics. This is my first yard in adulthood, having lived in the San Francisco flat for over a decade, the New York walk-up before that, dingbat apartments and glorified closets before that in other cities. Urban life. Artist life. Urtistic. Artbanic. TM that shit. Maybe a magazine, a blog, a vlog, a polywog, a movement to follow a name.

I wanted the outdoor space to be special, so I bought stone and ferns, a Japanese maple, and a porcelain birdbath, real on-the-nose. I dug holes for the pond. A project. My husband said, if we install a waterfall we'll drown out the noise from the main road. I wanted koi. He wanted a hot tub. We bought them all. Water, water everywhere. I designed the garden in the kayushiki teien tradition, meant to be strolled through, to stop at the pond and reflect, to cross the arching red bridge as if boats floated underneath. No boats here, though, just a slew of koi, one whom I call Big Jim. He's the fatty of the pond. The others follow him. Every time he swims in view I hear Macho Randy Savage's voice, *Snap into a Big Jim!*

I sip my wine. It is a Pinot from one of our club memberships, an old winery down the street with a large backyard and a small amphitheater for local cover bands that play Fleetwood Mac during club pick-up parties. I always thought it would be a great place to meet men with medium-to-large bank accounts, would tell my husband so, and he would roll his eyes and rest his palm on my knee, pretending to enjoy the music. The winery had really clean, fruity Pinots, but I'd drink their rosés on a sunny day, which was almost always. Rosé is versatile, adaptable, ready for anything.

I notice across the road my stilt-house neighbor looking out her kitchen window. Her and her husband are nice people but boring, one in real estate and the other in finance. They throw catered dinner parties for a curated few in the neighborhood. They discuss investment potentials and futures with acronyms that sounds like military orders. Asset classes, bull market, capital gain. So many numbers. How else could they afford a riverfront home, after all, even in this old Moonie stumptown that floods every decade? My husband and I scrounged to buy this house. We're both creatives. I told this to the couple, how hard it was for queer artists. We were sitting in their back patio overlooking the river, drinking an inky cabernet—a bit too bold for the weather and the overcooked Halibut—when I started grilling them: how much did they spend on the white leather living room suite, the mid-century retro kitchen appliances, the Oaxacan woven throw pillows? My husband tapped my hand with his finger. The wife picked up on what I was doing and asked if I wanted another glass of wine with her lips pried up the sides. I accepted and filled my mouth. Now, out the window, her lips are different, turned down, her eyes meeting mine like we are conspirators of some plan that we royally fucked up. I nod to suggest that maybe we did. She mouths something, a slow shaping of words muted behind glass and the rumbling of the earth. It isn't "I'm terrified" but I know that's what she means.

I brace my legs like I'm on my longboard, ready for the swell of ground, like I can ride the earthquake into safe harbor, preferably one with a sandy margarita bar and dogs bounding around sunken chairs, their tongues slapping their snouts. Safe harbor always was a beach for me, an edge of the world even as a child, when my older cousin drove me to the Outer Banks and taught me how to paddle, how to Cobra, how to Warrior Two at that instant the wave striped white under the board. We floated during the in-between, the jellyfish and driftwood, children's squeals skipping along the water-top. Summers at the Carolina shore were the closest thing to me like home. Correction: floating out on the ocean beyond the beach in Carolina felt most like home, where my feet didn't touch ground. People think earth is so solid, some kind of security, *keep your feet on the ground.* Not the case. They're fools to think the ground is a guarantee. But the water. If the NorCal Pacific wasn't so fucking cold, I'd float down this river on a piece of driftwood right now, a loose plank, any makeshift surfboard, down to the ocean's mouth, impervious to the convulsing ground. I'd keep going until there was no land left to spot.

Not that I surfed that much in New York, either. I could have taken the A train with my board pinching my armpit for the hour ride to Rockaway if I really wanted to. I never did. Maybe I didn't love surfing as much as I told people, as I told myself. That's not why we moved to California, anyway. We did it for the trees. The success came later, the professorship, the solo gallery shows, the intermittent accolades. But first, the trees. So many trees we had never seen on the east coast. The Monterrey Cypress, the Black Oak, the Redwoods. We both marveled, loved them, a mutual love. My husband thought they had an ancient aura. Prehistoric, he would say. I would roll my eyes and say, "All tree species are prehistoric. History is a human invention, how arrogant we are." I'd say it with my chin grabbing the sky, only vaguely aware of the irony.

A half dozen redwoods tower above the cabin, their fallen red needles forming soft mounds over which giant ferns splay their fronds.

The ground grows louder, windows shatter, and California pulls in: wind, leaves, pine scent, sap. I take a single step back to avoid contact and steal another sip. Both kitchen lunettes burst with strain. The living room bay window splinters. And just as more glass from somewhere downstairs makes a sound like a popped light bulb, the power goes out. Very little sun peeks through the canyon, but it's just enough for me to find a candle in the cabinets and light it with the stove. The rumbling continues, amplifies like the Earth's belly is wired to a volume knob.

That's when I see our dog—*his* dog—a huge American Bulldog mutt, sitting on her haunches, squarely in front of me, her mouth flaps jiggling with the quake.

"You're not supposed to be here," I say.

We found her on the shoulder of the freeway, trotting along the 101 like she was paid to do it. My husband pulled over, opened the back-passenger door, and she without hesitation leapt in, and that was that, like it was scripted. She's too big to live in our apartment, I argued. She sheds too much. She slobbers everywhere. Her bark scares people away from becoming our friends. But my husband was in love. *I'll take her for long walks, I'll brush her often, I'll clean the floors, fuck those people.* I acquiesced, but complained every other day. He pretended not to hear me. The dog was endearing, though, in that dreadful sort-of way, giant dragging jowls that drooled, pirate rings circling her eyes. She curled her ass to my chin in the bed, farted loud enough to wake me, my arm wrapped around her torso.

"Whole lotta shaking going on," she says. The voice coming from her big face sounds a lot like post-*Moonstruck* Cher.

"Is that your attempt at humor?" I ask.

"You drink too much wine."

I look down at the glass, as if I forgot it was in my hand. There is a small fruit fly struggling not to drown.

"I never thought you cared," I say.

"That's rich coming from you," she says.

The dog was the first thing my husband took when he moved out of the cabin. You can have it all, he said, stuffing his sneaker collection and all 100 pounds of the dog into his Mini Cooper, and drove off. I told him I felt suffocated, by the chores, by the domesticity, by the commitment. I couldn't make art. I felt like I was paddling out to open water, only to be pulled back in by his tide. I needed to be an artist. I was drunk on a bottle of rosé.

Then be an artist, he said.

The dog walks over and stands next to me at the window. It is almost pitch-black outside, so I only see my faint cracked reflection and the dog's, but I keep staring out.

"This house is musty," she says.

"It's perfect, and you don't have to be here," I say.

"Why do you like this house so much?" she asks.

"Because I earned it," I say.

"You knew that answer way too fast," she says.

"I know what I want," I say.

"How are want and earn the same thing?"

"It's a causal relationship," I say.

"You never listen to anyone," she says.

"I think I preferred when you only barked," I say.

She cranes her head up towards me. Those big pirate eyes always look so sad. A line of slobber suspends from her mouth flaps.

"You're a ridiculous animal," I say.

"Yeah, that appears to be the truth of things," she says.

The dog starts fading. At first, I think it is the waning light, the ongoing rattle muddling my sight. This earthquake is going on for a long time.

"I've worked hard," I say, gesturing around me. "For this."

"Lord," she says, and lifts her chin and howls.

"I don't speak dog," I say.

"That's where you're wrong," she says.

"It must be so disappointing that I don't understand," I say.

"Now that you mention it, yes."

EPICENTER

I didn't say: I feel like everything's against me. I want everything to quiet down, stop moving for a while and let me catch up.

She looks at me with those big pirate eyes again, and my throat tightens. The bay window breaks open in an exploding shatter and, with a huff—as if expecting it—the dog leaps through the newly gaping hole and disappears.

The darkness redoubles, the rumbling intensifies. A pulsing vibration sings along the edges of the ceiling; I remember the sirens that would slice through my neighborhood in New York, the promise of someone dying so nearby. At the sound, I would rub my palms on my thighs, pull a glass of wine to my lips and pretend to understand impermanence. My husband would rest his hand on the back of my neck and squeeze lightly.

The hardwood floor opens up with a cracking boom, a wide jagged gap from kitchen to living room under the wall and out towards the garden. The wall parts like a curtain. The cherry red bridge collapses into the koi pond. I suck in a breath. I built that bridge, carved the bevels into the balsa by hand, sturdy enough for a big man to walk across, to look over for what floats underneath, seeking the traveling boat, the koi, all following Big Jim. *Snap into a Big Jim!* The koi would be the metaphor, the microcosm of humanity in its flex, of endless machination and making, moving and maneuvering. A strong bridge I built, and now merely flotsam.

The water bubbles and a head slowly emerges from the ink of the pond—hair, a face, then shoulders, a man, a broad chest, a thick torso reflecting what light is left, a naked man with a significant and floppy cock. One of my mother's old boyfriends.

The water flattens the dark hair to his head, his chest, his belly, some of the pond scum leeching his skin. He grins, a front tooth missing. I wonder if someone punched it out. He tip-toes through the gap in the wall and right up to me, then stops a mere six inches from my body.

"You've grown up," he says.

"You got old," I say.

He laughs. "Yeah, maybe a little. But I still got it!" He flexes

150

Miah Jeffra

his arms. They are well-muscled, the way I remember them as a boy, his whole body an artifact of power. Gray hairs stipple the cavity of his chest.

"Do you want some sweatpants, or Speedos?" I ask.

"Why, do you think I need them?" He grins.

"Suit yourself." I shrug, but I don't move an inch. Seeing this man after all these years freezes me in memory. The first one is the time he caught me rubbing my dick against a pillow. He had slept over that night and my bedroom door must have been ajar. I was only beginning to discover my changing body then, twelve or thirteen when he was dating my mother. They dated for about two years. Two long years. At one point I looked up from the pillow and he was peering through the crack in the door, a huge grin on his face. Then it disappeared. After that, I would often find him walking around the apartment in his underwear, the bulge so prominent, the outline of his glans clearly pushing against the white cotton, his balls a round, needful harvest. Huevos. I would sneak long looks when he stretched, the V of his body revealed, the tufts of armpit hair, the crest of his cum-gutters. It would get me so hot. And then I would catch him grinning at my stares, and I'd escape into my room and read Edgar Allen Poe, my whole body crackling with salacity and cold fire. Somehow, he knew what I was before I did.

"How's your mother?" he asks, and all that recalled desire drains from me. What remains is an urge to spit.

"You don't get to ask that," I say.

"Oh, come on, that was a long time ago. It's good to see you."

"I don't fuck pillows anymore, and you're shanking in prison."

He looks around the breaking house, and back at me. He grins. I want to slap it off his face. It doesn't hold the same dominion it did when I was a kid.

"This house is nice. You've done good for yourself."

"I worked hard."

"Yeah, it appears you say that a lot."

"Because it's true." I gulp my wine, anything to put something between us. I try not to look down, and settle my gaze on his suprasternal notch.

"There's value in a man earning his way," he says, peering into the quaking darkness.

151

"And what did you ever earn?" I ask.

"A man can know a thing without ever being a thing," he says.

"Why did you hurt her like you did?" I ask, a sudden wave of anger rising into my throat.

"I was a drunk. I loved your mother," he says.

"You beat her up."

He looks down, scratches his head, peers back up and squints. "Yeah."

"That was it? You were drunk?"

"Why are you standing here?" he asks.

I remember one night he stumbled home wasted. This was not unusual. He was singing a Credence Clearwater Revival song. He was in a good mood. So it was a surprise when, out of nowhere, he picked my mother up by the neck with his right hand, just to see if he could do it, he said. Lifted her body towards the ceiling. Kissed her with mopey lips, laughed, then dropped her like a laundry bag, and headed to bed. She remained frozen, crumpled on the ground, her hand wrapped her neck, staring at the closed bedroom door, then at me, back at the bedroom door, the shock painting her face. It is no wonder he is serving time for murder, another lover years later, not long after he dumped my mother for someone else.

But not before he completely fucked her up. My mother was possessed by a hydra of fear—fear of his body, fear for her safety, fear that she failed somehow, in her choices, as a mother, as a protector of her child; it could have been any of those and all of them at once. Whittled a crystal carapace for herself with one sharp edge of that fear. I watched her immobilize in the prism, all of herself refracted, but I could not reach her, could not find the precise place to smooth back the errant unwashed hair, calm the twitching fingers, the darting eyes of a prey animal. Shame is a hunting and a haunting; it comes in from all sides.

Since I couldn't reach in, I faced out. I learned to make dinners that she would spear and shift on the plate, learned to forge her name on checks to pay utilities past due, help her dress for job interviews she would bomb, her woeful apologies a soundtrack to my adolescence. I knew she was sorry, I wanted to forgive, and maybe I did. But I used anger to motivate me. Watching her sit unbathed on the couch for days—reruns of *Friends* and *Wheel of Fortune*—fired me into the rest of the world. I scored the first job I could, fast food at fourteen, paid for my books at school, saved for a 1992 Ford Escort with a rusted-out floorboard. Insurance. When we needed something, I figured it out. And now with wheels, I could get away from her apologies, her pathetic reasons for her soul-freeze, would take off, drive wherever, through the weekend. When I returned, she would ask where I had been. I would tell her—the beach, Chapel Hill, a truck stop—and I hoped she would forbid me from doing it again, say that I was too young to disappear for days on my own, that she was my mother. But she didn't. She was too afraid to do even that.

The crack in the floor expands, and we topple. My mother's ex-boyfriend lands square on top of me, his hard beef of a body. I turn my head away, but his breath crawls along my cheek.

"Why aren't you on the other side of this chasm?" I ask.

I can feel his grin without seeing it. I can feel his cock growing against my leg. The house is a giant splinter.

"Why don't I hate men?" I ask.

"You are a man now, too," he says.

"I do hate you," I say. "I do."

He glances at the giant crack in the floor, its pure lightlessness. "Then push me in," he whispers.

"Where does it go?"

He emits a falling whistle from his missing front tooth, his breath surprisingly clean-smelling, like crushed thyme leaves.

"Do what you want," I say.

"Oh, no," he laughs. "It's not about what I want. You of all people know want, yes? Isn't that right?"

I stare into his eyes, his humorless face so close, and something loosens in my chest.

"I don't know."

"What's that?" he whispers.

"I said." I swallow the heat in my throat. "I don't know." And the tears come.

He lets out a long, slow breath. It parts around my lips and cools my ears. For a following instant, he is completely still, silent, our bodies pressed flat against one another.

There are so many beings stirring the air at any given moment, all directions a unique decision, a compound of this-ways and thats. And the knowledge of those infinite and subtle and not-so-subtle exploits moves me. More tears come, different tears, altogether a cooler temperature.

And then, with one arrangement of muscle, my mother's ex-boyfriend leaps off of me, pulls his mouth wide, and wordlessly launches into the abyss.

With that, the widening gap splits the koi pond right down the middle. The water rushes into the crack and right through the house. It continues, flows out to meet the river. The rushing is fast in the fissure, and I watch Big Jim and his friends zoom past, pine cones, twigs, and then shit from the neighborhood, a trash can, a rake, a Rubik's Cube, two ugly Christmas sweaters, a plastic flamingo floatie, a Kentucky Fried Chicken bucket, all hurtling toward the river. The new stream in my cabin rises with more water, from swimming pools, from hot tubs, kitchen sinks and showers, whooshing down to the bank. It spills out into the cabin. Murky water lugging burger wrappers, toothbrushes, and real estate magazines heaves into the corners, filling fast, globs of turf, gobs of leaves, shellac. Knee deep in seconds. I grab my wine, clomp out the back door to the redwood tree just beyond the deck, and climb. My thighs grip and pull, forearms hugging. Grip, pull, hug. I reach a large burl, cancerous looking, but now a convenient shelf. I haul myself up and squat, sigh. I survive again. And not a drop of wine spilled, you better believe it.

Then, suddenly, the rumbling, the sound, the water, the careening detritus, it all ceases.

Everything goes dark and still, like the whole world has fallen away, once yowling sound then silence, sloughed like boiled chicken meat off a bone. Like I'm perched at the edge of the universe. There is nothing left.

I work to adjust my eyes. They adjust to more dark.

The moment calls for a laugh, a chuckle, a "well...*shit*." A sip of wine, a fold of my glass-holding hand to the chest, a graceful pose that signifies either my sophistication, or an irony I can't quite clarify.

If a forest disappears and there is only one person around to witness it, has it really disappeared? Something like that.

And then I hear my husband, somewhere below me. Well, not hear exactly, but I sense his breathing, his living, his particular arrangement of molecules, his unique life in proximity, the wake of the world making way for his presence. A soft warmth flows through me. I didn't realize I was cold.

From somewhere in the pitch, I hear him ask, "Do you need help?"

"No," I say. "I got this," and tighten my legs around the tree, my feet perching the burl.

"It doesn't appear that way," he says.

"Well, nothing is apparent at the moment."

The rutted ridges of the burl bark press into the arches of my feet.

"You can ask me for help."

"I can't do that."

"Why?"

"It's not fair."

"Why?"

"I made you leave. I'm on my own now." Then I add quickly, "I want to be."

"That's not how it works," he says.

I peer out at the blackness. It's matte, not deep or abyss-like, but flat, like I'm in a velvet box that refuses all light. My legs ache from squeezing the tree trunk.

"All you need to do is ask me to help you."

"I'm not going to do that."

"But you'll fall."

"Then it'll be my own fault. That's the consequence."

"No, the consequence will be that you die."

I look out into the dark, and toss my wine glass, more to see where it goes, or better yet *how* it goes. But I experience neither. It merely disappears as soon as it leaves my hands. I stare at my hand for a long time, longer than I ever allow, longer than I understand.

Then, I realize that my feet are no longer balancing on the tree's burl, but instead on my husband's extended hands above his head, like a candelabra. His hands are generous, softer, more pliant than the bark.

Years before, when we first toured the cabin, tucked below the forest canopy, we both instantly knew it was what we wanted. My husband knew the moment he saw the pitched ceiling of rich wood, that color where red and brown confuse each other in their mutual depth. He said it made him feel wrapped up in a warm blanket. He said it was the room he wanted to breathe his last breath in, when the time came. For me, it was the trees, the six redwoods posted around the house like sentries, towering into the sky. Years before that, the first time I visited the west coast, I declared that I wanted to live in the redwoods, and this house delivered on my promise.

We stay like this for a while, my husband and I, his hands straight above his head, still propping me up. I want to say something, I know his arms must ache, but the oblivion feels good. My husband hums a showtune. It's familiar, but aren't they all? I wish I hadn't tossed my wine away, imagine it on my lips, its warmth or comfort, I don't know. Somehow the air outside feels inside-like, carries upon it no sound, like a held breath. My heartbeat slows.

"Do you want to come down?" he asks.

"To what?" I ask. "Everything's gone."

"That's not true," he says.

"What then?" I ask.

"Remember when you pulled your back out surfing in Mexico?"

"Totally seized up, I don't know how I swam back to shore," I say.

"It was impressive," he says.

"Adrenaline. The true pain came after, lying in bed."

"You yelled at me," he says.

"Well, yeah! I was angry. My body had failed me."

"That wasn't it."

"Enlighten me, then, Obi-Wan."

"I was helping you get to the bathroom. You kept insisting you could do it on your own."

"And I fell trying. It hurt. I was mad."

"No. You couldn't deal with it. It made you furious."

"I needed the bathroom. I wanted to get there."

"Need, want, earn."

"I'm stubborn," I say.

"They're different words, you know."

"So, now that we've been split up for two days, you've finally figured me out?"

"Come down. Put your foot on my shoulder, then the other.

Let me get you."

That's when my throat seizes, no breath, no spit. Only a sound, a croak, a creek, like a door opening that has been jammed. It's an ugly sound, and I don't know it. I don't know it. I stare out to the black, and then below me. My husband is the only thing I can see. There doesn't appear to be ground below him. Yet, he stands solid, his arms overhead, as if he's made of wood. I start, slide my body down along his body, and steady my feet on top of his feet, wrapping my arms around his torso. My husband and I embracing, like lovers.

After more silent rise-and-falls of his chest to count, my husband grabs my shoulders and softly shifts me beside him. I seize up in panic, worried once my feet leave the tops of his they will slip, along with the rest of me, down into the groundless dark. But my feet settle upon the black without give, like an infinity floor.

Standing side by side, my husband's hand in mine, we look out to the emptiness. Or maybe the suchness? I have read many books on Zen philosophy, and what of it? The futility of my answers. He softly glides his finger back and forth in my palm.

I laugh. "That was one hell of a quake," I say.

"The big one," he says.

"What is left?"

"Plenty," he says.

"Any trees?" I ask.

"I think they're out there," he says, and hums another showtune, maybe the same one.

That's when I see them; there they are, barely visible, dark vertical outlines against dark—close, far, all around. Pitch black, the trees are what's left, and us. My husband's hand in mine. Our mutual presence. The trees.

AFTER THE STORM

Mina Manchester

The first time I drove Anders' pickup, the Ford F-150 with dents along the side panels and the short bed, it was late November, getting close to Thanksgiving, and although there had been rain almost every day for the last three months, and each was gray and hard to love, on this day the skies were darker and more threatening. There was a sense in the air that shit was about to go down.

I took the keys off the hook in the hall and closed the swollen door that never shut right— it either slammed or stuck—and paused for a moment outside the house in the glen of evergreens, feeling the soft bed of dry needles under my duck boots and smelling the wind. The trees were shivering around me, their leaves and branches swaying as if they were limbering up for the dance to come.

My family's lake house was at the base of an extremely long, windy, narrow gravel driveway hacked in by handsaw through hundred feet tall evergreens. It was one in the afternoon by the time I was ready to drive two and half hours each way to pick up an antique dry sink some guys were selling on Craigslist. I'd hired a real estate agent to appraise the place and she said the kitchen needed to be upgraded, that's what sold houses. My dad didn't have the money to buy anything new, so I started scouring the Internet.

It's amazing what people give away or sell for a song. For my entire life, the cabin was a dumping ground for discarded or half-broken things, and now, for the first time in its history, we were changing that. We'd replaced all the old dented cheap furniture with antiques found at estate sales or the Goodwill.

The solid wooden furniture we'd acquired was made by hand, perhaps outdated, scuffed and dusty and out of vogue, but I loved how each piece seemed outside of time. I found myself drawn to something my brother talked about just before he died, the Latin word *linde*, meaning the limits of things. At the time, I'd thought he was talking about gender, and how he was a transboy, but now I was starting to think he'd meant something else entirely, something bigger, about what you can change and what you can't. The dry sink, from the 1900s, was being sold for one hundred dollars, and would replace the scratched Formica countertops with a marble top I planned to polish myself.

The front door of the cabin opened, and my dad came out. "Weather report says it's going to rain," he said. "Better take the tarp." It was thoughtful the way he'd folded it into tight squares and neatly coiled a rope for me to take. I could tell he cared.

"I'd go with you but I've got to finish installing the new showerhead. Better get it done before the open house tomorrow. It better sell or I'm on the street." Dad was joking, but not really. He'd used up all his savings to pay for Anders' rehab, and when that hadn't worked, the funeral. This house, a cabin really, was all he had left. We had to get it in saleable condition or he'd lose his last remaining asset.

I hoisted myself up into my big brother's truck and remembered how he'd told me before he died to shift into four-wheel drive to make it up the hill.

When I arrived on Whidbey Island three months ago, I'd only intended to stay for Labor Day weekend. It was clear when I got there Anders was in a bad way, and Dad was hanging in. Since I was the only one who'd gone to college and knew my way around a spreadsheet from my job at the Capital Group in New York, I took it on myself to tally the receipts and take over the finances. Dad never had any money, and they were running this operation on a shoestring, as usual. I worried it was going to run into the ground like pretty much every other hare-brained business idea Dad had during our childhood, so I stayed. I emailed my boss and took a two-week vacation. Those first two weeks in the house were claustrophobic with my dad and Anders bickering all the time, but it was worse in the emptiness he left behind. After his death, I took an unpaid leave of absence from my job in New York with no end date specified.

I shifted into four-wheel drive and gunned it up the hill. At the top, I made a series of left turns and found my way by memory to the highway. I had spent countless weekends here as a kid with my dad and Anders and I remembered each curve as though it were one of the stuffed animals on my childhood twin bed. Although my eyes were no longer accustomed to driving long stretches of dark highway in the country, I was looking forward to it. Ever since my brother took his own life in mid-September, things had been grim at the house. Dad preferred to cry at night, over his whiskey in the woods. He didn't like me to see, but I always felt bad that both of us were so alone. Sanding doors, installing new floors, and painting the walls was blissfully mind-numbing, and my mind drifted. All I thought about was Anders and what we'd done wrong, or what we hadn't gotten right.

Growing up, we lived in a different house every year, sometimes multiple houses. When Anders was five and I was three, a thirty-foot wave knocked over a stack of crab pots on the Amber Marie where our father was working on deck and the heavy steel cages crushed his vertebrae. Dad started drinking and coming up with his ingenious business ideas, and Mom left shortly thereafter, for Reno of all places. We never heard from her again. Dad said she'd liked the big money from fishing and the drugs it bought even more. With a small insurance settlement, a check every year from Fisherman's Fund and Dad's disability, we barely scraped by. "Your old man was lucky," his fishing buddies always said to me. "Five other guys drowned when their boat went down."

Anders always said he was the reason Mom left, that she packed her bags the week after he cut off all his hair and refused to wear the dresses she bought for him. It didn't bother me or Dad that Anders said he was a boy. Dad had always wanted a son, I think, and I loved having a big brother who showed me how to do everything. No one at school knew, because we were always moving, and Anders was always private about himself. He looked like a boy. Whether he sought out testosterone shots when he hit puberty was between him and Planned Parenthood.

When I first came home, and Anders was still alive, it seemed we were doing better than before. The cabin, the land, it had potential, though no one saw it but us. No one else wanted to do the work, and there was a lot to be done. It was a real bitch, that's for sure. Even though many days we fought, I thought overall it brought us together. That's the real reason I stayed.

But now, without Anders, I wasn't sure I wanted to be there. I loved the lake, I loved the land, I loved my Dad. The way it smelled, slightly mossy, like wet grass dragged through silt, got into my hair and skin and nails, and it was in the water we drank, and now it would be in the dry sink and the shower and the laundry; no matter how much Tide I used, I wouldn't be able to get it out.

Despite the ominous clouds, it was a beautiful drive. Miraculously, a CD started to play, and my ears were surprised by Anders' music. I hadn't realized he'd gotten into classical. I stared out at the bigleaf maple, paper birch and cedar trees that seemed to shimmy, their leaves fluttering against the backdrop of Tchaikovsky's Piano Concerto No. 1. Better known as the beginning of *Swan Lake*.

My mind cleared as the stiff cold breath of the oncoming storm entered the steel shell of the truck, scattering my worries to the corners of the earth. The music made me think about contrasts, and swans, and how Dad always said anything bad that happened was a Black Swan even though they piled on and on. I was thinking about the last conversation I had with my brother. It was the morning after Anders and Dad drank too much and Anders got mad and stormed off.

I, of course, went after him. I grabbed a flashlight, realizing too late it was Dad's headlamp, which was about five sizes too big, but I adjusted the strap and felt the saturated earth squish beneath my feet as I climbed the steep driveway in the dark.

It was a moonless night, where the blackness between trees

felt thick and impenetrable. I didn't notice a single creature, no green reflective deer or racoon eyes blinking back at me from behind the woodpile. Walking along the road by the lake, I went left, thinking the public beach a natural choice. That's where I would have gone if I wanted a quiet place to think and throw rocks.

At this time, sometime after midnight, the beach was quiet and deserted. The shore lapped softly against the sand and round pebbles. I didn't find Anders.

Returning to the cabin, after giving the other side of the lake a thorough searching, I was cold through my flannels and into my bone flesh. Dad told me Anders drove back to the mainland, despite Dad telling him he was too drunk to drive and trying to take his keys. Anders drove home without incident, to the rodent and roach infested shit box he lived in above a bar owned by one of Dad's friends.

It always bothered me that Dad maintained his friendship with the landlord when it was his negligence that kept Anders living in squalor. I knew what Dad would say, though, that it wasn't his friend's fault, it was Anders'.

The next morning, Anders was sitting at the kitchen table I'd bought at Habitat for Humanity. He held his head in his hands, drinking coffee I'd set out in the machine the night before. I looked out at the lake.

"Why'd you get so upset?" I said.

"I'm sorry," he said. He looked so despondent, so filled with shame and self-hatred.

"Where'd you go? I looked everywhere for you, I went over to the public beach and then halfway around the lake on the other side." Although I was angry, I never could stay mad at Anders.

"I don't fit here," he said. "You don't know what it's like, being afraid all the time." I watched the wind make little ripples on the lake. There were no strong currents. It wasn't that big of a lake, although I surmised from swimming it flowed clockwise from the underground spring that fed it.

Now, the music in Anders' truck swelled to a crescendo. I pictured Anders standing at the edge of a big darkness, looking out at nothingness. I could see him so clearly, the oversize black hoodie with the white crab logo from the dive bar in Anchorage he'd been kicked out of for picking a fight with a townie. When he told me about the experiences he had up in Dutch Harbor and on the Bering Sea, he spoke as if it were a prison.

"You don't understand. There's nothing there. No bookstores, no bowling alleys, no restaurants, no coffee shops, no libraries, no hotels, nothing but strip clubs, dive bars, and bad weather." All the time alone, he said, he'd gotten into reading, finally.

When he came back from Alaska for what turned out to be the last time, he seemed changed. Quieter, calmer, if that was possible. He'd always been reserved, except when he drank. He was exactly like Dad that way.

"I think I'd like to write," he said, "but I'm too scared." The implication, not that I didn't face it, but that my darkness wasn't as dark, wasn't lost on me. All I could tell him was that it was true, I didn't know what it was like.

Outside the wind was howling now, but inside the truck, the seat heater was on, and my butt was warm. The contrast put me on edge. I couldn't shake the feeling that the line between keeping it together and losing it was dangerously thin. I was scared it was going to slip away from me, that there was going to be a crackup. I think that's why Anders left, because he was afraid it was going to happen to him, but I wasn't totally sure. Hedging his bets, I guess. Now I wanted to ask him what to do with the rest of it, the in between that wasn't changeable or unchangeable. "Leave it alone," I imagined he'd say. "Best left undisturbed for your own sanity. You've gotta make peace with it, Sis."

By the road's lip, the sea slapped the shore. Many whitecaps littered the water's rough surface. I was driving along a two-lane highway that would eventually lead to a dramatic suspended bridge over Deception Pass. After Anders died, Dad and I drove back to the cabin and got to work. We had nothing else to do.

The only thing that brought me back to myself was the vibration in my hands while I was using the chop saw, and the kickback of the oversize clippers I used to trim back the wildness that was the landscaping. It didn't take me that long to understand I liked making things, taming things, setting them according to my vision. The esoteric theoretical world of nebulous and poorly understood financial products, which is what I'd been spending my time on day in and day out at Capital Group in New York, was starting to seem more and more like a strange fever dream.

I took in the view from the road, where the open ocean met the land, where Whidbey Island was a bulwark against all that wildness, a point of stability where you could walk, run, and live. Any endeavor that didn't support flourishing in the natural world seemed more than just a criminal enterprise; it was a damn tragedy. What was the fucking point of adding up the zeros and ones, of blindly following the route of material ascension, when the entire world was unjust and there were ginormous trees ringing escarpments, such as the liminal one I was currently piloting this truck along? I thought again of *linde*. The literal translation is the limits of things, but colloquially—I looked it up online in the Oxford English Dictionary—over the centuries, it's become known as the concept of timelessness, of being made to last.

I drove and drove. I prayed my cellphone wouldn't die because I had fuck all idea of where I was. My destination, a tiny town called Alger, which struck me as too close to algae for the locals to take themselves seriously, was in a part of unincorporated Island County. At the entrance to Deception Pass, I rolled onto the high bridge over the Strait of Juan de Fuca, one of the most glorious natural wonders in the whole Pacific Northwest. Of course, on this particular day, the bridge was down to one lane, and construction workers were roped in.

I let my eyes drift out over the Sound, trying not to imagine my body going over the edge.

It was a popular tourist destination, and equally so with the suicidal part of the population. It wasn't where Anders chose to die, though. He did that with pills and booze in his own apartment, the same one that didn't have a working stove and got bitterly cold at night because it wasn't properly insulated, but still cost eight hundred and fifty bucks a month.

By the time I got to Alger and pulled up to the house where the guys were selling the dry sink, it had started to rain. I texted the number listed on the Craigslist post, and out from the enormous garage came two young men who told me they were brothers. The one who shook my hand and introduced himself as Steve "from Craigslist" had close cropped black hair and wore a flannel shirt and wide leg khakis. The second one was Dan. Dan had long sandy blonde curls, flipflops, and a nose ring.

"Aren't you cold?" I said, pointing to his bare feet.

"Nah, I'm always hot," he said, and he reminded me of Anders, how everything seemed to roll off him, until it didn't.

The dry sink was in the corner of the garage, which was immaculate and stocked with neatly organized tools of every kind. My dad would have loved it. I inspected my purchase. It was oak, barely a scratch on it. The sink was a porcelain bowl without so much as a single chip. It depictured figures in repose at the seashore in blue ceramic glaze. I wondered why they were getting rid of it, and as if reading my mind, Steve said, "It was from our cabin. We're selling it." I met his eyes and thought I detected a sadness that wasn't there before. Why is it you always have to give up what you love? I handed him one hundred dollars in twenties in a damp white business envelope. He counted it and nodded to his brother.

The three of us maneuvered the heavy sink onto a dolly, and then Steve wheeled it onto the bed of the pick-up. Dan hoisted it up and together they laid it carefully to rest. Steve gently unscrewed the porcelain bowl and marble top and handed them to me. I wrapped them in towels and set them on the backseat, putting the brass hardware in the cupholder. Then I got the tarp and ropes and the three of us tied down the magnificent old furniture.

"How far do you have to drive?" Steve asked.

"Two and a half hours," I said.

"Whoa," Dan said, "you better make it back quick before the storm comes in or it's going to get all wet."

I checked my phone for the time and to my dismay saw Google maps drained the battery to red. I hoped Anders left a charger in the glovebox. It was already four, if I dallied any longer it would be dark for the last part of the drive, the most dangerous part, around the hairpin curves of the highway over the cliffs. Sunset came early in this part of the country, at this time of year.

I looked out towards the road I'd driven in on as though I were a sea captain trying to anticipate the height of the waves.

"It'll be fine, you're all strapped in, and you've got the tarp," Steve said. I looked down at Dan's feet and saw his big toe was bleeding.

"You cut yourself," I said. What kind of idiot doesn't wear proper shoes in this weather? I looked self-consciously at my duck boots. But Dan didn't seem to mind. I offered him a Band- Aid from the First Aid kit in the back of the truck, but he declined.

Steve tipped his head to me in a friendly thank you, and they waved, their black lab following me with his wizened old eyes as I headed off. Driving back to the highway, I couldn't help wondering if it was tragedy or a death that prompted the brothers' family to sell their cabin. The place I'd been to, presumably their parents' house, as they seemed a few years younger than me, was well-kept. They were a fishing family, too, that was obvious from the boat trailers and piles of nets and crab pots stacked in the garage. It was clear they'd made different choices along the way though. They had a bigger, nicer house than we'd ever lived in, but it was out in the boonies, where my dad never wanted to be. He claimed he wanted us to go to better schools, but I thought the real reason was it was harder to find a babysitter and drinking buddies out in the sticks.

I wondered about the brothers. If they got along, though they appeared very different.

Anders and I were always more alike than we were separate. We both loved watching *Forensic Files*. There was something about a team of scientists who collected all the evidence and found the perpetrator in the end. I guess we liked the fiction that even horrible things could end well.

I missed our long walks around the lake talking about what kinds of dogs we'd get.

Anders always wanted a pug to carry around and snuggle with. I wanted a border collie, because they were smart, and their fur was soft. Most of all I missed how Anders felt like an extension of me. That's what siblings are, more the same than anyone else. And now my only mirror, the person who laughed at my terrible dark sense of humor, the only person who could tell me that everything would be alright, even when we both knew it wouldn't, was gone.

But there wasn't time to do any more thinking. I had one job, to get the dry sink back in one piece.

The first part of the drive was fine. I found Anders' cellphone charger in the glove box and plugged in my dying phone. I reversed the directions, although I was feeling confident I could retrace my steps by memory if I had to. This probably wasn't the truth, since I had a terrible sense of direction, but I tried to comfort myself with the notion anyway. I wondered if Dad had finished installing the showerhead, and if it would work by the time I got back.

By the time I rounded the path to Deception Pass again, I didn't even notice the view.

The whole truck was shaking in the wind. My hands were dry and cold from gripping the steering wheel. I checked the rearview mirror and saw that, despite the brothers' promises, one of the ropes had come undone and bottom corner of the tarp was blowing around. I was scared I'd be pulled over. Then I thought there were worse things than a cop stopping me; at least they'd probably help me re-tie the tarp. The worst part would be if the weather was so bad the police weren't even out.

About ten cars ahead I saw flashing red lights and a highway patrol setting out cones. A giant tree was blocking the entire highway. I tried to peer around the semi-truck directly in front of me. All the vehicles came to a complete stop. The wind rushed at the truck, shaking it from side to side. Fat raindrops pelted the windshield. Tchaikovsky's *Dances of the Swans* blasted from the speakers. All I could think of was how lucky it was the tree hadn't landed on anyone's car. Literally no one was hurt. People were getting out of their cars and putting on their raincoats, peering out under their rubber hoods and looking at each other.

I thought back to the late summer weekend when the arborist came out to the property and gave us a bid to take down three evergreens. "They're all rotten," he said. "It happens on these properties close to the lake, the roots get wet and eventually they're eaten away." I pictured the big trees lying on the squashed cabin, recalling pictures from the devastation of tropical storms, houses reduced to sticks on the ground. I couldn't stop my mind from following the thought all the way to the most extreme imagining: that everyone in my family, the only people I'd ever really loved, was dead.

"What do you think about when you're out there, all alone on the ocean?" I'd asked Anders.

"Things you love," he said.

"Ah," I'd said, as if I understood, but the truth was I didn't, because at that time I felt if you loved something, then you just loved it, and you didn't have to think about it. Even if other people did, hour by hour and minute by minute, you just didn't have to. But then, when Anders died, I got it. I saw what he saw, that suddenly one day you looked up and you'd gotten so far away from the thing you loved, it started to turn away from you in return.

But the question I was curious about now was, then what do you do? Do you have to find new things to love, or somehow chart a course back? How perilous that journey was, and what you'd lose along the way scared the shit out of me. So maybe now I knew what Anders was talking about. The fear that kept you hiding, head under the covers, afraid of starting anything because it was going to hurt.

I felt for the first time in months, ever since I'd touched down on the tarmac at Sea-Tac International Airport, that Anders' fear was justified. This was the kind of storm where a giant tree could just land on you. And it wasn't just today, it was always.

It was ten thousand dollars to remove the rotten trees and, of course, we didn't have the cash. Dad was saving up, and, in the meantime, doing everything by hand. "We're doing things the old-fashioned way," he said. The only way we could afford.

There was no cell service at the cabin, so I tried the landline, but it wouldn't even ring.

Fuck, the power was out. I had to get back, urgently.

But first I had to tie down the tarp. I piloted the truck over to the shoulder, pulled my raincoat up over my head, and climbed into the bed. The rear rope was gone, it must have flown away in the wind, and I didn't have any more. In desperation, I tucked the corner end of the tarp underneath the sink, hoping that the weight of the furniture would hold it in place, knowing I was deluding myself to think it would stay.

Then I followed a line of cars and trucks that were pulling U-turns and heading for the alternate highway, which was just a regular road, and not well maintained. I searched the map on my phone, eyes popping up to glance warily at the trees swaying above. I was out of my depth. I had no idea where I was. I was over an hour out, somewhere on an island in the middle of a storm, and trees were falling.

I gripped the steering wheel tighter. My neck was starting to ache from angling over the dashboard. Eventually, after much teeth gnashing, the road I was on came to a T and joined back up with the highway I'd been on to begin with. At least I knew where I was again.

Rounding the big S curves on the cliffs the *Pas de deux* was starting. I tried to focus only on the music, following the dynamics, marking it in my mind when it got soft and when it got loud. I did not let myself look over the edge. I was so intent, time went by quickly, and then I was at the top of the hill, heading down the driveway, and forgot to shift out of two-wheel drive. The truck skidded a bit on the wet gravel. At the bottom of the hill, the house stood perfectly intact. The rotten trees towered, barely even swaying. I parked the truck and ran, rain accosting my shoulders as I scraped dirt off my duck boots on the steps. Inside, Dad was sitting on the sagging leather couch, thumbing through a showerhead installation manual.

"I got the sink," I said. He swiveled to take me in, and we went to move it inside.

"The generator's out," Dad said. "We won't have power tonight. What took you so long?"

"A tree fell across the road," I said. "Right by Deception Pass." His face bore an expression of surprise and perhaps a tiny bit of awe that I'd made it back in one piece.

"Was the Craigslist guy okay?" Dad said.

"Yeah, it was two brothers and they helped me tie it down, but one of the ropes came off in the storm. I hope the sink didn't get wet."

"Sorry you had to go by yourself," he said. We carried the dry sink inside piece by piece, taking the bottom two drawers out so it wouldn't be too heavy to lift by hand. We didn't have a dolly. When we got it all inside the cabin, Dad took one of the drawers and slid it in. I lifted the other and tried to fit it in but it wouldn't go. "It doesn't fit?" he said. "Did you check it before you bought it?" He looked up at me, disgusted. Dad studied the drawer and the hole in the bottom of the dry sink as if the fact that it wasn't going in was beyond comprehension.

"I did check it, everything worked when I inspected it."

"It can't be, it doesn't fit!" He stared at the drawer again, as if in disbelief.

"I promise, I made sure it worked!"

"Did you try both drawers?" He met my eyes accusingly.

"I didn't slide them both out, but they were both all the way in before we loaded it in the truck." I could hear the whine in my voice. I sounded petulant, like a child. But it was the truth.

Dad ran his calloused fingers over the sides of the drawer. "This is all wet, that's why! Wood that gets wet gets warped. It's never going to fit. Now what are we going to do? We have no kitchen sink, and the open house is tomorrow!"

"I'm sorry, the tarp came undone in the storm, and I didn't have any more rope to tie it back down. I tried my best."

"You ruined it!" I stood still. He had never yelled at me with this much rage before. Then he seemed to realize what he was doing. A change came over his body and it seemed as though he was willing himself to calm down, relaxing his muscles one by one.

"When I was helping my old man, if I got a part that didn't fit, he threw it in my face." When he spoke, it was as though he was transported back in time. He got a funny look on his face, as if he were no longer in the cabin with me, but far away, both in time and space, with his own long-dead father. I wanted to say, *I'm sorry, Dad. I'm so sorry that happened to you,* but for some reason, I didn't. Now I understood what Anders had to put up with when I wasn't there, why he got so angry all the time. Anders deflected all of Dad's rage, all his generational trauma, and spared me.

I still felt wronged and in the right. But a knowing dread came over me as well, like a stomachache. Shivering in the cold I thought of warming up in the sauna. Then it occurred to me, the sauna, like everything in the cabin, was built by hand, from wood. Handmade, imperfectly built, no two the same. Linde. Meant to last. Without hesitating, I took the drawer. It might dry the wood enough to gently sand until it fit. Then I could re-stain it. It wouldn't be perfect, but it would work. "I'll get it to fit," I said.

"The sauna?" Dad said. I nodded. "Good idea," he said. I

turned to go downstairs. "When Anders was in Alaska, he was raped," Dad said.

"What?" I said. I turned my head over my shoulder to look at him, the drawer still in my arms as though it were a heavy baby.

"It was a friend of the skipper. He found out about him, about his gender. One night, he waited for him in the engine room."

I set the drawer on the floor. I felt my body collapsing.

"He had to work alongside his rapist for three more weeks before he came home."

"I didn't know; he didn't tell me," I said.

"There was nothing I could do to protect him." My dad slammed his fists against the wall.

I thought about Mom. I rarely ever thought about her. I remembered her light brown hair in feathery curls against the sides of her face. That one rainbow striped sweater, which in my three-year-old memory is possible I mixed up with my kindergarten teacher's.

"You did as well as you could. No one did better than you, Dad." It wasn't the whole truth, but it was the truth of my father's life. I went to him and put my arm around his humped shoulder; it was awkward, but not really.

On the sauna bench, the drawer glistened. I made a small fire underneath the rocks and hand dried the rest of the dry sink with an old towel. Upstairs I made a polish for the marble top with baking soda, lemon juice, and vinegar. As I rubbed a nubby cloth across its surface in concentric circles, the grime and dust of the last century came off in my hands, giving an untarnished veneer to something old.

Later, after I'd sanded the drawer and applied a coat of stain, Dad made a fire in the fireplace, and I kept thinking about how the rotten trees didn't fall. We sat in our bathrobes in the living room drinking Franzia out of mismatched coffee mugs. The power was still out, the generator still dead. I absorbed the honeyed pine wood around us, illuminated by two white pillar candles, the kind they put on church altars.

AFTER THE STORM

My dad talked about his childhood, how after his father died, he had to step up as the head of the house. I felt bad for the little boy he'd been, and the big man he'd become, someone who could fix anything, even if he'd never done it before. Anders and I heard Dad's tale of woe many times. When we were growing up, he never liked coming here to the cabin. He didn't want to sit around all day and fish. It was too quiet, he said.

I thought about when I'd first arrived at the cabin, and it had looked exactly the same as I'd remembered. How I'd walked down to the lake and put my fingers in the water, even though it was late, and I'd wanted to see my family and rib Anders about getting a dog. It'd been a chilly yet sunny Sunday, and it had felt like being in church, except I'd never believed in God anyway.

"Do you feel differently about being here now?" I asked Dad. Because it seemed he did. I thought there was something he wanted to say.

"I've been here for six months," he said. His voice choked up. "The lake, every day, how it changes from hour to hour, it's amazing."

My father was crying at last, moved by impermanence. As he spoke, his words reminded me of the moment after the storm ends, the calm release. The way the air smells after all the scents of cooking oil and garbage dumps, diesel engines and sewers, are washed away, and there is nothing left, just pure air.

All I could think of was my future, my future, my future.

SNOW CRANES

Anil Classen

Mikoto found the diary on the coldest morning of winter. Her hands were still stained from the beetroot she had peeled earlier, making the crime even more evident, blood-stained, indicating possible violence. The bright yellow edge of the notebook beckoned like light escaping under a door. It was the yellow of the omelette she had managed to perfect over the years, folded over and over in the narrow square cast iron pan her mother had handed to her when she left her childhood home for a new life with Akira.

She sat for the longest time on the tatami with her feet folded beneath her body. The book was balanced on a pillow in front of her like an unexpected gift that could either bring joy or pain. Mikoto would only allow these two possibilities. Her brain was spinning with what could lay between the pages of a book her son had clearly wanted to keep from her. She thought about opening it. Maybe if she limited herself to only one page it would not trouble her afterwards? It reminded her of that moment when she had discovered her sister's secret cache of candy. Mountains of worm-like rolls, squashed into the thinnest rice paper. She could still see the cheerful rabbit on the wrapper as she nibbled, the milkiness reminding her of pudding. She remembered wrapping the remainder of the sweet and pushing it to the back of the one drawer she owned, the one she knew her mother snooped through from time to time, this made clear by her underwear arranged in straight towers as opposed to her usual untidiness.

Mikoto decided to leave the book on the pillow and made herself a pot of tea instead. She looked out her window as the kettle boiled, bringing crackling noise into her silent apartment. Her neighbourhood was covered in an oblong cloud that looked like an alien invader, a battleship that had descended unexpectedly over the residents who would surely look up into steely grey, wondering what had robbed them of sunlight.

173

SNOW CRANES

The tea was a good distraction. Preparing supper would have been better, but since Hari had left for university, there was little point to slaving over a selection of dishes like she had in the past. She knew that the waste would only sadden her before irritation set in. The leftover congealed sauce would only look up at her like a drying oil spill.

The first week alone had been the worst. She cooked meals as if her son would walk through the door, throwing his oversized backpack on to the floor before kicking off his sport shoes. She had learned to decipher the subtle art of each thump of soiled athletic wear. She could even predict the mood attached. The softer the sound, the less annoyed he was. The closer in time each shoe fell signalled his level of frustration. When her husband left to venture into a new, colourful life without them, Hari slipped permanently from her grip. His silence scared her because it was smooth, impossible to grasp no matter how many tricks she tried. Her hand would only skim the surface and make her feel foolish for not understanding the person she had not only created but also loved more than anyone else.

"You can't go to Okinawa," she said when Hari told her about his acceptance letter.

He thoughtlessly held it up to her face as if she needed an official stamp, documented proof of her impending loneliness.

"Why?"

"It is too far away."

She heard her tone. She knew that it would make him angry. Could she blame him? How can you encourage a bird to love its wings and then insist it not use them?

"It is not forever," he offered in a voice that made her feel small.

"I know."

"I need to better myself. I need to take care of us."

That sealed it. Those were the words of a father and not a son. Mikoto knew then that their roles had unknowingly switched. Akira had left her like a helpless child. She would never have guessed she could feel so lost simply because a man had left her.

She circled the date on her calendar in red. She watched as time swallowed the days. On Hari's last night, they sat on opposite sides of the low table in the living room that doubled as her bedroom. She watched him eat the soup she had taken a lot of time with, the one she knew they could not afford because

174

of the fresh scallops she placed in at the very end. She knew he loved the muscled firmness of it, the way it yielded to the softest nibble before releasing a smooth and sweet flavour no other seafood could replicate.

When the tea had finally gone cold, the rest of the Oolong now turning bitter in the black teapot in front of her, she sighed, trying to focus on an idea for supper. Her mind flitted like a window blind stuck in the wind, knocking the slats up and down at irregular intervals. She could feel the curiosity grow inside her. She knew that it was wrong, but nothing could stop her feet leading her to the bedroom. Nothing could stop her hands reaching for the book and opening it. Nothing could stop her eyes from recognising the precise handwriting she had watched with quiet adoration as Hari's confidence grew. She sat down on the tatami and folded her legs once again until all her weight was balanced on the base of her spine. Then, after a long, painfully held breath, she read the lines she knew she would later regret.

We had planned the outing for the longest time. It felt like a holiday as we sat in the train, the town disappearing behind us. I wanted to turn back. The opening fields filled me with quiet dread. I wanted to tell Yoshida this, but I knew he would only laugh at me. He would listen to me intently, like he always did, with his eyelids low, the way they were when he was about to fall asleep. He always looked sleepy. His long fringe that was permanently brushing his eyebrows added to this effect. He told me his aunt had been threatening to cut it. She warned him about taking a pair of scissors herself and chopping the offending hair off. Yoshida laughed out loud when he spoke of this. He jumped up and performed the scene, first his aunt, this made clear by him crouching low to show her trying to pin him down before he jumped right back up, acting out his reaction, ducking and diving like a ninja. He even added sound effects to make it more real. I loved his stories. I could never tell stories the way he did. The fear of my jokes not being laughed at made me silent. It was easier to keep the words safe in my head where no one could judge them as boring.

His uncle, Koshiro, had invited us for a weekend trip into the northern part of Honshu, in the Aomori prefecture. We would be staying in his cabin. Yoshida had already warned me that there would be no electricity. I could not imagine something so old fashioned. So the trip became even more exotic, like a scene out of Indiana Jones or maybe James Bond, but then again, James Bond always had gadgets and they needed electricity or batteries at least. Yoshida told me that it would not be comfortable but that his uncle was the coolest person he knew and being invited to see the cranes was an honour in their family.

I did not need him to tell me that the reason he had been invited was because his mother had died the summer before. Yoshida's family had tried to give him as much support as possible, but eventually they gave up. His grief was like a door he would never open, no matter how hard you knocked. Okan went over even though I begged her not to. I knew that she wanted to help like any mother would want to, but I also knew that Yoshida would see the pity and die on the inside. There would be nothing worse than having to smile through such a visit. I had to do the same when my father left. People showed up as if they wanted to investigate the crime, to see if it was real. I wanted to rip off the doorbell. I wanted to be left alone and all they wanted to do was inspect the sore to check if it was still hurting.

Mikoto snapped the book shut. She could not bear to read about the sadness. She knew that Hari had tried his best to be stoic. He had that wonderful way of shaking his head and raising his right shoulder when she asked him if anything was troubling him. It was a game of pretence. Both of them knew it, but circling the pain was simpler than poking it with a stick from the side where there was still a risk it could flare up and lunge towards them.

She decided to grind the komenuka as a distraction. This task was getting more and more difficult. She realised that the time was soon approaching when she would have to buy the ready-made version because her hands were no longer as strong as before. The labour involved in preparing the rice bran was quite strenuous. She remembered how her mother would take out the smallest pot they owned, the white and green flowered enamel one, before boiling the rice until the water became murky. After straining, she would add milk and honey to the mixture until it formed a thick enough paste, one that required a lot of patience and effort. Her mother would spread the sticky mass over all her children's cheeks in hard strokes because she believed this brought even more glow into their faces.

Mikoto had done the same with Hari. Now, looking at the small blue and white ceramic bowl in front of her, she could still see his eager eyes looking up at her, waiting for her fingertips. He always sighed happily when the paste touched his cheeks for the first time, sitting patiently still as more and more was applied until she was satisfied. Looking up into the mirror, her tired face greeted her before she dipped her fingers into the paste. There was something soothing about pulling the mixture across her own skin. It felt good doing this solely for herself. She did not think about turning another man's head, grabbing attention so that she could still feel the flutter of hope again. This ritual was for her alone. Still, Hari's words would not leave her. She sat and watched her skin as the paste dried slowly. She knew that the diary was toying with her. It would not let up. After she slipped into her pajamas, she rattled the front door handle, ran a hand across the window ledge to check the locks and turned out all the lights. The city beamed through the kitchen window at her, opaque yellow and white dots that were shrouded in fog, a sign of impending cold weather. When she sat down on her bed, the diary was on the nightstand, waiting patiently to be read further.

Today there was new light in Yoshida's face as he looked out of the window at the passing farmland. The sea of white was almost blinding. It felt like the world had decided to cut us off somehow, covering the once green with an arctic intensity that made my eyes sting. Yoshida stayed glued to the window, though. He rested his chin on his arm and for once he was not making a joke or teasing me. Instead, he watched men in yellow vests, carrying even brighter yellow shovels as they cleared snow from the tracks to keep the flow of traffic running on the Tsugaru railway.

I could finally look at Yoshida's face without him slapping the attention away. The scar on his cheek had become hollow and soft. It was from that time we had planned a siege on Mr. Kiwanara's property. His plum tree had stood too enticingly in the summer heat, the ripening red fruit almost expanding before our very eyes. Yoshida's sleeve had caught on a branch on the way down as plum juice trickled from his mouth. Neither of us were prepared for the crack of wood, followed by him tumbling. The mark on his cheek was a battle scar, he later told me as I pressed a cloth to the blood even though my stomach turned.

But today, there were no lines lacing his forehead. He had the smallest smile that caused his lips to pucker. It would not be long before we changed trains, but for now, he was silent.

His uncle fetched us from the station. His boots seemed to overpower the rest of him, bright red soles that you could probably see for miles when he walked through snow. His cheeks were bright pink. I don't know if it was from alcohol or the cold. He nodded at us both before patting Yoshida's shoulder roughly. This would be the only sign that they were kin for the rest of the day. He watched us occasionally from the safety of his side of the truck as we drove towards the cabin that I knew would be magical. And it was. Yoshida felt it too, I am sure. His eyes widened as the woods parted, revealing the tiny structure that stood wilfully on its own. When his uncle opened the wooden front door, it was clear where we were sleeping. In the opposite corner were two rolled up mats. I was relieved to see that his uncle was generous enough to place us close to the oven. Such a simple act of kindness in these temperatures was more noble than gold.

The sun was already starting to dip, so we set about starting our dinner. I thought it would be impossible in the small space. But his uncle cracked open plastic containers and from nowhere, a meal appeared. All we had to do was wash our hands and watch the simplest fish and rice take centre stage on the tiniest table I had ever seen. Okan would be insulted if I told her how good the food was. Even writing this feels like a betrayal. She has fed me all my life and then one day, in a cabin, in the middle of nowhere, a simple dish wipes the slate clean.

"After we wash up, we will start preparing for bed. Early start tomorrow," Yoshida's uncle said.

He looked at us sternly. My mouth was so full, I couldn't answer, so I nodded instead. I think he preferred this.

The next morning, it was still dark when we were pulled from our sleep. Outside was that strange dark I had only seen a few times, once when we visited my grandparents in Hokaido. It was still too early for the sun to take centre stage, but the snow was so bright, it created enough illumination to make you feel like you were still asleep, maybe dreaming. The silence stood like a wall around everything I looked at. It kept the sounds far away. It muffled any possible noise with an invisible force. It bent everything to its will. In front of the cabin, the snow was smooth. No animal had run across it. There was no trail of tiny dots and indentations to make us think about what had been active in the hours when we were asleep. For a moment, the loneliness of it all made me feel sad. Then Yoshida came up behind me and nudged me with his elbow, motioning towards his uncle who was clearly impatient.

We drove for a few minutes along the edge of an embankment lined with trees that seemed to lean towards us. Maybe they wanted to warn whoever was passing of impending danger. I forced myself to look at the road ahead that seemed to stretch into mirage-like nothingness. How Yoshida's uncle knew where to drive was a mystery. There were no tracks, no visible tread marks he could follow. Yet, there were determined turns of the steering wheel, a sigh that was followed by him looking left and right as if traffic would appear out of nowhere. Eventually, the truck staggered up a small hill until it came to a stop. The loud click of a seatbelt made me look up. It was clear that we had to get out and follow him. He pulled a bag out of the back seat and stood in the open doorway while fishing out a camera with an impossibly long lens. Yoshida was the first one out. I heard the hiss of his boots sinking in the snow. He turned back, his fringe brushed to one side. He smiled lightly before it merged into a yawn. His face was still sleep-compressed. The puffiness would relax over time and reveal a smoothness that turned heads in the street. He was that good-looking.

The sky had already changed. The marbled effect teased at possible daybreak. It felt like a gift. It felt like something only I could see. But then I heard a laboured breath and Yoshida's uncle stormed passed me, making his way up the hill before standing on the cusp like an adventurer claiming virgin land. His head followed the horizon and both Yoshida and I watched, waiting to be called when it was safe. After an extended second, he motioned towards us but pressed a finger to his lips. I'm ashamed to write that I felt annoyed. I was hungry. My body felt sore from sleeping on a mattress that was indeed too thin. I wanted tea, like at home, brewed slowly until the bitterness had evaporated as if by some magical force.

"Enough."

Mikoto heard the sadness in that one word she said to no one except herself. It hung in the air, suspended like a moth flickering air around its wings in the hope of keeping the gossamer moving at the correct speed.

"He would die if he knew."

She turned out the light and curled up on the futon. She welcomed the darkness. It hid her well from any reflections she may have seen in passing mirrors or shiny surfaces. She knew that if she looked at herself, she would see the guilt there, the lack of respect for Hari's privacy. She was unprepared for the lack of constriction in his writing. The words felt foreign, yet there were nuances there that sparked memory. But there was an edge to it, like meeting someone who resembled a childhood friend. There was the automatic temptation to assume they were exactly like the person you knew even if this later felt silly.

The next morning, she forced herself not to look at the diary. She busied herself with getting ready. It was Wednesday, so it was her day for reading. While her friends could not understand her sitting alone in the dusty local library, Mikoto enjoyed having the space to herself.

When she returned home, she purposefully turned on the radio, the hollowness of the living room begging for sound. She even found herself humming as Masato Shimon's "Oyoge! Taiyake-kun" filtered into the kitchen. It reminded her of summers on her bedroom floor, playing the one rare vinyl her sister allowed her to touch. But the diary still lingered in her mind. Perhaps it had been unwise to visit the library that morning, surrounded by volumes of literature, words that made her think of Hari. It was inevitable that she found herself sitting on his bedroom floor, cross-legged like she did as a child, only this time, the diary felt heavy in her small hands, like an encyclopaedia holding too much truth.

I did not want to be almost knee deep in snow in the middle of nowhere, even if Yoshida beckoned with an outstretched hand that I grasped at too quickly. I was unprepared for what I would see next even if I knew why we were there. It should not have felt like a surprise and yet, it did. Maybe it was the cold, or the lack of energy, because I wanted to turn in the opposite direction, away from the vapour escaping my lips. I did not anticipate my breath catching in my throat when it became clear what I was looking at. Maybe it was the silence, the light even, that wrapped each feathered body in a luminosity I was unprepared for. It could have been the elegance of their movements, the way they sidestepped each other before turning back as if to give a lingering glance that asked to be followed. All I knew was that it was a spectacle of outstretched wings, lines of black and white folding in and out of each other like a parade of flags that clapped open and shut as if choreographed.

It was Yoshida who broke the silence. He leaned in and pointed towards two cranes bowing in front of each other.

"Look."

The escaped word crashed around us for a brief second. His uncle turned from his camera. His enlarged eyes made us shrink in our boots. I turned back to the birds. The two Yoshida had pointed out were still off to one side. This time one of them flicked out a wing at a curved angle, allowing the pointed feathers to reach out as if demanding even more attention, like an extended, chivalrous hand requesting a dance.

I could feel my smile as I turned back towards Yoshida. He nodded but did not return the smile. It did not confuse me. He was like this. He did not force anything he was unprepared to give. It only increased the value of every gesture.

It happened on the way back to the truck. His uncle was still taking photographs, but Yoshida started walking away from the ridge. My large strides overtook his quickly. It was just before the door that I turned around and misjudged the snow, my ankle leaning dangerously to one side, ready to freefall into a wobble. I felt the loss of balance and the uneven ground sucked me down quickly. I did not hear him run towards me, or the laboured breath. I only felt the hands on my wrists before I landed on him, both of us sinking into the snow soundlessly.

I was the one to lean forward. I trusted the moment, the way everything seemed to lead to such proximity. How could I not? Afterwards I lied to myself. I tried to push reason to its limits. I wanted it to be his fault. He had led me on, made me see the glimmer of something that I could hold on to. Even writing this now makes the lie burn deep like it should. I deserve nothing less for wanting to blame him for something I had brought upon myself.

It was not that simple. I know this. I know that him pulling back while I closed my eyes was something I should have reckoned with. How presumptuous I was to think he would melt into the moment like I did. I was unprepared for his eyes that told me I had overstepped. Blunt, open hurt. I had silently said something that could never be retracted. I felt the shame hit me like a sucker punch, like some idiot in a film caught unawares when he should have been paying attention. I knew the cues. I knew him. How could I have been so foolish?

Mikoto closed the book slowly. It had been silly to turn off the radio, something she always did to save electricity. Without the familiar choruses of pop music in the background, she could hear her own breathing quite clearly. It was heavy, air squeezed almost painfully out of her lungs, a sound that should have been light and easy. She felt her stomach twist. Was it nerves? Hunger? She decided on the second.

The plan was to prepare a plate of unagi, something Hari hated. Now she had the freedom to cook the glistening eel that lay lopsided in a bowl of fresh water on the kitchen sink. She opened the cupboard to prepare the tare sauce, but her heart sank when her hands searched in vain for kezurikatsuo, a necessary ingredient. She would have to run out and buy the pricey fermented bonito from the store down the road. She sighed at her own thoughtlessness and threw a large shawl over her shoulders before slipping her feet into the pair of white tennis shoes at the front door, the only footwear she wore because her bad back dictated her fashion choices now. When she walked into the grocer, there was a commotion at the back. Two children, clearly panicked, had run into a display of canned lychee, causing their mother to break out into a hushed rant that was followed by heavy prodding that only caused the girl, in pigtails and a bright pink anorak covered in tiny white sheep, to break out into a convulsion of crying. Her pretty face was stretched and contorted to such a degree that her younger brother could only stare at her in open amazement.

Mikoto was so caught up in her search, scanning labels, that she did not notice the approaching footsteps. It was not long before she collided with the stranger. She looked up, startled after the impact. Yoshida's familiar face, only this time with enlarged eyes, greeted her with a shy smile.

"Sorry," she said as he almost bowed towards her.

Mikoto could not help looking at the swaying fringe, returning to her son's words before the guilt slammed the innocent observation down like a fly swatter hitting linoleum.

"No," Yoshida answered quickly. "I should have been watching where I was going...are you looking for something in particular?"

"Hmm."

Her gaze wandered back to the rows of accurately stacked cans and jars. She wondered if this was his hard work. Was he that accurate and diligent in his job? Or was he like the boys who loitered on the street outside in baggy dark jeans and oversized black sweatshirts, a pack of matte crows laughing at everything conceivable, even at an honest day's work?

"Have you...heard from Hari?" she asked slowly.

Her eyes remained purposefully on the shelf in front of her to avoid cornering him. She was scared he would run off.

"No."

"You are not alone," she sighed. "He is suspiciously silent."

"He must be busy...school and all."

"Hmm."

"Can I help you look for something?"

She turned back to the embarrassed eyes that were almost hidden behind thick black spectacles, another trend she had observed in the trains she was forced to travel to get out of her neighbourhood, seeking freedom from the enquiring looks of neighbours and friends who were permanently worried about the woman now living on her own.

He forced a smile, making her feel another flash of guilt.

"Kezurikatsuo," she said softly.

"What?"

"I'm looking for kezurikatsuo...for dinner tonight." Before she could stop herself, she asked, "Do you like eel?"

It was a mindless question. She could tell that it caught him off guard. His mouth twitched slightly before he smiled.

"My mother used to make it. She was known in our neighbourhood for her unagi."

"Come after work, then. I won't take no for an answer."

He looked down at his shoes, scruffy black trainers that she knew he could have taken better care of, but he was like Hari, always busy, eyes always glued to a screen.

"I can't."

"And why not?"

"I..."

"You are not going to allow me to eat on my own, are you?" Mikoto asked with a smile that he looked at briefly before his lips rose ever so slightly.

When the doorbell rang after seven, she almost jumped. She had prepared the table, her heart shifting an inch when she positioned the second plate on the mat where Hari would normally have sat.

"Hello," she said in her most cheerful voice.

He slipped his hood down, revealing wet hair as he bowed quickly.

"It started raining. Here." He smiled, handing her a brown paper bag.

Inside was a box of purple and cream packaged Panapp desserts. How did he know it was her favourite? Mikoto loved the textured vanilla ice cream layers that sandwiched the most delicious grape jam. The mixture always clung to the roof of her mouth like thickened toffee, offering a lingering taste that forced her eyes to close in silent satisfaction.

"Come in. It is already icy outside."

He slipped out of his shoes, his white socks in stark contrast with the dark carpet at the entrance. As she gestured towards the table, he bowed slightly before slipping through the doorway, his head almost touching the top of the cut-out wall. Hari was a lot smaller, Mikoto thought, as she followed him.

They ate in silence. She used the time to watch him, to look at his face as he tasted her food. He closed his eyes during the first bite and nodded to himself. Mikoto wondered what he was thinking. Was it a return to something he knew? Was it totally different to his mother's? Was it too salty? Too much soy sauce? Either way the silence was thankfully not a barrier between them. It was comforting to see the food disappear without apprehension.

"I miss him, you know," Mikoto said slowly.

Her sudden sentence was startling, causing him to almost drop a chopstick.

"Do you think he will come back soon?" she asked carefully.

"I don't know."

She could feel her fingers curl into a fist on her lap at his answer.

"He would come home if you asked...just for a visit."

He looked out the window, at the rain now running down the glass in thin lines. The clouds were light and grey, the colour of the underbelly of a duck. It made Mikoto think of fingers disappearing between feathers that curled to touch, awakened by warmth and curiosity, surprised by the lightness that presented itself without warning.

"No, he wouldn't," he finally said, just as she was about to stand up and fetch more water.

"You're wrong," she said deliberately, her eyes finding his. "He'd do anything for you."

She saw his throat twitch at the blunt honesty. Another flash of guilt. This one was perhaps even more unfair than all the others. And then the unexpected, a nod that sent his fringe into a sway so slight, it made her think she had imagined it moving.

After he left, trying in vain to push away the offered container of leftover food, Mikoto looked at the empty dining room table for the longest time before turning off the light. She replayed the visit in her mind over and over again. She tried to pinpoint a possible moment where she had reached through to Yoshida, maybe turning him towards the possibility of contacting Hari. When she sat on her bed, the diary in her hands once more, she patted her chest to steady her heart before opening to where she had stopped the last time. The words sprang up towards her once again. Hari's presence was suddenly there. It felt like he was reading his words with his eyes flitting between the text and her, trying to see a reaction.

When Yoshida's uncle returned to the car, we were both sitting in silence. If he noticed this, he never showed it. His face was rosy and carefree. I assumed the photographs he needed had been captured and we could make our way back to the cabin, to warmth, to food, away from where I had been embarrassed. Yoshida and I sat side by side in the truck and I began to dread every bump in the road, every curve that could accidentally push our bodies together on the tight backseat. I half expected Yoshida to climb over the gearbox and sit up front with his uncle. But he didn't. He stayed put. He kept his eyes on the slanting scenery that remained stiff in colour, changing only in shape and mass as we made our way towards the woods.

I was glad to come home. Even Okan's incessant questions did not bother me. The lies came easily enough even though they chipped away at the memory I tried to rewrite in my mind. Yoshida's shocked eyes woke me in the middle of the night. They pulled me from my sleep, forcing me to sit upright in my bed.

I was happy when the letter arrived. I knew from the weight of the envelope that it would mean an escape. Okan watched me from the bedroom doorway. I knew she would not come closer and read over my shoulder. She would allow me this privacy in a home she had tried to make as lovely as she could. It wasn't easy. I knew the sacrifice. I saw how the other women eyed her with open scrutiny. It was so brutal. They should have felt shame had they any decency. And now, the reward stood before her, a future she could half call her own.

Yoshida came to the small dinner my mother put together. It felt like an ending when it should have been an applause for a beginning. I watched him talk to our friends who laughed at his jokes like they always did. He had the same mannerisms, the same lightness to his eyes until he looked at me. His eyes darted away, and I felt a wave of anger, something so uncharacteristic to what I normally felt around him. I wanted to walk over and push him roughly. I wanted to say that he was being unfair. I should have been the upset one. My pride was the one burned and left discarded like a firework that should have brought joy but now only lay on the ground as litter. But Okan came to the rescue, unknowingly. She plated more food than we could eat, pushing us towards having a good time even though my spirit wanted to flip the table over and walk out.

When everyone assembled at the front door to leave, there were awkward goodbyes. Okan stepped out because there was too little room for everyone slipping into their jackets and coats. The light laughter was followed by nervous smiles and promises to keep in touch.

I wanted Yoshida to stay a second longer, but he didn't. He waved a hand as if we would see each other the next day before turning towards the door hurriedly. His hair was already tucked beneath the bright red beanie we had bought together. In the store I told him that it complimented his face, and he smiled even more broadly at my praise before punching me on the arm. It was terrible seeing the back of him, watching him disappear through the door with the others as if he were heading out to better things. When I was alone, I stood there a moment longer, watching the door, questioning why I had not run after him, why I had not forced him to speak to me.

The next day Mikoto threw her feet over the side of the bed, her hands searching for her glasses before she even opened her eyes. The room felt hollow, the furniture almost floating before her hands gripped the curtains, casting out the darkness in favour of light. The ring of the telephone took her by surprise.

"Okan?"

"Hari? Why are you calling? Did something happen?"

"No."

She heard the hesitation, the intake of breath.

"I was thinking of visiting. Will you be home over the weekend?"

"Where else would I be?"

"Don't be silly," he said.

Mikoto did not have to see him to know that his lips were curled in the softest of smiles.

WEREWOLVES

John Copenhaver

Archie wove through clusters of men toward me. The Chicken Hut usually buzzed with chatty patrons knee-to-knee and arm-in-arm, imbibing cocktails, ordering dinner, and listening to Miss Hattie play deranged cabaret tunes on the piano. "Wait 'Till the *Son* Shines, Nellie" was a favorite. But tonight, the room vibrated with anxiety, and men were leaning toward each other, whispering. The news was spreading.

"Hi ya, Dave." He settled into the chair across from me.

I glanced at my beer bottle, not wanting to show him my raw eyes.

"Say, what's the matter?" He drew his chair closer. "You look like you lost your last friend."

"Christ," I groaned. "Haven't you heard?"

He shrugged. "Something's up for sure." He scanned the room. "Is the Hut expecting a raid tonight?"

"Pete's dead." Saying it out loud stirred the thick, soupy sadness pooling in me.

"Oh, God." His eyes grew wide. "How?"

I shoved today's *Washington Post* at him, spinning it around and jabbing my finger at a headline: "Suspect in homosexual sting operation takes fatal leap." I gulped my beer to ward off tears.

He scooted closer, peering down at the article. "Jesus."

"The night before last, some pretty-faced vice cop made him in the Lafayette Square restroom. You know the routine—the decoy winks and waves his dick around, invites the mark back to his place for beer, and arrests him outside, all in the name of the Pervert Elimination Campaign," I said, my chest tight with rage.

"I can't believe it."

"They were going to print his name in the paper, like all the average Joes and Janes they arrest, his private life a fucking public record. Then, that's it—no job, no career, no prospect for employment." I fiddled with the corner of the Schlitz label. "He jumped from his window, eight floors up. He went through someone's cloth-topped convertible. Just like Petey—going out in style." I chuckled. "Christ."

"Since Eisenhower barred us from government jobs, it's so much worse," Archie said, shaking his head. "They should be worried about Joe McCarthy, not commies and queers." He dropped his hand on my knee. "I'm sorry," he said, squeezing it. "It's crushing news."

Archie was in his late twenties, wiry, handsome, with a swirl of dark hair and bright, roving eyes. But he didn't seem to know it—a desirable trait in most people, but in him, unsettling, needy. He pushed you away when trying to draw you in. I never knew how to avoid sending mixed signals. Do I lean in to give him a boost or back away for fear of leading him on? I moved my knee from his grip. "Come on, Arch, you didn't even like him."

"Okay," he said, throwing up his hands. "Pete and I—we're very different sorts. You're right. His cavalier behavior rubbed me the wrong way. But I wouldn't have wished this on him. Ever. I hate the decoy cops who did this—wolves in sheep's clothing!"

I shouldn't have snapped. "I'm in a state. It's a lot to take in. Pete and I—"

"I know," he said softly, "you loved him."

"I did—I *do*."

"I never understood you two," he said, his hazel eyes flickering with pity. "You're such an upstanding and loyal fellow, and Pete was, well ..."

"Eager to fuck."

He smirked. "His dalliances in the restrooms were a risk, especially considering he clerked at the State Department."

"I'm not surprised the cops got him, not at all." I circled my fingers around the bottom of my bottle. "But I don't know why he ended things."

"He's far from the only one."

"It's just not like him."

I conjured Pete standing at the window in his living room,

alone and broken, tears streaming, staring at the city twinkling in the night. What had he been thinking? Why didn't he ask for help? Was he afraid I'd judge him? Grief twisted in me, but before it snarled, I smoothed it out, flattening it into something sharper and more durable. "If I knew where to find the vice cop who suckered him," I said. Archie's face was white, eyes fixed, absorbing. "If I knew what this apple-cheeked asshole looked like, I'd grab him and sort him out. Payback for Petey."

"It'd be dangerous."

"These cops are destroying us, then going home to their wives and puffing out their chests, like, 'I bagged another queer, honey! Maybe I'll get a promotion.' Fuck them."

"Do you think this persecution will ever end?" He rested his hand on mine; I didn't pull away.

"If we don't fight back, they'll crush us." I looked at him. "They've been whispering this asshole cop's name around the bar. Wyle. Have you heard of him?"

"No," he said. "Let me ask around."

I took a swig of beer. The liquid was warm, flat, and bitter. "Will you?" I said, my mind clearing and filling with purpose. "Do it for Pete, okay?"

He patted the top of my hand. "Give me a day or two."

It was true. Petey was insatiable. We'd been an item for years, more or less. When I turned thirty last fall, I asked him if we could be exclusive, just him and me. He balked and handed me a drink. "Honey," he said, "your big shoulders and dreamy blue eyes are something else, but I'm not a one-guy kinda guy." He drifted to the bar cart, swaying to Jo Stafford's "Fools Rush In." He wasn't rejecting me, just monogamy. I couldn't be angry—or didn't think I should be. I'd dated other men, but none like Pete, and I didn't want anyone else. So, to stay together, I had to learn to share him. It wasn't easy. Over time, distance grew, and I moved out, but if he walked into a room and smiled, his eyes sparking with mischief, I'd return, and the crazy cycle would begin again. All that excitement and frustration didn't matter now, erased and replaced by a single note: the low hum of vengeance.

When Archie knocked on my door, I pulled myself from the window, where I'd been smoking and watching evening settle over the trees of Meridian Hill Park. I answered, and he introduced me to a sheepish 20-year-old in tight dungarees. Sam Trucco. Our witness. He could identify Wyle, the cop who had robbed Pete of his life.

"What can I get you, gents?" I asked. "A drink or a smoke?" They chose bourbon.

Archie and the kid sat on the sofa across from me, tumblers in hand. I caught Archie's eyes on my body. I'd kept myself fit since the war. I was wearing a thin tank top, and my dog tags dangled down the groove in my chest—a turn-on for him, I imagined. I folded my arms.

"So, Sam..." I asked, "what can you tell us?"

The kid glanced at Archie, who nodded, giving him the go-ahead. "I knew Pete a little from Lafayette Square and Franklin Park." He checked with Archie again. "We, uh, *interacted* a few times."

Sam was a good-looking kid with sandy blond hair, slate-blue eyes, and smooth, tanned skin. A thin scar artistically marred his upper cheek. I understood Pete's attraction. "We had an understanding, Pete and me," I explained, attempting to put him at ease. "I'm not jealous, and he needed...well, he needed *a lot* of attention."

Nudging him along, Archie asked, "So, you've seen this cop, right?"

"Wyle? I sure have. He works out of the First Precinct." He took a sip of his bourbon. "Officer Jake Wyle, or at least that's what the guys think he's called."

"We need more details."

"If you have a pencil and paper," the kid said, "I can sketch him for you."

"Sam's an art student at the Corcoran," Archie explained, widening his eyes at me.

"In my third year," Sam remarked. "Have no idea what I'm going to do with it."

"Engineers always need good draftsmen," I said, grabbing paper and a pencil from a small writing desk across the room.

After a quick swill of bourbon, he began sketching. His delicate fingers fumbled at first, then flipped to the eraser for corrections. Eventually, he found his rhythm, and his strokes grew confident.

While he worked, Archie's hungry glare fell on me again. If he wanted to look, I wasn't complaining. To track down Wyle, I'd need his help, especially when I showed the devil how I felt. I grabbed my smoldering cigarette, took a drag, the ash flaring orange, and leaned back, stretching out my arms, giving Archie my chest. We locked eyes, and I let a ribbon of smoke slip between my lips. He melted a little. Good.

When the kid finished, he turned the sketch around and said, "That's him." The face in the drawing was older than I would've guessed. Maybe early forties? Not Pete's type. He had a broad, plain mug, a bank of bushy dark hair, full cheeks, and a trim full mustache. His eyes were hard. God, was Petey *this* desperate?

"I've seen him in the Square several times," Sam said, "then the other night with Pete before—"

"Before he was arrested," I finished, anger blooming.

"I'm sorry," the kid said gloomily. "Don't blame yourself."

"I wasn't planning to," I snapped, tossing my cigarette in the ashtray. But I *did* blame myself. The night Pete was arrested, I told him I'd meet him at the Chicken Hut, but I'd been waylaid at work. He'd wandered off to the park restrooms before I could get there.

"Thanks, Sam." Archie inserted himself. "This is what we needed. Don't worry. We won't let on you're the artist."

I picked up the drawing. "Yes," I murmured, scanning the picture and imprinting every detail. "Thank you."

Archie gave him a few bucks—drinking money—and escorted him out.

With the door closed, he said, "We have the asshole's picture. What now?"

I didn't answer him.

He studied me, stepping close. He was flushed, horny even. "What are you going to do? Go to the precinct substation, wait for a shift change, tap him on the shoulder, and slug him?"

I wanted to kill Wyle, but I could barely say it to myself, much less to him. "It has to be more than a few loose teeth," I grumbled. Under the surface, I possessed a soldier's uncanny knowledge that life was easy to snuff out, even if the impulse to kill didn't come naturally.

He moved closer.

Nonsensically, I shook my head and said, "I want to find him."

"And?"

"I want to take him somewhere, and, and—"

"*Scare* the hell out of him."

"Yes."

He leaned into me suddenly, but I pulled back, startled. Undeterred, he grabbed my arms and pressed his lips to mine. I could have resisted—he wasn't my equal in strength—but confused, I gave in. I tasted bourbon, reminding me of Pete's love for Manhattans. Yet his eagerness was frantic, unlike Petey's slow, alcoholic lovemaking. Archie scrambled up me like a rock, hands everywhere. I shoved him away. He stumbled, stray hairs falling across his forehead. "Sorry, Arch," I said. "Not now."

"Don't be sorry," he said, frowning and adjusting his hair. "I understand."

"All I can think about is Pete, about what they did to him."

"Well..." He sniffed and straightened up. "Let's do something about it."

We decided to take turns watching the First Precinct on Indiana Avenue, home of the vice squad. It was a busy station, so we'd use Sam's drawing to identify Wyle and track his movements before acting. Once we knew his habits, we'd follow him in my black Buick, grab him away from the crowds, force him into the car, and drive him to Archie's boarded-up family farm in Virginia. There, in the quiet, we'd make him feel what Petey felt. I'd carve it into his bones.

While Archie staked out the precinct the first night, I entered Pete's apartment with my spare key. On the coffee table sat an upright cocktail shaker and an overturned martini glass with an olive gathering mold—his last drink. Beyond it, the window where he'd jumped framed Georgetown and the Potomac. I imagined the sound of Pete's navy-blue silk robe, rippling like a flag as he fell. Shaking off the thought, I went to the bedroom and searched for his Colt 1911 service pistol. I'd discarded mine to forget the war, but using Pete's gun to force Wyle's compliance felt right. Pete's ghost lingered in the gunpowder.

While I was at the apartment, Archie saw Wyle leave the

precinct and head west to catch a streetcar on 7th Street. He followed on foot. Wyle switched lines to reach Mt. Pleasant and walked home through quiet, tree-shaded streets—the perfect spot to grab him. After confirming his routine, we made our move.

While we waited in the Buick at Wyle's Mt. Pleasant stop, I handed Archie Pete's gun. "Feel its weight," I said. He gripped it, mystified, as if it were a relic. "Do you know how to use it? Just in case."

"My father taught me to shoot on the farm," he said. "He insisted all men should know their way around a gun. He sensed I'd disappoint him. He hoped shooting a gun would, somehow, straighten me out."

"Maybe he wanted you to learn how to protect yourself."

Archie's brow wrinkled, unsure if I was joking. "Well, it didn't straighten me out." He smiled, and I thought of our kiss the other night. I didn't want to go there again—it was too confusing. He glanced at the gun in his palm. "It's funny Pete didn't use this to...you know."

"He'd never have done that," I said. "He was proud of his service. He'd see it as...sacrilegious."

"Sorry," Archie muttered, handing it back. "Morbid thought."

Right on schedule at 10:20 PM, Wyle stepped off the streetcar, his black mustache visible in the streetlight, and headed away from Mt. Pleasant Street into the quiet neighborhood. He wore a dark, ill-fitted suit, with a pistol holstered at his hip.

Archie slid on his flimsy dime-store Halloween mask, a black-hatted witch with green skin, a warty nose, and a cackling grin. "I'll get you, my pretty," he said, chuckling. He'd bought one for each of us at Woolworths to conceal our identities. Not wanting to draw attention from passersby, I left mine up, resting on my head—a werewolf with bright orange fur and blood-dipped fangs. I hopped out of the car, and Archie started the engine. I hurried to catch up to Wyle as he turned into a shadowy neighborhood street.

I carried Pete's Colt low on my hip as Archie drove beside Wyle, rolling down the window and calling, "Hey, do you know the way to Lafayette Square?"

Wyle didn't hear him or ignored him, so Archie called again. This time, Wyle looked over, and I yanked down my mask— trick or treat!

"You're off track, bud," Wyle said, stepping toward the car. "That's downtown—" He froze when he saw the witch mask, then backed into my gun.

"Stop right there," I growled. "Arms up and don't move."

"What the—?"

"No questions." I cocked the gun. "Do it!"

He raised his arms.

"What do you want?"

"No questions."

I slipped his revolver from his holster and tucked it under my belt. "Open the back door and get in."

He obeyed, and I followed, keeping the Colt trained on him. Archie threw the Buick into gear.

"Do you know who I am?" Wyle asked, a crack in his voice. "I'm police." His hands were still up.

"We know," I said, slamming the door. "We're here to help you understand your police work, to enlighten you."

"What do you mean?"

"We're avenging angels."

His eyes narrowed with scorn. "More like Halloween freaks."

"Do you want a bullet in the head?" I snapped. Then to Archie: "Drive. Now."

On the way out of the city, I bound Wyle's hands behind him with his cuffs and pulled a flour sack over his head, allowing us to remove our masks. I also tossed his police issue .38 on the front passenger's seat. We arrived at the farm outside Culpeper after midnight, the moon a pale sliver in the sky. Archie's parents were dead, but he couldn't bear to sell or live on the farm. It was abandoned, crumbling among overgrown fields. His childhood sounded tough.

At the end of a twisted drive, the Buick's headlights lit up a two-story barn, the perfect location for our lesson in fear. We didn't want Wyle seeing anything that could identify Archie.

With the Buick running, Archie retrieved three gas lanterns and a rope from the trunk and waded through knee-high grass to the barn's doors. The crisp night air and smell of dead leaves wafted in through the windows. Wyle mumbled something, but I shoved the gun into his ribs. We'd silenced him on the drive to stay focused.

Archie unlocked the rusty chain on the doors, and it hit the ground with a thud. He waved me over. Using terse commands, I led Wyle out of the car toward the barn. He stumbled, cursing.

The barn stank of rotting hay and bat droppings. Archie lit a lantern, casting light across the space. Cobwebs covered every corner, and rusted tools leaned against the walls. No one had been here for years. He lit the other lanterns and spread them around to maximize light, though the darkness above pressed down on us.

After clearing cobwebs, Archie found a sturdy chair and placed it in the center. I led Wyle to it, holding the gun as Archie tied him up. "Why are you doing this? What did I do to you?" Wyle whimpered under the mask.

Archie stood back, observing. Wyle looked like an offering to a Pagan god. We put on our Halloween masks, lurid in the lamplight. I yanked the sack off his head, sending flour into the air. "Jesus Christ!" he blinked. His coif and mustache were dusted white. "Where am I? Let me go!" He struggled, but the chair wobbled.

I crouched, the werewolf mask a thin barrier. "You're going to answer for what you and vice do to men in Lafayette Square. You've destroyed lives—and why? Because of McCarthy's fearmongering?"

"What is this?" He scowled.

"Does it make you feel like a man?"

"Is this about perverts?"

A violent urge shot through me. "Because of you," I said, stepping back, "a good man is dead."

"What 'good man'?" he said, full of scorn. "The men loitering in that park for their disgusting sexual appetites? They aren't good. They're sick. Twisted." He huffed. "Sucking cock behind the White House. The White House!"

I drew Pete's Colt from my waistband and shoved the barrel into his cheek. He jerked back, his eyes glistening. The muzzle left a ring in the film of flour. Until now, he'd been confident, cocky. Now, he was afraid. "I get it," he said, wilting. "You're fags."

"We are," I said softly. "You ruin our lives and brag to your buddies about getting us, those fags." I shoved the barrel toward him again. "You see this?" Pete's pistol danced in front of his flour-covered face.

His eyes widened.

"It belonged to the man you entrapped, arrested, and killed. You seduced him, then pushed him to the edge—" My grief cracked my speech. "You pushed him and shoved him over." My eyes were wet, my hand trembling.

"I don't know what you're talking about," he said defiantly.

"You lurked in Lafayette Square, peeped through a hole, made eyes, or unzipped your pants—then flashed your badge and humiliated him."

"Who?"

"Pete Lessing."

"Never heard of him."

"You're full of shit."

"I'm telling you. I don't know him."

I wanted to kill him. It'd feel good, a righting of the universe. "You do, and you're going to pay for it."

Archie was at my side, hovering. I sensed he was worried about how far I'd take it. I wondered too. The only thing stopping me was fear of police retaliation against other gay men. We were interchangeable to them, like one organism.

"Tell me." Wyle squinted. "When did this happen?" His tone shifted, more relaxed.

"Don't play stupid."

"Recently?"

I stared at him, which he took as a "yes."

"I'm a sergeant," he said. "I don't do that work. You have the wrong man."

I thrust Pete's pistol at him. "You're Officer Jake Wyle."

"No." He smirked, shaking his head. "I'm Jim Frost. Sergeant Frost."

I lowered the gun.

"If you don't believe me, check my wallet."

I locked eyes with Archie—Werewolf to Witch. Had we made a mistake? Had Sam? If this was the wrong guy, what did that mean? "Search him," I said, nodding to Wyle, Frost, or whoever he was. "We need his wallet."

Archie didn't move. He didn't seem to want to. I thought of our kiss. I hadn't liked it, but it had bound him to me, to this task. Maybe it wasn't enough. Maybe I'd been unfair to use him. Still, now wasn't the time to retreat. Hiding my frustration,

WEREWOLVES

I handed him the gun. "Aim it at his dick."

I leaned into our captive to pat him down. After searching his left side with no luck, I shifted to his right, blocking Archie's view. Seizing the chance, the cop shot up from the chair, the fragile wood snapping under his bulk, and the ropes slid down. He drove his head upward, slamming his skull into my jaw. I flew back into Archie, who braced my fall, only to stumble, drop the gun, and hit the floor with a thump. The cop made a frantic dash for the door but tripped over the ropes and chair debris, pitching forward. Unable to break his fall with cuffed hands, he smacked the wood with a grunt. Ignoring my throbbing jaw, I scrambled for the gun and snatched it off the floor. Adrenaline kicking in, I bolted across the room and kicked him hard enough to roll him over. His face, red and wet with agony, was covered in straw. I shoved the pistol in his mouth to stop his moaning. I dug into his lapel and pants pockets, but there was no wallet or ID.

"Where's your fucking wallet?" I barked at him, but he couldn't answer. He was still sucking on my gun. His eyes were teary, and his lips trembling. I pulled my gun out and stood up, keeping it aimed at his head. "Arch," I called over my shoulder, "I can't find his wallet."

He didn't answer, so I turned to him. His face was blank, frightened. "Your mask," he said, swallowing. "Where is it?"

I'd lost it in the scuffle. Jesus. I spotted it on the floor, its empty eyes and fanged snarl glaring into the gloom beyond the rafters. Our captive could identify me. My senses sharpened, and I held the Colt tighter, the trigger's crescent shape alive under my forefinger, as if it, not me, pumped with blood. This was no longer a kidnapping, no longer a lesson in fear. We'd have to kill him. What choice did we have? If we let him go, we were dead. Minutes ago, hours ago, days ago, I would've wanted nothing more than to plant one between his eyes or send him over the side of a building, but that was an idea forged by anger, not a deep-seated impulse. From the war, I knew the reality of killing. Pete knew that reality, too. This stunt was a fantasy. Until now. The second I no longer wanted to kill him, I had to.

"Where is his wallet?" I asked Archie.

"I don't know."

"Look around."

He stood there, maybe the horror of what we had to do was

198

also working its way into his bones. If we had to make this man vanish, I wanted to know if he was Wyle, Frost, or whoever. I killed too many men whose names I didn't know in the Pacific. "Maybe it's in the car," I said.

"Go. Check it out."

Archie nodded as if waking from a spell.

After he left, our captive begged, "Please don't do this. This won't end well for you. It will follow you forever."

"Shut up." After checking the handcuffs, I tucked the gun in the back of my pants, grabbed him by his lapel, and propped him against a support post, his new home until our next move. Straw stuck out from the folds of his clothes, his disheveled hair, even his bushy mustache.

As I began to wind the rope around him, he whispered, "You should know. The witch, he lifted my wallet while tying me up."

I paused. "I don't believe you."

"Why would I lie?"

"A million reasons."

"If he has my wallet, he knows who I am."

"Why would he lie?"

"I don't know. But he's keeping something from you."

I finished wrapping the rope, pulling it tight, and tying it off with a double knot. "Another thing," he murmured, barely audible. "His voice is familiar."

The door creaked behind me. I looked up and snatched Pete's Colt from my waistband. Archie stood at the opening. The sickly green witch mask was eerie in the lantern glow, his hazel eyes catching the light. He was empty-handed. "You didn't find it?"

"I searched everywhere."

"Shit. Where is it?"

"Maybe he didn't have it."

"I had it," he said, shifting against the splintery pillar. "I always keep it in my left lapel pocket."

"He lost it somewhere along the way, then," Archie said, stepping in and closing the door with a clang. "I don't know what to tell you."

I studied him, doubt washing through me. Was he lying to me? Why would he lie? I glanced at the cop, who returned my gaze with a penetrating glare. If this was Frost, Sam—or even Archie—had led us to the wrong man. Was it a mistake? No.

Sam's drawing was so accurate—even on the nose. The man in the drawing was the man we grabbed, but it didn't mean the man was Wyle.

"Archie," I said. "Take off your mask. If he's seen my face, he might as well see yours."

He didn't respond.

"What's wrong?"

"I'd rather keep it on."

"Why?"

"He almost got away once. He can ID you, but not me."

"I'm not escaping," our captive piped up. "You've got me."

"I want to keep it on."

I stepped toward him, adjusting my grip on the gun. "Take it off."

The witch shook his head. "Dave, please don't."

"He knows your name. Archie West. Archibald West. Now, take it off."

"No."

"Fine," I said, closing in. "Let me search you for the wallet."

"I'm telling you the truth." I detected a wobble in his voice. "Jesus."

"Let me search you." I edged closer. "Earn my trust."

"I thought I had."

The cop barked a laugh. "Ha!"

"Shut up," Archie said, shaking. "Shut the fuck up."

"I got it!" our captive cried gleefully. "Your voice—you're Jake Wyle. You're queer bait." When truth is spoken, it rings like crystal. In an instant, I knew I'd been lied to, that Archie had orchestrated all of this, but my mind couldn't catch up—or maybe my heart? The distraction gave him a second to pull Frost's revolver from his waistband. Somehow, I remember seeing his face, or maybe the mask became his face.

Snapping to, I lunged for him, trying to knock the gun away, which made no sense. We had to kill Frost anyway. But I didn't want him to do it. It wasn't his to do. Archie dodged me. Before I recovered, he aimed—his farmer father's training on display—and shot our captive below the right eye. The man's head hit the pole, blood dribbling down his cheek.

✚

Although I'd missed Archie, I didn't lose my balance. I quickly recovered and held Pete's Colt between us, its muzzle sketching small circles in the air. "Drop the gun!" I yelled, breathless. "Now!"

He stood there, silent, with a blank expression. His arms hung by his sides, and Frost's police-issue revolver stayed in his hand like he'd forgotten it. Was he in shock? At some point, he'd removed his mask and discarded it. When? I wasn't certain.

I repeated: "Drop the gun!"

He obeyed, releasing the grip finger by finger.

It hit the boards with a thud. I kicked it into the shadows of a dim stall.

"You're Jake Wyle," I stated as if it was a fact.

He pondered it, wrinkling his nose, and replied: "Yes and no. It's just a name. No one is Wyle."

"Give me a straight answer," I demanded, my temper rising. "Did you entrap Pete? Did you drive him to his death? Are you Wyle?"

"You're missing the point." His voice grew hotter, but fear tinged its edges. "Frost commands the squad that patrols Lafayette Square. He put together the vice cops and civilian operatives who trap men and destroy lives—lives like Pete's."

"So, why was everyone whispering Wyle's name at the Chicken Hut, not Frost's?"

"Wyle is a name some decoys use. A screen between our real identities and this dirty work. A name for restrooms, park benches, and seedy hotel rooms."

"So, you are a decoy." My grip tightened around the Colt. I wondered: Could I kill him?

His dark eyes grew distant; his face went pale. "I'm ashamed of it. It was either become a decoy or be ruined. I would've lost everything."

"But Pete would've recognized you, and he wouldn't have been into it—into you."

Archie chuckled bitterly.

"He didn't like you."

He rolled his eyes. "Come on, Dave, he 'liked' everyone," he said with despair. "But you're right."

"How did it happen? I need to know."

"Sam is a decoy, too," he explained. "Frost and his superiors blackmailed him. He's from a prominent family in Charleston, South Carolina. When they caught him last spring, he wasn't exposed like Pete. They called his father, a senator, and struck a deal. A generous donation to the MPDC pension fund and Sam's agreement to act as a decoy while attending art school. They weaponized his looks." His expression darkened. "When I first saw him, I knew he'd be the siren call for many men."

I narrowed my eyes.

Archie looked away. "I was the one who lured him in."

"Jesus."

"It's a never-ending chain of dominos." He sighed deeply. "And you thought the worst they could do was out us and rip away our jobs and lives. No, the worst is when they force you to betray your own."

Anger stirred in me. "No one made you."

"Frost was the real monster," he said in a controlled tone. "We cut off the head of the beast."

"Another will grow back." I eased my trigger finger and lowered the gun; the fury was draining from me. "Why didn't you tell me? Why keep this from me?"

Pain flickered in his hazel eyes. "Shame," he said, the lines on his pale forehead deepening. "I was scared you'd blame me for Pete's death, and I don't want you to hate me, Dave. I like you. I've always liked you. You know that. So, I asked Sam to draw a picture of Frost, but say it was Wyle. It wasn't entirely a lie. Frost and vice created Wyle—all the Wyles."

A confusing swirl of emotions churned inside me. Archie was both victim and villain. He was trapped yet complicit— foolish, yet somehow, clever. I couldn't untangle it now, so I shoved the gun into my waistband and surveyed the room: the flickering lanterns, the broken chair, and Frost's body tied to a post, blood soaking through his shirt collar. I felt a pressure radiating from the barn's dark corners, like the accusatory gaze of an unseen Greek chorus. "What do we do?" I asked. "How do we clean this up?"

"We need to get rid of the body," he said. "Far away from my family's farm."

"We could toss him into the Potomac."

"Maybe…" he said, lost in thought.

Frustrated, I nudged him. "Well?"

"We should make it look like a suicide."

"What?"

"Make him one of us. That would be poetic justice." His eyes glimmered with excitement, shedding the remorse he showed earlier. "We could even grab a copy of *Physique Pictorial* and leave it at the scene."

"We're not staging a gay suicide," I snapped. "I'm tired of that tired old story."

"But it's a story everyone believes."

"That's why I hate it."

"You're not supposed to like it, Dave," he said, shaking his head. "You're supposed to believe it. The fragile, broken queen sipping martinis and swan diving out of a—" He cut himself short, seeming to realize he'd crossed a line. "My point is: it happens."

Disliking Pete was one thing, but mocking his death was another. "Don't ever say something like that again. Ever. Pete deserved better."

Stung, Archie's face sagged. "I'm sorry." He hung his head, looking like a scolded puppy. "I didn't mean to be so careless."

The word "careless" sent a chill through me. He should have said "thoughtless."

"What do you mean 'careless?'"

Archie glanced up, and for a fleeting moment, fear—no, dread—flashed across his face. Then, something in him clicked on like a light, and he smiled, but it was a sad smile. However unintended, it came off as patronizing. "I'm sorry for being careless with my words. If I hurt you, I'm sorry."

I realized what had gotten under my skin. It wasn't the word "careless." It was that he had been careless. "How did you know Pete was drinking martinis before he died?" I remembered the spilled glass on his coffee table and the moldy olive.

"I didn't," he said, his shoulders tensing. "I don't."

"You were there."

Archie didn't respond at first; he just locked eyes with me. I became more aware of the layers of shadows surrounding us, the night creatures scuttling in the loft, rafters, and along the walls, the musty scent of rotting hay, and the acrid odor of lamp oil.

"Yes," he finally admitted, exhaling. "I was there."

"Petey didn't kill himself."

He scowled. "Of course, he did," he said, seething. "Jesus, Dave. He was killing himself every time he tricked, every time he went into those restrooms in Lafayette Square, the Y, and the Chicken Hut. Every time he betrayed—yes, betrayed—your love. Your devotion to him. You didn't deserve him."

WEREWOLVES

"You pushed him out the window," I said, my words like blades. "You set him up with Sam, but that was only the first step, right? To finish 'the story everyone believes'—your own words!—you made sure his story was one of despair, not survival."

"Why not?" he snapped, the lines around his eyes and mouth deepening with rage. "Pete was a disaster. When I went over there after he was arrested, he was drunk out of his mind, ranting about his life, how it was over, and how he had nothing left but you. 'I have Dave,' he told me. 'He's everything to me, my heart. I can count on him. I always have.' I couldn't take it, don't you get it? It was unbearable. He was going to destroy himself, and you, too. So, I opened the window for air, led him to it, and—" He moved closer to me. I reached for Pete's gun, and he froze. "I did it for you."

"I loved Pete. I still love him." My grief felt lighter now, more clear. More sure. "I'll always love him. You had no right to take him from me. To take his life."

"He screwed anything with a dick," Archie spat, righteous anger flashing in his eyes. "He was completely out of control." His eyes were red, glistening.

"He craved love," I said. "He needed all that love."

"So do I!" Archie cried. His lips quivered. "I crave your love! And that's all I want. Don't you see?"

"You can't steal love."

I drew the gun and stepped forward. Something crunched beneath my foot. I glanced down. The yellow and orange werewolf mask stared up at me, its snarl distorted by my shoe. Straw poked through its eye holes. "You should've been the werewolf, Archie."

"What?" He sniffled, wiping away tears.

But I didn't respond. Instead, I kicked over the oil lantern by my foot. Its oil seeped out and ignited. Archie yelped and stepped back. I moved swiftly to another lantern and, keeping him in my sights, picked it up and hurled it against the closest wall, where it exploded into flames. The hay and dry wood caught fire instantly. Soon, the barn would be a blaze. I crossed to the third lantern, pivoting as I moved, not allowing Archie to escape, keeping him in the center of this burning circle. I grabbed the lantern off the floor and smashed it against the pole above Frost's head. Oil spilled out, and flames followed, engulfing the dead Sergeant.

Archie remained motionless. Was he terrified or simply resigned? "Stay here and burn away your sins," I said, "or come with me and take responsibility for what you've done. Your choice." He didn't move. The fire crept closer, and smoke began to thicken the air. I pulled my shirt over my nose. The crackle of burning wood grew into a roar. It was time to leave. The werewolf mask twisted and curled in the fire. "Archie," I shouted, "I never would've loved you. It doesn't work that way."

He looked stripped bare, vulnerable.

"But I could've been your friend."

His eyes sparked. "I don't want a friend," he said. "I want you."

Sadness broke over me, not for Petey, but for what Archie had become. The flames were closing in fast.

"Goodbye," I said, coughing, the smoke stinging my eyes. I turned, closed the door behind me, and ran to the Buick. I started the engine and drove away, bumping over the rutted road and patches of grass.

About fifty yards away, I glimpsed the blaze in the rearview mirror and, for a moment, thought I saw Archie's silhouette against the firelight. I pulled over, got out, and scanned the horizon. The wind had picked up, the smoke billowed, and the strange, soft noises of the night seemed somehow louder and more overwhelming. Was Archie out there somewhere in the field? Did he choose to live or die? Why did I even care?

I turned away, got back in the Buick, and drove.

OUR FINEST GIFTS

David Pratt

Thing one, he was *not* "little." He was seventeen, well over the age of consent in Galilee. Ergo, thing two, he was not a "boy." I am not, either. Not anymore.

The drummer part was true, for sure, but, Jesus Christ, the "pa-rum-pa-pum-pum" bit? Nuh-uh. He played his drum for me. For me, too. And it was *way* more than pa-rum-pa-pum-pum. The drum was part of him. The song makes him sound all innocent and sweet, but he was deep and he was kind of weird. He was obsessed with that drum. And he knew what to do with it. He knew what to do with some other things, too, okay?

So, a little background. It was spring of Nisan, 3764, and there's all these rumors. "It's Moshiach! M'shiḥa!" Blah-blah-blah. "Just like Isaiah said!" They're like, "It must be real 'cause there was a star," but, um, the woman was a virgin? And an angel spoke to some shepherds? Well, you know what? I read Isaiah's column in the Nazareth *Shofar*, "20 Ways You Can Prepare for a Savior Now," and it was bo-o-oring, and I read that article, "Isaiah Owns Goliath in Just Three Words," but Goliath is a Philistine—I mean, an actual one. The people in this backwater will believe anything, just so they don't have to deal with their own mediocrity. I can't *wait* to get out. I'm going to Jerusalem. I'm going to be an actor. They're doing this totally amazing musical, *Ark!*—about You-Know-Who—and I'd be so-o-o-o perfect for Japheth, the youngest son. The lead is going to be this total hunk, Hamish Yated, and, I mean, I would love to look on his nakedness, pardon my Aramaic. Plus he's got this song, Japheth does, "I Have Seen You," and it is *right* in my range. Sorry. I know. I do go on.

Anyway.

And I knew my parents wouldn't care. They wanted to get rid of me. Especially my abba. I tried to stay out of his way.

So, everyone's all, "Moshiach, Moshiach!" and one evening the weather's nice and I'm outside, smoking, which my mom gets bent out of shape if I do in the house, even though my abba and my brother-in-law do it *constantly*. She's like, "The baby! The baby!" My sister's little boy was like, *the* cutest thing. It felt so-o-o good to hold him and just, like, sing to him or whatever. He was only a few days old. I could practically hold him in the palm of my hand. So, I'm like, "If it's bad for the baby, tell Abba to stop." And she's like, "Don't tell me what to do!"

So, I'm out there, I see this guy coming up the street, hunched, kind of dragging along. Exhausted and dirty. I knew he didn't come from here. I mean, after eighteen years, I knew everyone. Plus, even at that distance, he was...attractive. Not Hamish Yated hunky. More like...*compelling*. The first time I kind of thought that about a guy. Before with me, it was always hot/not hot. Now I was discovering something more. Different. Hard to describe. I stepped into the street and said "Hey."

And he looked up and stopped and said, "Hey."

And I'm like, "Are you okay? Looks like you could use a rest."

And he really looked at me. All he said was, "Thank you," but he was so focused and real, and, as you may have gathered, I did not get appreciated very much. It was never, "Thank you for whatever." It was always, "Why didn't you do it *better*?

He said "thank you" like he *recognized* me. So I wanted to have, like, the best mattress, best food, warmest water, everything. I said, "Come in." And I said something that, looking back, was kinda tactless—"What are you carrying that around for?" meaning the drum, which was slung over his shoulder on a strap—but he didn't seem to mind. He said he was going to Bethlehem. I was like, *Oh, great, another one!* But I wasn't going to stick my foot in it again, so I didn't say anything.

Then he says, "I'm going to play my drum for Moshiach."

So I'm like, okay, "Wow. So. The rumors are true."

And he's like, "I don't know. But people are going. So I had to."

We came around the side door so my folks and the servants wouldn't see. "Why?" I said. And I was getting interested in the idea of helping him wash up. Not like getting a look or getting a feel, but that maybe taking care of someone, giving them, like, dignity, is sexy? Even if you don't see or touch anything?

And he said, "If it is Moshiach, so, I've been practicing my drum all my life. It's the most important thing to me. I go to bed thinking what I'll play tomorrow, or I'll wake up thinking about a whole new idea for a way to play. Sometimes I get up in the middle of the night." I resisted saying, "Bet the units love that." He said, "So, if he really is the King of the Jews, I have to play for him. Plus, it's all I have. People are taking gold and sheep and stuff, but we're poor, my amma and me. I didn't even think I should go, because of leaving her alone, but she said, 'You have to.' She says she knows I'm going to be a big success with my drum. She packed food for me. She said I had to give my gift and He had to receive it. So, here I am. But I ran out of food, though. Do you know how much farther it is to Bethlehem?"

"I have food," I said. He was so, I dunno, quiet and alive. Knew just what he was doing. I wanted to touch him, but I didn't know how that would go. I thought I saw him kind of looking me over. I got hot water for him, plus some water to drink, and some old clothes I had, and I deliberately said I'd leave him alone while I got food.

When I came back, he was naked, with his back to me (I think modesty is kinda hot in a guy), splashing himself. He was beautiful. It wasn't so much his body, which was nice—there was only one lamp and I couldn't see much anyway—it was the way he did stuff. So, like, conscientiously, carefully, not worried about being naked but not showing off, either. He trusted me, even though he just met me. That made me a little swoony, and I also wished there was more food, more and better of everything. I thought we lived pretty well, my family and me, but I wanted him to have so much more. My nephew cried in the other room. I told the drummer all about how sweet he was and how I got to hold him sometimes. Then he smiled at me. "That's really nice," he said. He understood, even though he didn't have nephews or nieces himself. Or anyone, except his amma. I hoped she was okay and not too lonely, back there in wherever.

I put down the lentils and pumpkin and tahini I had, and I gave him a clean levush takhtona and gleema. He began dressing himself. I apologized for the food. He was surprised. He said it was perfect and smelled good. He said that, after he ate, he would play his drum for me—quietly, he promised— to repay my kindness. I didn't get called kind a lot, either.

Honestly, I didn't know what the big deal was. Someone's tired and starving, isn't this what you do? "Not always," he said. Some bad shit had happened to him on the road. He wouldn't say much about it, but I think he got thrown out of some places or beat up. "Thank God the drum was okay," he said. I didn't want to tell him he was here, now, in part 'cause he was so cute. But, like I said, he was more than cute. Anyone would want to help him. I dunno what's the matter with people. My parents probably would've let him go right on by, or maybe they would have let him eat out back or sleep on the roof.

He ate slowly for someone who was hungry. He looked almost, like, regal, with the gleema around him, and this shy smile. I had to say (I mean, obviously, I didn't say it), I wasn't looking forward to a one-person drum concert. I like some melody with my lentils, right? Was he just going to bang and I had to imagine bells and a harp? But he was intent on doing this for me. In his eyes I could see, he was about to do—to share—the best thing in the world. In *his* world. If someone asked me to share the best thing in my world, I don't know what I would do. Show them my nephew, maybe. I'd be too nervous to sing or act by myself. It was more a thing I was *going* to do, when I got to Jerusalem. I guess I could sing the tenor part of "I Have Seen You": "Father I have seen you; Father I know who you are."

It's funny. You say, if the baby is Moshiach, the drummer should play his best for him. But I think—and I know it's not logical—if he plays his best, his absolute best, the baby *will be* Moshiach.

Yeah. Fuck.

He put the bowl aside and washed his hands. He took the drum, and I thought he was going to say, "Here's a song from..." or "Here's a song by..." Although they wouldn't exactly be "songs."

So I'm talking away (what else is new?), and he puts his finger to his lips. I'm like, "What?" He smiles. Then I saw. He had started. He was making circles on the drum with his fingertips. It barely made a sound, but if I was totally quiet, well, I guess total quiet was the point. And he went through, like, every possible way of, like, caressing a drum with your fingertips. Fast, slow, one fingertip, two, five, ten, both hands, each hand a different speed. Then he threw in little taps. He'd rub and tap at the same time. He hit the rim with his thumb. Then scratched the center with his nails. Then more tapping.

Then back to fingertips, swirling, like wind at night, like the Siruqu, dunes in moonlight, tip-taps representing, like, people, a traveler, two thieves, voices from a tent, kids playing inside the light. All I loved about this place. Vast spaces, night, people making their way, breezy green palaces, fires, stars, pumpkin and lentils, crumbly loaves charred on one side. A baby sleeping. It even made me love my little town, which, like, don't get me started.

His hands were so gentle, so sure, so skilled and loving, I wanted to be the drum. How would he touch me? Would I cry? I thought an angel would appear. Maybe one did. And the joy on his face, like he was the tent and children played inside him. With one hand still circling the drum, he reached over and placed two fingers lightly on my eyelids. I closed my eyes. I laid back, lost in his swirling desert. Then I realized he had stopped. I opened my eyes. He smiled and put the drum aside.

He bent down and kissed me, his lips soft, accepting. I pressed gently back. Then our tongues played, like children in a tent. Then our whole mouths worked, rhythmically, tongues digging, and we began to shed clothes. His hands swirled over my skin as they had swirled over the drum. Here was a man, barely a man, not "little" at all, who loved and knew what to love. How to be with what he loved. I felt like I was better, too, at all of that, as though I myself were the drum, though this wasn't exactly my strong suit. I'd had only a couple of experiences, awkward and aggressive, like what I had imagined drumming to be like. Banging. But he was leaves on my skin. Safe for me to let go. "I have something for you," I whispered. And I came. "There. It's for you." He scooped up some and licked it off his fingers. Then he kissed me, so I tasted it, too.

"I have something for you, too," he whispered.

"You already gave me so much," I said.

"But I've never given this to anyone," he said. The way he clutched at me when he came, I believed it. I ate it, even though I thought I wasn't so crazy about that kind of thing. It was delicious because it was his. Filling because it was his.

We washed each other, then slipped naked under my big blue and purple blanket. "What if your parents come?" he whispered.

"They never do."

"Or, like, servants?"

I shook my head. "No one cares."

"That's not true."

I caressed and kissed him. "It isn't," I said. "You care. I see why you're going to Bethlehem." I shared with him the idea that he would not play well for Moshiach, but that his playing would *make* Moshiach who He was.

"Why do you say that?"

"You play...divinely."

"I ask God to play through me," he said. "Allow me to play what you want me to. Let me be your messenger. It is the greatest honor. Everyone is supposed to have a divine experience." Could I ever sing "I Have Seen You" or sing anything in the way he was talking about? No matter how much I asked God? He added softly, "I don't know how much longer I'll be able to do it."

"What? Why?" I panicked. His drumming had to be in the world forever. It had to.

"'Cause we're poor. I can always play a little, but my amma's been so good. She lets me play hours at a time. Soon, I'll have to earn a living. I'll have to do what men do."

"You can make money from your drum," I said.

"An itinerant drummer?"

"In Jerusalem!"

He shook his head. "I can't leave my amma. Besides, even the ones who really make money, it's not all that much."

"But you have to!" I said. This was an emergency!

He put his finger to his lips, then lay his hand on my heart. "Just enjoy what we have. It was nice coming with you."

"Same here." I snuggled back down and kissed him some more. I heard wailing far off. Then in the next house. "Your amma." I said. "Does she, like, *know*?"

I was going to ask again when he said, tender and a little sad, "I love my amma. I wonder if she can imagine..."

I thought about that. Neither one of us said anything more.

In the morning we came again, and he let me give him some dates and bread and an orange, then he had to go. He promised to come back, after he had seen the baby, Moshiach, M'shiḥa, King of the Jews, whoever it was. It didn't much matter. Him going was what mattered. Even if he didn't find a baby or even if the baby was just a baby. Just his going, his wanting. But if he didn't play, if he had all those duties to his amma and all that adult stuff to do and he stopped playing his drum, then God would go out of the world. And coming from me, that's big, 'cause I don't take a lot of that God stuff seriously. Like, He's out there, but does He have so much to do with us? Does He have a Plan and expect a list of this and that from us? I think you've just got to make it up as you go along—like my drummer did—and hope. Be a vessel, I guess. I wonder if I can be? I don't feel like one, except sometimes. Maybe it's stupid of me to go to Jerusalem and sing. If I could sing like my drummer played, I would in a second. Maybe there is some truth to the God thing, because where did that insane playing come from?

I don't want to tell you what happened next. I was hoping you'd guess and I wouldn't have to say it.

Suddenly there was, like, all this gossip about how that whole family—the parents plus little Moshiach—had fled somewhere. Some people said Jordan, some said Egypt, some didn't know. So they weren't even *here* anymore.

Then the soldiers came. It's one of those things where, like, you just hear someone yell or see them standing a certain way in the street, and you know. And the next minute everyone's everywhere and stuff is happening that can't be happening. I heard screams like I'd never heard, then more, and pounding on doors and then our door and then they were in our house, and I don't know if I saw them take my precious, sweet little nephew from my sister's arms, but I do know that I saw them cut his throat and then, just for fun, dash him against the wall.

My sister was so insane that I had to pick him up. The soldiers had left. On to the next house to do the same thing. I picked him up and held him. What was left of him. Blood all over me. I just screamed and sobbed and swore and said maybe I could feel his breath or his little heartbeat, but I couldn't. Then there were neighbors in the house. There were screams everywhere outside. They said it was because of Moshiach. Herod was jealous. He'd ordered every kid under the age of two to be killed (some said it was one), just to be sure. That's why the family fled. So they were fine. They were fine, and I was holding the dead body of the sweetest little boy ever in world, and my sister was screaming like she'd never stop and women and men were screaming everywhere, and I just thought, Fuck you, King of the Jews. Fuck you fuck you fuck you fuck you! I hope they find you. I hope they find you and cut your throat, and smash you into a wall. I'd do it myself. You probably aren't even King anyway. But you got to go to fucking Egypt!

We had funerals. Dozens and dozens. One long funeral, one endless scream, all day, all night. My sister tore her clothes. She could hardly stand. I was on one side of her, our amma on the other. The funeral was the hardest thing I ever did. Harder than picking up his little body 'cause that was, like, a reflex. I didn't believe it. Then we went to funerals for other kids. I didn't try to count. It was the end of the world. The crying went on. All because Herod was so fucking sensitive. All because of one guy. I thought I'd run screaming into the desert and never come out.

The crying slowly quieted down, I guess. I can't really remember. I sat on the roof, smoking. More funerals. Tomorrow and the next day and the next.

And then one day I saw, at the end of the street. That walk. The drum over his shoulder.

I climbed down.

He ran into my arms. I just wailed. I hadn't known it was all still in me. "I know," he said. "I know I know."

No one in the house noticed him. Amma sat with my sister all day, and they wept. I don't know what my abba did. Drank, probably. My brother-in-law, same.

I took fish and bread from the kitchen. The drummer was dirty and I washed him, took his levush takhtona and gleema and lent him new ones smelling of aloe. They fell beautifully over him and he moved in them like water.

He didn't play. We just went to bed, lay in each other's arms, and kissed but did not come.

"Did you see him?"

"Yes."

"And?"

"He was lovely."

I felt my heart, like, contract. Lovely, like the boy I lost. How come he had to die so this "King" could live? "Is he the King?"

"He is something."

"Like what?"

"He listened when I played. You could see. I played the best I ever had. God really played through me. And He smiled. He knew. Other people thought it was weird. They gave stuff they could really use, the family. I explained the drum was all

I had. Finally she nodded. His amma." He nestled closer and wrapped me in his arms. "I'm so sorry about your nephew. I kept thinking I had to get here and see you. But it was everywhere. The wailing. I stopped and played for people, if they let me. It's why I took so long." I felt so much I practically crashed into him. His hands were the hands of a drummer as he caressed my shoulder, stroked my hair, outlined my ears. "The world is insane," he said. "But He is something. You should have seen Him. So radiant and still, watching, listening. Knowing. Isaiah said he'd break the yoke of our burden."

"I read that. Isaiah's all like, 'Toldja so!' It's more like he *caused* a burden."

"But 'the people who walked in darkness shall see a great light.'"

"They're always saying stuff like that."

"Yes, maybe," he said. "Maybe they are."

"Always," I said.

"Yes," he said. "Your nephew was radiant, too. A great light. Your love for him was holy and beautiful." He held me close. He kissed my cheek and then my mouth. "I love you for it." I didn't get hard, though. We nestled close, but we did not make love. As our breathing grew regular, he whispered, "We shall speak no more of Moshiach." I clung to him. For some reason I began to shake. I shook and shook for what seemed like a long time, and he held on until I fell asleep.

"You going home?" I asked in the morning. I had been afraid to ask before.

"No," he said. "My amma's gotta be outta her mind. She must've heard rumors like everyone else, and she doesn't know what to believe. And there's work at home."

"I could come and help." He didn't say anything. "For a while. I can't stay around here. I can't! I can come with you and help your amma and…I love you. You teach me how to be good."

He scoffed. "I can't teach you that," he said. "You know how to be good. You shared your food with me, your blanket, and you listened to my drumming. You're very good. Besides, you have to go to Jerusalem. Not yet, maybe. Your family needs you more than you think. They can't lose you now. But when the time comes, you have a dream in Jerusalem."

For a while I said nothing. Then: "I think maybe you are Moshiach."

He blinked. "What?"

"They got it wrong. It was you. It *is* you. Not that little kid. You played the drum. You gave life. You are our Savior."

He rolled his eyes. "No, no." He kissed me. "But you are sweet."

"Isaiah said it in the *Shofar*!" I protested. "M'shiḥa will carry our sorrows. You carry sorrow. The drum on your back! 'He will teach you with parables.' I've heard you play. You teach. Your fingertips. The sounds. You play parables."

He grinned. "Very nice! You are too kind to me. But I am a poor boy, and I must go and care for my amma. I will play the drum all I can. I promise. But Amma must come first."

"She'd have to understand," I said. "If you went to Jerusalem. It seems impossible, but the way you play, the way you *are*, people would…well, they'd pay, you'd be famous. You are Moshiach, I just bet. We could be in Jerusalem together."

"You don't bet on Moshiach," he said. "He is or He isn't. As for you, you have to go to Jerusalem alone, and what happens, happens. Or does not. I might go someday. Drumming…I love it. I can't imagine one day, one hour when God would not speak through my drum." He stroked my hair. "You go. Maybe we will see each other again. That would be nice."

I was disappointed how easily he let go of me. I couldn't do without him. I thought I had to make him stay, or I had to make him take me. I knew I couldn't. I lay awake, so conscious of my arm around him, my hands on him, because these were our last hours. Near dawn I fell asleep a little bit. When I woke up, he was awake and washed and dressed, and he was kissing me.

I felt awful. He had water and ate a piece of bread, and I cried. He held me and said we could be together again. Just not now. "It's not like we won't ever see each other again." I nodded but found nothing to say. Nothing to hope. He was leaving me with a grieving house that didn't want me.

My brother-in-law had actually told me to stop spending time with my sister. "I am her husband, not you," he said. He apologized later, in a stiff tone, like she told him to. He didn't care about me, but my amma said I had to listen to him. I told her, "If I were different, you wouldn't dare say that." And she was all like, how could I be disrespectful at a time like this, didn't I have any decency, blah-blah-blah? I said, "I guess I'm not human. Mystery solved."

The dawn was in the street. A couple of vendors. I wished

he'd go. He hugged me a long time. I was the drum for maybe the last time. "You have many gifts," he told me. "That's what I learned in Bethlehem. Looking in his eyes. You are precious." Well, he didn't have a family like mine. I hugged him back and told he was precious, too. He was a wonderful lover and a genius on the drum. "You're the chosen one," I said. "It doesn't matter if it's Jerusalem or not, or some other place. You owe it to God"— I couldn't believe I said that, I mean, *me*!—"to play every chance you get."

He looked me in the eyes, his hand on my shoulder. "If you say so," he said, "it must be true."

He hugged me one more time, then I watched him till he disappeared.

The crying gave way to silence. People stayed indoors. The children that were still alive asked where their brothers and sisters were, and we shushed them and said, "Heaven." Men went about their business like before. On Abbat, the songs were dreary and broken.

We had another blow-up, my brother-in-law and me. He was bent out of shape that I took my nephew and held him after the soldier killed him. He was all in my face like, "*She* is his *mother*!" pointing at my sister, "she should have held him!" Then it got totally weird. My sister told him to stop, and he told her to shut up. He made like he was going to hit her. Then he went back to me, and it was kinda hard to follow, but what it seemed like he said, in all seriousness, was, if I hadn't been "fussing over" my nephew, he wouldn't have died. Like me holding him had something to do with Herod's soldiers.

My sister was right there and Amma was right there, and all they said was, "Calm down."

I asked how he could say such a thing, and I repeated it back, and even before I was done, Amma was like, "Shhhhhh! That's not what he's saying." Then she wants me to apologize to him. "You must not accuse your own family—"

I said, "He is not my family." I did not say, "He's the handsome asshole who made you all gaga, so you gave him your only daughter."

He made a face and growled real low. "It is a good thing that you and I are not blood. I might have the sickness you have, and be an abomination in the eyes of God."

And you know what Amma said? "Stop it...*you two*."

You two???

216

And he's like, "At least I made a child. At least I *can*." Then he's coming at me, and he says, "You don't care if children die, because you can never make one."

And again, Amma was like, "*You two* stop it!"

"You see?" he says, pointing at Amma. "She pretends that what's wrong with her son is my fault." Then he turns all quiet and respectful and says, "I will do as you wish, Khamta. I will stop. But he will always be an abomination. I pity you, Khamta." And walks out.

I said to her, "I am your son. I am your *real son*."

She was like, "I don't know what you *mean*!"

I spit in the direction he left and went to my room.

I started packing my knapsack for Jerusalem. Slow, like. I mean, would I really do it? Walk out? Get there how? No one was giving me a camel or a donkey. I didn't have a lotta money and I couldn't ask *them*. When I got there, I wouldn't know anyone. My drummer said I should go, but he didn't know it would be like this. I kept packing.

Then Amma's in the door to my room. There's shouting. Always shouting. "Please," she says. "Tell me it isn't true." She holds out the hand of death. "Tell me it isn't." I wanted to cry. How blind she was. How men controlled her. How they pushed my sister around. How horrible this was for her. I thought one day I'd just disappear. Now that day had come, and she was so wrecked. She came at me, put her hooks into me. I was not myself. I was a doll broken left on the floor.

It was like when the soldiers came. One second, silence. The next...

Abba was there, coming at me, knife drawn. Amma was on the floor. Before I could ask how she got there, Abba slammed me up against the wall, the knife blade touching my neck, his insane eyes, his drunk breath in my face. All around me, the maelstrom. "Is it true? Is it true?"

All I could say was, "Yes! It's true. It was Him! The King of the Jews! M'shiḥa! He fucked me! And loved me! You'll see. We'll have a baby. He'll come back. We'll save the world!"

With a wail Abba looked up, mouth open to Heaven as though receiving celestial fire, then releasing that fire on me. Amma was on him. She clawed and yanked at him. I fell. Flailing, he turned on her. "You made him this way!" he shrieked. "It was you! Witch! My son-in-law had to tell me. My son-in-law! In my *own house*! This fucking, shitty disgrace!" He turned to me again. "I will rectify!"

She grabbed the hand with the knife. He burst into a frantic dance, wheeling and swinging. An arc of blood painted the wall and she screamed and I screamed, and then it was painted everywhere, dripping red hills on the walls of my room. When he had no more hills to paint, silence fell and the hills wept over my amma's still body.

I could do something. I could do one more thing. I could die myself.

Or run.

I ran.

Panting, sobbing, a few coins and the clothes I was wearing, hurling myself out, away, screams fading behind me. By now, my sister had found her mother mortally wounded and her father covered in blood. She would never know what really happened. And I ran, past her scream, past what any God or love could do. Past any King of the Jews. Past the last house, out among the jackals, past the last light. I ran and ran. I remembered what Isaiah said in his last column, "Five Things You Can Do to Feel Better Right Now."

"If you're looking to be more active, try mounting up with wings like eagles. That way, you can run and not be weary. Or, for a (literal) change of pace, try walking, and you won't faint."

I walked to Jerusalem.

Jerusalem was wild. Bright and busy and everyone doing everything. It made it easy to forget. My nephew's death, my mother's death, all now part of me. I found an apartment with some other guys. I couldn't get an audition for *Ark!*, but I got cast as a herdsman and I understudied the male ingénue in this little show off the Qarithā Zamira.

I stayed up long after the show cam down. I couldn't sleep, only lie there thinking of them...

And him. I looked for him everywhere. I missed being the drum terribly. I got a job in customer service for a tent maker. On the way to work, I looked for him, and on the way home. I looked for him on the way to the theater and on the way back.

He wouldn't come. Ever. He was the kind of guy who'd be

poor and stay by his mother till her last breath, not leaving her even then.

Then one day, I saw him. Yes! I blinked. Yes! It was him! On the Jaffa Road. He was selling this calligraphy he'd made. A grin spread across my face. I ran toward him. But something wasn't right. He didn't look up at me. Then I was there and finally he looked up, and he smiled. But it wasn't...or was it? It seemed like him. He had those long, beautiful hands. But he was a little stooped, and he had no drum. Like I said, he was selling calligraphy. His fingers were stained with the ink. I stared at them. Then he looked up and said, "Hi." I looked him in the eye, and I told him I had searched for him everywhere.

Then he smiled at me. "Why were you searching for me?" he said. "You knew where I would be."

2025 CONTRIBUTORS

Izzy Beach (they/them) is a Brooklyn-based horror writer, and recent graduate of Sarah Lawrence's MFA in Writing program. Originally from New Jersey, Izzy spent their childhood playing mermaids and reading books about very traumatized magical children. Prior to completing their MFA, Izzy lived abroad in Paris, France where they received their BA at The American University of Paris. There they majored in Creative Writing and double-minored in Comparative Literature and Gender Studies. Izzy's work is interested in the beauties and horrors of the body, complex queer relationships, mothers and daughters, folklore, fantasy, monstrosity, and angry femmes.

Anil Classen is a German South African writer of Indian descent based in Switzerland with a background in psychology and journalism. Avid follower of fashion, street food enthusiast, and bookworm, he swapped city life for the countryside where he found his love of writing. Winner of the Writing District and Parracombe Prize, his work has been shortlisted for the Wells Festival of Literature Competition and Anthology Short Story Competition.

John Copenhaver is an award-winning author whose latest novel, *Hall of Mirrors*, was named a New York Times Crime Novel of the Year. His debut, *Dodging and Burning*, won the Macavity Award, and *The Savage Kind* earned the Lambda Literary Award. A founding member of Queer Crime Writers, he teaches at Virginia Commonwealth University, mentors in the University of Nebraska MFA program, and lives in Richmond, VA, with his husband, artist Jeffery Paul Herrity. www.johncopenhaver.com

Laura Corin (they/she) is a genderqueer writer, Lambda Literary Fellow, and Tin House alum who lives on Dena'ina land in Anchorage, Alaska, with their wife and daughter. Publications include *The New York Times, The Guardian, The Writer, Anchorage Daily News*, the anthology *Building Fires in the Snow: A Collection of Alaska LGBTQ Short Fiction and Poetry*, and small literary publications. When not writing, Laura can be found running along Alaska mountain trails, singing Broadway show tunes off-key to alert bears to her presence.

J. Duncan Davidson writes for the same reasons others might knit...for quiet comfort and discovery. His interest in "holding on" narratives has become a hallmark of his work, as have stories exploring the machinery of intimacy. His recent fiction touches on the delights of found beauty, issues of aging bodies, and the natural complexities of relationships matured over a long, full life. Davidson lives with his husband in Seattle.

Lewis DeSimone's most recent novel, *Exit Wounds* (Rebel Satori Press, 2024), tackles the complexities of growing older in a society that is transforming at record speed. "Funny, surprising, thoughtful and sad," writes Felice Picano, "DeSimone's *Exit Wounds* is his love letter to San Francisco and a long overdue paean to the sustaining nature of gay male friendships." Lewis's previous novels include *Channeling Morgan*, *The Heart's History*, and *Chemistry*. After a quarter century in the Bay Area, he now lives in Minnesota, where he's working on his next novel and remembering how to shovel snow.

Alfred P. Doblin has spent most of his professional career working as a journalist. He has been recognized by numerous state and national journalism associations, including the American Society of News Editors (ASNE) award for excellence in editorial writing, the Society of the Silurians, NLGJA: The Association of LGBTQ+ Journalists, and was nominated four times for the GLAAD Media Award for Outstanding Newspaper Columnist. He was a runner-up in the Saints+Sinners 2024 Short Fiction Contest, and his debut book, *Tales of the Lavender Twilight*, a collection of 11 interrelated short stories, will be released this spring by Rattling Good Yarns Press. Doblin lives in Brooklyn, NY.

Marcy Rae Henry is a multidisciplinary Latina/e artist from the Borderlands and the author of dream life of night owls (Open Country Press), *We Are Primary Colors* (DoubleCross Press), *the body is where it all begins* (Querencia Press), and red delicious (dancing girl press). Her book *death is a mariachi* won the 2024 May Sarton NH Prize for Poetry and will be published in 2025. Other work has received a Chicago Community Arts

Assistance Grant, an Illinois Arts Council Fellowship, a Pushcart nomination, and first prize in Suburbia's Novel Excerpt Contest. MRae is an associate editor for RHINO Poetry. marcyraehenry. com

Miah Jeffra is author of four books—most recently *The Violence Almanac* (finalist for several awards, including the Grace Paley and Robert C Jones Book Prizes) and the novel *American Gospel*, finalist for the PEN/Hemingway Award—and is co-editor of the anthology *Home is Where You Queer Your Heart*. Work can be seen in *StoryQuarterly, Prairie Schooner, The North American Review, ANMLY, DIAGRAM, storySouth* and many others. Miah is co-founder of Whiting Award-winning queer and trans literary collaborative, Foglifter Press, and teaches writing, decolonial studies, and cultural theory at Santa Clara University.

Reginald Kent (he/they) calls both Seattle and Singapore home. He holds an MFA from The University of Washington's program in Creative Writing and is currently continuing his scholarship in UW's English Ph.D. program in Literature and Culture. They have work featured in The Best Asian Short Stories 2022 collection and QLRS. He was a fellow of the 2023 American Short Fiction Workshop as well as the Lambda Literary Retreat for Emerging LGBTQ+ Voices 2024. Reginald's creative work and scholarship focuses on contributing towards and celebrating the literature and performances of queers of colour. Find him at: https://english.washington.edu/people/reginald-kent

Mina Manchester received her MFA from the Sewanee School of Letters. Her short stories and essays have been finalists for awards and published in: *Electric Literature, HuffPost, The Master's Review, Santa Fe Writers Project, Columbia Journal, The Evergreen Review, The Normal School, Pinch Journal, New Millennium Writings*, and *The Bellingham Review*. A Scandinavian American originally from Seattle, she's an Editorial Assistant for Delphinium Books in Los Angeles.

Meagan Perry (she/her) grew up in Alberta, Canada. Her work has been published in *The Saint Anne's Review, Carolina Quarterly, Another Chicago Magazine*, and others. Her audio work has been heard on English-language public radio around the world, and also on many podcasts. She was on the organizing team for Queer Sightings, the first gay and lesbian film festival in Edmonton, and now lives with her partner in Toronto. She wants every worker to have decent wages and union protections. For more: meaganperry.com.

David Pratt is the author of the Lambda-winning *Bob the Book* (Chelsea Station Editions), *Wallaçonia* (Beautiful Dreamer Press), *Todd Sweeney* (Hosta Press) *Looking After Joey* (Lethe Press), and a story collection, *My Movie* (Chelsea Station). His stories have appeared in several periodicals and anthologies, including SAS's *New Fiction from the Festival 2025*. He has performed work for the theater in New York City and Michigan. In 2020-2021 he published *The Book of Humiliation*, an "anti-novel" in 16 zines.

Ever since his teens, **Tom Semmes** has exhibited a talent for the visual arts, studying painting at RISD and building a career as a graphic and web designer. Now retired, he looked for fresh sources of inspiration and found it in community theater and a daily journaling practice. Two years ago, Tom started a writer's group called Spark Plugs, which meets weekly and holds him accountable to finish the stories he starts. Tom is a resident of Frederick, MD.

Charlie J. Stephens is a queer, non-binary writer from the Pacific Northwest. Born and raised in Salem, Oregon, and current resident of Port Orford on the southern Oregon coast, they are the owner of Sea Wolf Books & Community Writing Center. Charlie's short fiction has appeared in *Electric Literature, Best Small Fictions Anthology, New World Writing, Original Plumbing*, and elsewhere. Their debut novel, *A Wounded Deer Leaps Highest* was published by Torrey House Press in 2024 and their new collection of short stories will be published by Buckman Publishing in spring 2026. More at charliejstephenswriting.com.

ABOUT THE EDITORS

Morgan Hufstader is a writer of queer mysteries and thrillers. Originally from New York City, she has since grown roots in New Orleans and commits herself to supporting the local literary and arts community. With over a decade in literary marketing, she has spoken at the Saints+Sinners Literary Festival to demystify digital marketing for authors. She has also had her works published in previous anthologies. Currently, she is studying in the Creative Writing Workshop graduate program at the University of New Orleans.

Paul J. Willis, Executive Director/Project Director, has over 29 years of experience in nonprofit management. He earned a B.S. degree in Psychology and a M.S. degree in Communication. He started his administrative work in 1992 as the co-director of the Holos Foundation in Minneapolis. The Foundation operated an alternative high school program for at-risk youth. Willis has been the executive director of the Tennessee Williams & New Orleans Literary Festival since 2004. He is the founder of the Saints+Sinners Literary Festival (established in 2003), and has edited various anthologies including the most recent *Saints+Sinners: New Fiction from the Festival 2025*. He was the 2019 recipient of the Publishing Triangle Leadership Award for contributions to the LGBTQ+ literary community.

FINALIST JUDGE

Greg Herren is the author of over 40 novels, 50 short stories, and has edited over 20 anthologies. He has won several awards for his writing and editing, and has been nominated for a multitude of others, including the Shirley Jackson, the Lefty, the Agatha, and the Anthony. His next novel, *Hurricane Season Hustle*, will be released in fall 2025.

OUR COVER ARTIST

Timothy Cummings, represented by Catharine Clark Gallery in San Francisco and Nancy Hoffman Gallery in New York, journeyed to a French Quarter pied-à-terre overlooking Armstrong Park in the Fall of 2017 as part of a My Good Judy Residency. The My Good Judy Foundation provides residencies for artists seeking to produce a body of work or performance in New Orleans that address culture making from an LGBTQ perspective. The residency was established to also honor the work of author and activist Judy Grahn. The subjects of Cummings' work are often children and adolescents struggling with issues of sexuality and sexual orientation in an adult world. In 2013, he was an artist-in-residence and subject of a solo exhibition at Transarte in Sao Paulo, Brazil. His paintings are also part of the collections of singer, songwriter, and composer, Rufus Wainwright, Whoopi Goldberg in Los Angeles, CA, and Tomaso Bracco, and Sara Davis in Milan, Italy. Timothy enjoyed his time in New Orleans, where he received inspiration from the spirits of his favorite writers, Tennessee Williams and Truman Capote. "They shaped my early adolescence. They offer a magical telling of the spirit of this place. The darkness and humor of life and the queer Southern aesthetic shows up in my work as well. Williams' 'garrulous grotesques', replacing the bleak mundane of the world with a lush queer poetic eye for the shadows is part of my focus," Cummings said. He graciously created an original painting of Tennessee Williams to be used as the cover art for the COVID-cancelled 2020 Tennessee Williams & New Orleans Literary Festival. For the 20th Anniversary of Saints+Sinners, Timothy created the original painting, *Incident at the Carousel Bar*, featuring a young Tennessee Williams and a mysterious masked companion. We are so proud to use his artwork on our Festival program book covers, and we thank Timothy for the generous donation of his paintings to the Festival's fundraising efforts. He resides in a tiny house in Albuquerque, New Mexico.

You can see more of Timothy's work at: www.cclarkgallery.com/artists/series/timothy-cummings and at www.nancyhoffmangallery.com/artist-timothy-cummingss

SAINTS+SINNERS LITERARY FESTIVAL

The first **Saints+Sinners Literary Festival** took place in May of 2003. The event started as a new initiative designed as an innovative way to reach the community with information about HIV/AIDS. It was also formed to bring the LGBTQ+ community together to celebrate the literary arts. Literature has long nurtured hope and inspiration, and has provided an avenue of understanding. A steady stream of LGBTQ+ novels, short stories, poems, plays, and nonfiction works has served to awaken lesbians, gay men, bisexuals, and transgendered persons to the existence of others like them; to trace the outlines of a shared culture; and to bring the outside world into the emotional passages of LGBTQ+ life.

After the Stonewall Riots in New York City, gay literature finally came "out of the closet." In time, noted authors, such as Dorothy Allison, Michael Cunningham, and Mark Doty (all past Saints' participants), were receiving mainstream award recognition for their works. But there are still few opportunities for media attention of gay-themed books, and decreasing publishing options. This Festival helps to ensure that written work from the LGBTQ+ community will continue to have an outlet, and that people will have access to books that will help dispel stereotypes, alleviate isolation, and provide resources for personal wellness.

The event has since evolved into a program of the Tennessee Williams & New Orleans Literary Festival made possible by our premier sponsor, the John Burton Harter Foundation. The Saints+Sinners LGBTQ+ Literary Festival works to achieve the following goals:

1. to create an environment for productive networking to ensure increased knowledge and dissemination of LGBTQ+ literature;
2. to provide an atmosphere for discussion, brainstorming, and the emergence of new ideas;
3. to recognize and honor writers, editors, and publishers who broke new ground and made it possible for

LGBTQ+ books to reach an audience; and

4. to provide a forum for authors, editors, and publishers to talk about their work for the benefit of emerging writers, and for the enjoyment of readers of LGBTQ+ literature.

Saints+Sinners is an annual celebration that takes place in the heart of the French Quarter of New Orleans each spring. The Festival includes writing workshops, readings, panel discussions, literary walking tours, and a variety of special events. We also aim to inspire the written word through our short fiction contest, and our annual Saints+Sinners Emerging Writer Award sponsored by Rob Byrnes. Each year we induct individuals to our Saints+Sinners Hall of Fame. The Hall of Fame is intended to recognize people for their dedication to LGBTQ+ literature. Selected members have shown their passion for our literary community through various avenues including writing, promotion, publishing, editing, teaching, bookselling, and volunteerism.

Past year's inductees into the Saints+Sinners Literary Hall of Fame include: Dorothy Allison, Carol Anshaw, Ann Bannon, Samiya Bashir, Nancy K Bereano, David Bergman, Lucy Jane Bledsoe, Maureen Brady, Jericho Brown, Rob Byrnes, Patrick Califia, Louis Flint Ceci, Bernard Cooper, Timothy Cummings, Michael Cunningham, Jameson Currier, Brenda Currin, Mark Doty, Mark Drake, Jim Duggins, Elana Dykewomon, Amie M. Evans, Otis Fennell, Michael Thomas Ford, Katherine V. Forrest, Nancy Garden, Mary Gauthier, Lawrence Henry Gobble, Jewelle Gomez, Judy Grahn, Jim Grimsley, David Groff, Tara Hardy, Ellen Hart, Charyl Head, Greg Herren, Kenneth Holditch, Andrew Holleran, Candice Huber, Fay Jacobs, G. Winston James, Saeed Jones, Raphael Kadushin, Michele Karlsberg, Judith Katz, Moises Kaufman, Irena Klepfisz, Joan Larkin, Susan Larson, Lee Lynch, Jeff Mann, William J. Mann, Marianne K. Martin, Paula Martinac, Stephen McCauley, Val McDermid, Mark Merlis, Tim Miller, Kay Murphy, Rip & Marsha Naquin-Delain, Michael Nava, Achy Obejas, Frank Perez, Felice Picano, Radclyffe, J.M. Redmann, Lance Ringel, David Rosen, Carol Rosenfeld, Steven Saylor, Carol Seajay, Martin Sherman, Kelly Smith, William Christy Smith, Pamela Sneed, Jack Sullivan, Carsen Taite, Cecilia Tan, Justin Torres, Noel Twilbeck, Jr., Patricia Nell Warren, Don Weise, Jess Wells, Edmund White,

Paul J. Willis, and Emanuel Xavier.

For more information about the Saints+Sinners Archangel Membership Program, visit www.sasfest.org. Be sure to sign up for our e-newsletter for updates for future programs. We hope you will join other writers and bibliophiles for a weekend of literary revelry not to be missed!

FICTION CONTEST SPONSOR

The John Burton Harter Foundation is a nonprofit organization that promotes John Burton Harter's art and the interests he cared about. JBHF provides resources to nonprofit organizations that advance the arts by featuring Harter's Work.

John Burton Harter (1940-2002) established the foundation through a charitable trust to ensure the visibility of his art and fulfill his creative vision. In keeping with his wishes, JBHF has supported exhibition, catalogues, publications, and initiatives with funding or gifts of original Harter works since 2002. Recipients include non-profit institutions and organizations, from major art museums to local groups.

John Burton Harter, known as Burt to friends, was born in 1940 in Jackson, Mississippi, and raised in Louisville, Kentucky. He received a BA in Art History in 1963 from the University of Louisville and an MA in Painting from Louisiana State University, Baton Rouge in 1970. He also took courses in South Asian Studies at the University of Pennsylvania, Philadelphia, and studied Field Archaeology at The Hebrew University of Jerusalem, Israel. From 1967-74, Harter worked as Assistant Curator of Paintings at The Historic New Orleans Collection, but then returned to the Louisiana State Museum, where he was Assistant Curator of Visual Arts from 1974-86 and Curator of Collections from 1986-1991. He has had solo exhibitions at the Leslie-Lohman Museum of Art in New York; Wadsworth Atheneum Museum of Art in Hartford, Connecticut; Louisiana State Museum; and The Historical New Orleans Collection. Harter was found murdered at his New Orleans home in 2002 by an unknown assailant.

"Saints+Sinners is hands down one of the best places to go to revive a writer's spirit. Imagine a gathering in which you can lean into conversations with some of the best writers and editors and agents in the country, all of them speaking frankly and passionately about the books, stories and people they love and hate and want most to record in some indelible way. Imagine a community that tells you truthfully what is happening with writing and publishing in the world you most want to reach. Imagine the flirting, the arguing, the teasing and praising and exchanging of not just vital information, but the whole spirit of queer arts and creating. Then imagine it all taking place on the sultry streets of New Orleans' French Quarter. That's Saints+Sinners—the best wellspring of inspiration and enthusiasm you are going to find. Go there."

— **Dorothy Allison**, National Book Award finalist for *Bastard Out of Carolina*, and autho of the critically acclaimed novel *Cavedweller*.